J.R.R. TOLKIEN

THE LORD OF THE RINGS
comprising:

BOOK ONE
THE RING SETS OUT

BOOK TWO
THE RING GOES SOUTH

BOOK THREE
THE TREASON OF ISENGARD

BOOK FOUR
THE RING GOES EAST

BOOK FIVE
THE WAR OF THE RING

BOOK SIX
THE END OF THE THIRD AGE

and

APPENDICES

THE RING
GOES SOUTH

BEING THE SECOND BOOK OF
THE LORD OF THE RINGS

BY

J.R.R. TOLKIEN

HarperCollins*Publishers*

HarperCollins*Publishers*
77–85 Fulham Palace Road,
Hammersmith, London W6 8JB
www.**fire**and**water**.com

Seven-volume edition 1999
1 3 5 7 9 8 6 4 2

First published in Great Britain by
George Allen & Unwin 1954
Second edition 1966
This new reset edition published
by HarperCollins*Publishers* 1994

 ® is a registered trademark of
The J.R.R. Tolkien Estate Limited

ISBN 0 261 10394 6

Set in Post Script Monotype Plantin Light by
Rowland Phototypesetting Ltd,
Bury St Edmunds, Suffolk

Printed and bound in Great Britain by
Clays Ltd, St Ives plc

CONTENTS

Three Rings for the Elven-kings under the sky,
  Seven for the Dwarf-lords in their halls of stone,
Nine for Mortal Men doomed to die,
  One for the Dark Lord on his dark throne
In the Land of Mordor where the Shadows lie.
  One Ring to rule them all, One Ring to find them,
  One Ring to bring them all and in the darkness bind them
In the Land of Mordor where the Shadows lie.

CHAPTER I

MANY MEETINGS

Frodo woke and found himself lying in bed. At first he thought that he had slept late, after a long unpleasant dream that still hovered on the edge of memory. Or perhaps he had been ill? But the ceiling looked strange; it was flat, and it had dark beams richly carved. He lay a little while longer looking at patches of sunlight on the wall, and listening to the sound of a waterfall.

'Where am I, and what is the time?' he said aloud to the ceiling.

'In the House of Elrond, and it is ten o'clock in the morning,' said a voice. 'It is the morning of October the twenty-fourth, if you want to know.'

'Gandalf!' cried Frodo, sitting up. There was the old wizard, sitting in a chair by the open window.

'Yes,' he said, 'I am here. And you are lucky to be here, too, after all the absurd things you have done since you left home.'

Frodo lay down again. He felt too comfortable and peaceful to argue, and in any case he did not think he would get the better of an argument. He was fully awake now, and the memory of his journey was returning: the disastrous 'short cut' through the Old Forest; the 'accident' at *The Prancing Pony*; and his madness in putting on the Ring in the dell under Weathertop. While he was thinking of all these things and trying in vain to bring his memory down to his arriving in Rivendell, there was a long silence, broken only by the soft puffs of Gandalf's pipe, as he blew white smoke-rings out of the window.

'Where's Sam?' Frodo asked at length. 'And are the others all right?'

'Yes, they are all safe and sound,' answered Gandalf. 'Sam was here until I sent him off to get some rest, about half an hour ago.'

'What happened at the Ford?' said Frodo. 'It all seemed so dim, somehow; and it still does.'

'Yes, it would. You were beginning to fade,' answered Gandalf. 'The wound was overcoming you at last. A few more hours and you would have been beyond our aid. But you have some strength in you, my dear hobbit! As you showed in the Barrow. That was touch and go: perhaps the most dangerous moment of all. I wish you could have held out at Weathertop.'

'You seem to know a great deal already,' said Frodo. 'I have not spoken to the others about the Barrow. At first it was too horrible, and afterwards there were other things to think about. How do you know about it?'

'You have talked long in your sleep, Frodo,' said Gandalf gently, 'and it has not been hard for me to read your mind and memory. Do not worry! Though I said "absurd" just now, I did not mean it. I think well of you – and of the others. It is no small feat to have come so far, and through such dangers, still bearing the Ring.'

'We should never have done it without Strider,' said Frodo. 'But we needed you. I did not know what to do without you.'

'I was delayed,' said Gandalf, 'and that nearly proved our ruin. And yet I am not sure: it may have been better so.'

'I wish you would tell me what happened!'

'All in good time! You are not supposed to talk or worry about anything today, by Elrond's orders.'

'But talking would stop me thinking and wondering, which are quite as tiring,' said Frodo. 'I am wide awake now, and I remember so many things that want explaining. Why were you delayed? You ought to tell me that at least.'

'You will soon hear all you wish to know,' said Gandalf. 'We shall have a Council, as soon as you are well enough. At the moment I will only say that I was held captive.'

'You?' cried Frodo.

'Yes, I, Gandalf the Grey,' said the wizard solemnly. 'There are many powers in the world, for good or for evil. Some are greater than I am. Against some I have not yet been measured. But my time is coming. The Morgul-lord and his Black Riders have come forth. War is preparing!'

'Then you knew of the Riders already – before I met them?'

'Yes, I knew of them. Indeed I spoke of them once to you; for the Black Riders are the Ringwraiths, the Nine Servants of the Lord of the Rings. But I did not know that they had arisen again or I should have fled with you at once. I heard news of them only after I left you in June; but that story must wait. For the moment we have been saved from disaster, by Aragorn.'

'Yes,' said Frodo, 'it was Strider that saved us. Yet I was afraid of him at first. Sam never quite trusted him, I think, not at any rate until we met Glorfindel.'

Gandalf smiled. 'I have heard all about Sam,' he said. 'He has no more doubts now.'

'I am glad,' said Frodo. 'For I have become very fond of Strider. Well, *fond* is not the right word. I mean he is dear to me; though he is strange, and grim at times. In fact, he reminds me often of you. I didn't know that any of the Big People were like that. I thought, well, that they were just big, and rather stupid: kind and stupid like Butterbur; or stupid and wicked like Bill Ferny. But then we don't know much about Men in the Shire, except perhaps the Breelanders.'

'You don't know much even about them, if you think old Barliman is stupid,' said Gandalf. 'He is wise enough on his own ground. He thinks less than he talks, and slower; yet he can see through a brick wall in time (as they say in Bree). But there are few left in Middle-earth like Aragorn son of Arathorn. The race of the Kings from over the Sea is nearly at an end. It may be that this War of the Ring will be their last adventure.'

'Do you really mean that Strider is one of the people of the old Kings?' said Frodo in wonder. 'I thought they had all vanished long ago. I thought he was only a Ranger.'

'Only a Ranger!' cried Gandalf. 'My dear Frodo, that is just what the Rangers are: the last remnant in the North of the great people, the Men of the West. They have helped me before; and I shall need their help in the days to come; for we have reached Rivendell, but the Ring is not yet at rest.'

'I suppose not,' said Frodo. 'But so far my only thought has been to get here; and I hope I shan't have to go any further. It is very pleasant just to rest. I have had a month of exile and adventure, and I find that has been as much as I want.'

He fell silent and shut his eyes. After a while he spoke again. 'I have been reckoning,' he said, 'and I can't bring the total up to October the twenty-fourth. It ought to be the twenty-first. We must have reached the Ford by the twentieth.'

'You have talked and reckoned more than is good for you,' said Gandalf. 'How do the side and shoulder feel now?'

'I don't know,' Frodo answered. 'They don't feel at all: which is an improvement, but' – he made an effort – 'I can move my arm again a little. Yes, it is coming back to life. It is not cold,' he added, touching his left hand with his right.

'Good!' said Gandalf. 'It is mending fast. You will soon be sound again. Elrond has cured you: he has tended you for days, ever since you were brought in.'

'Days?' said Frodo.

'Well, four nights and three days, to be exact. The Elves brought you from the Ford on the night of the twentieth, and that is where you lost count. We have been terribly anxious, and Sam has hardly left your side, day or night, except to run messages. Elrond is a master of healing, but the weapons of our Enemy are deadly. To tell you the truth, I had very little hope; for I suspected that there was some fragment of the blade still in the closed wound. But it could not be found until last night. Then Elrond removed a splinter. It was deeply buried, and it was working inwards.'

Frodo shuddered, remembering the cruel knife with

notched blade that had vanished in Strider's hands. 'Don't be alarmed!' said Gandalf. 'It is gone now. It has been melted. And it seems that Hobbits fade very reluctantly. I have known strong warriors of the Big People who would quickly have been overcome by that splinter, which you bore for seventeen days.'

'What would they have done to me?' asked Frodo. 'What were the Riders trying to do?'

'They tried to pierce your heart with a Morgul-knife which remains in the wound. If they had succeeded, you would have become like they are, only weaker and under their command. You would have become a wraith under the dominion of the Dark Lord; and he would have tormented you for trying to keep his Ring, if any greater torment were possible than being robbed of it and seeing it on his hand.'

'Thank goodness I did not realize the horrible danger!' said Frodo faintly. 'I was mortally afraid, of course; but if I had known more, I should not have dared even to move. It is a marvel that I escaped!'

'Yes, fortune or fate have helped you,' said Gandalf, 'not to mention courage. For your heart was not touched, and only your shoulder was pierced; and that was because you resisted to the last. But it was a terribly narrow shave, so to speak. You were in gravest peril while you wore the Ring, for then you were half in the wraith-world yourself, and they might have seized you. You could see them, and they could see you.'

'I know,' said Frodo. 'They were terrible to behold! But why could we all see their horses?'

'Because they are real horses; just as the black robes are real robes that they wear to give shape to their nothingness when they have dealings with the living.'

'Then why do these black horses endure such riders? All other animals are terrified when they draw near, even the elf-horse of Glorfindel. The dogs howl and the geese scream at them.'

'Because these horses are born and bred to the service of

the Dark Lord in Mordor. Not all his servants and chattels
are wraiths! There are orcs and trolls, there are wargs and
werewolves; and there have been and still are many Men,
warriors and kings, that walk alive under the Sun, and yet
are under his sway. And their number is growing daily.'

'What about Rivendell and the Elves? Is Rivendell safe?'

'Yes, at present, until all else is conquered. The Elves may
fear the Dark Lord, and they may fly before him, but never
again will they listen to him or serve him. And here in Rivendell there live still some of his chief foes: the Elven-wise,
lords of the Eldar from beyond the furthest seas. They do
not fear the Ringwraiths, for those who have dwelt in the
Blessed Realm live at once in both worlds, and against both
the Seen and the Unseen they have great power.'

'I thought that I saw a white figure that shone and did not
grow dim like the others. Was that Glorfindel then?'

'Yes, you saw him for a moment as he is upon the other
side: one of the mighty of the Firstborn. He is an Elf-lord of
a house of princes. Indeed there is a power in Rivendell to
withstand the might of Mordor, for a while: and elsewhere
other powers still dwell. There is power, too, of another kind
in the Shire. But all such places will soon become islands
under siege, if things go on as they are going. The Dark Lord
is putting forth all his strength.

'Still,' he said, standing suddenly up and sticking out his
chin, while his beard went stiff and straight like bristling wire,
'we must keep up our courage. You will soon be well, if I
do not talk you to death. You are in Rivendell, and you need
not worry about anything for the present.'

'I haven't any courage to keep up,' said Frodo, 'but I am
not worried at the moment. Just give me news of my friends,
and tell me the end of the affair at the Ford, as I keep on
asking, and I shall be content for the present. After that I
shall have another sleep, I think; but I shan't be able to close
my eyes until you have finished the story for me.'

Gandalf moved his chair to the bedside, and took a good
look at Frodo. The colour had come back to his face, and

his eyes were clear, and fully awake and aware. He was smiling, and there seemed to be little wrong with him. But to the
wizard's eye there was a faint change, just a hint as it were
of transparency, about him, and especially about the left hand
that lay outside upon the coverlet.

'Still that must be expected,' said Gandalf to himself. 'He
is not half through yet, and to what he will come in the end
not even Elrond can foretell. Not to evil, I think. He may
become like a glass filled with a clear light for eyes to see
that can.'

'You look splendid,' he said aloud. 'I will risk a brief tale
without consulting Elrond. But quite brief, mind you, and
then you must sleep again. This is what happened, as far as
I can gather. The Riders made straight for you, as soon as
you fled. They did not need the guidance of their horses any
longer: you had become visible to them, being already on the
threshold of their world. And also the Ring drew them. Your
friends sprang aside, off the road, or they would have been
ridden down. They knew that nothing could save you, if the
white horse could not. The Riders were too swift to overtake,
and too many to oppose. On foot even Glorfindel and Aragorn together could not withstand all the Nine at once.

'When the Ringwraiths swept by, your friends ran up
behind. Close to the Ford there is a small hollow beside the
road masked by a few stunted trees. There they hastily
kindled fire; for Glorfindel knew that a flood would come
down, if the Riders tried to cross, and then he would have
to deal with any that were left on his side of the river. The
moment the flood appeared, he rushed out, followed by Aragorn and the others with flaming brands. Caught between
fire and water, and seeing an Elf-lord revealed in his wrath,
they were dismayed, and their horses were stricken with madness. Three were carried away by the first assault of the flood;
the others were now hurled into the water by their horses
and overwhelmed.'

'And is that the end of the Black Riders?' asked Frodo.

'No,' said Gandalf. 'Their horses must have perished, and

without them they are crippled. But the Ringwraiths themselves cannot be so easily destroyed. However, there is nothing more to fear from them at present. Your friends crossed
after the flood had passed and they found you lying on your
face at the top of the bank, with a broken sword under you.
The horse was standing guard beside you. You were pale
and cold, and they feared that you were dead, or worse.
Elrond's folk met them, carrying you slowly towards Rivendell.'

'Who made the flood?' asked Frodo.

'Elrond commanded it,' answered Gandalf. 'The river of
this valley is under his power, and it will rise in anger when
he has great need to bar the Ford. As soon as the captain of
the Ringwraiths rode into the water the flood was released.
If I may say so, I added a few touches of my own: you may
not have noticed, but some of the waves took the form of
great white horses with shining white riders; and there were
many rolling and grinding boulders. For a moment I was
afraid that we had let loose too fierce a wrath, and the flood
would get out of hand and wash you all away. There is great
vigour in the waters that come down from the snows of the
Misty Mountains.'

'Yes, it all comes back to me now,' said Frodo: 'the tremen-
dous roaring. I thought I was drowning, with my friends and
enemies and all. But now we are safe!'

Gandalf looked quickly at Frodo, but he had shut his
eyes. 'Yes, you are all safe for the present. Soon there
will be feasting and merrymaking to celebrate the victory at
the Ford of Bruinen, and you will all be there in places of
honour.'

'Splendid!' said Frodo. 'It is wonderful that Elrond, and
Glorfindel and such great lords, not to mention Strider,
should take so much trouble and show me so much kindness.'

'Well, there are many reasons why they should,' said Gandalf, smiling. 'I am one good reason. The Ring is another:
you are the Ring-bearer. And you are the heir of Bilbo, the
Ring-finder.'

'Dear Bilbo!' said Frodo sleepily. 'I wonder where he is. I wish he was here and could hear all about it. It would have made him laugh. The cow jumped over the Moon! And the poor old troll!' With that he fell fast asleep.

Frodo was now safe in the Last Homely House east of the Sea. That house was, as Bilbo had long ago reported, 'a perfect house, whether you like food or sleep or story-telling or singing, or just sitting and thinking best, or a pleasant mixture of them all'. Merely to be there was a cure for weariness, fear, and sadness.

As the evening drew on, Frodo woke up again, and he found that he no longer felt in need of rest or sleep, but had a mind for food and drink, and probably for singing and story-telling afterwards. He got out of bed and discovered that his arm was already nearly as useful again as it ever had been. He found laid ready clean garments of green cloth that fitted him excellently. Looking in a mirror he was startled to see a much thinner reflection of himself than he remembered: it looked remarkably like the young nephew of Bilbo who used to go tramping with his uncle in the Shire; but the eyes looked out at him thoughtfully.

'Yes, you have seen a thing or two since you last peeped out of a looking-glass,' he said to his reflection. 'But now for a merry meeting!' He stretched out his arms and whistled a tune.

At that moment there was a knock on the door, and Sam came in. He ran to Frodo and took his left hand, awkwardly and shyly. He stroked it gently and then he blushed and turned hastily away.

'Hullo, Sam!' said Frodo.

'It's warm!' said Sam. 'Meaning your hand, Mr. Frodo. It has felt so cold through the long nights. But glory and trumpets!' he cried, turning round again with shining eyes and dancing on the floor. 'It's fine to see you up and yourself again, sir! Gandalf asked me to come and see if you were ready to come down, and I thought he was joking.'

'I am ready,' said Frodo. 'Let's go and look for the rest of the party!'

'I can take you to them, sir,' said Sam. 'It's a big house this, and very peculiar. Always a bit more to discover, and no knowing what you'll find round a corner. And Elves, sir! Elves here, and Elves there! Some like kings, terrible and splendid; and some as merry as children. And the music and the singing – not that I have had the time or the heart for much listening since we got here. But I'm getting to know some of the ways of the place.'

'I know what you have been doing, Sam,' said Frodo, taking his arm. 'But you shall be merry tonight, and listen to your heart's content. Come on, guide me round the corners!'

Sam led him along several passages and down many steps and out into a high garden above the steep bank of the river. He found his friends sitting in a porch on the side of the house looking east. Shadows had fallen in the valley below, but there was still a light on the faces of the mountains far above. The air was warm. The sound of running and falling water was loud, and the evening was filled with a faint scent of trees and flowers, as if summer still lingered in Elrond's gardens.

'Hurray!' cried Pippin, springing up. 'Here is our noble cousin! Make way for Frodo, Lord of the Ring!'

'Hush!' said Gandalf from the shadows at the back of the porch. 'Evil things do not come into this valley; but all the same we should not name them. The Lord of the Ring is not Frodo, but the master of the Dark Tower of Mordor, whose power is again stretching out over the world! We are sitting in a fortress. Outside it is getting dark.'

'Gandalf has been saying many cheerful things like that,' said Pippin. 'He thinks I need keeping in order. But it seems impossible, somehow, to feel gloomy or depressed in this place. I feel I could sing, if I knew the right song for the occasion.'

'I feel like singing myself,' laughed Frodo. 'Though at the moment I feel more like eating and drinking!'

'That will soon be cured,' said Pippin. 'You have shown your usual cunning in getting up just in time for a meal.'

'More than a meal! A feast!' said Merry. 'As soon as Gandalf reported that you were recovered, the preparations began.' He had hardly finished speaking when they were summoned to the hall by the ringing of many bells.

The hall of Elrond's house was filled with folk: Elves for the most part, though there were a few guests of other sorts. Elrond, as was his custom, sat in a great chair at the end of the long table upon the dais; and next to him on the one side sat Glorfindel, on the other side sat Gandalf.

Frodo looked at them in wonder, for he had never before seen Elrond, of whom so many tales spoke; and as they sat upon his right hand and his left, Glorfindel, and even Gandalf, whom he thought he knew so well, were revealed as lords of dignity and power.

Gandalf was shorter in stature than the other two; but his long white hair, his sweeping silver beard, and his broad shoulders, made him look like some wise king of ancient legend. In his aged face under great snowy brows his dark eyes were set like coals that could leap suddenly into fire.

Glorfindel was tall and straight; his hair was of shining gold, his face fair and young and fearless and full of joy; his eyes were bright and keen, and his voice like music; on his brow sat wisdom, and in his hand was strength.

The face of Elrond was ageless, neither old nor young, though in it was written the memory of many things both glad and sorrowful. His hair was dark as the shadows of twilight, and upon it was set a circlet of silver; his eyes were grey as a clear evening, and in them was a light like the light of stars. Venerable he seemed as a king crowned with many winters, and yet hale as a tried warrior in the fulness of his strength. He was the Lord of Rivendell and mighty among both Elves and Men.

In the middle of the table, against the woven cloths upon the wall, there was a chair under a canopy, and there sat a

lady fair to look upon, and so like was she in form of woman-
hood to Elrond that Frodo guessed that she was one of his
close kindred. Young she was and yet not so. The braids of
her dark hair were touched by no frost; her white arms and
clear face were flawless and smooth, and the light of stars
was in her bright eyes, grey as a cloudless night; yet queenly
she looked, and thought and knowledge were in her glance,
as of one who has known many things that the years bring.
Above her brow her head was covered with a cap of silver
lace netted with small gems, glittering white; but her soft grey
raiment had no ornament save a girdle of leaves wrought in
silver.

So it was that Frodo saw her whom few mortals had yet
seen; Arwen, daughter of Elrond, in whom it was said that
the likeness of Lúthien had come on earth again; and she
was called Undómiel, for she was the Evenstar of her people.
Long she had been in the land of her mother's kin, in Lórien
beyond the mountains, and was but lately returned to Rivendell to her father's house. But her brothers, Elladan and
Elrohir, were out upon errantry: for they rode often far afield
with the Rangers of the North, forgetting never their mother's
torment in the dens of the orcs.

Such loveliness in living thing Frodo had never seen before
nor imagined in his mind; and he was both surprised and
abashed to find that he had a seat at Elrond's table among
all these folk so high and fair. Though he had a suitable chair,
and was raised upon several cushions, he felt very small, and
rather out of place; but that feeling quickly passed. The feast
was merry and the food all that his hunger could desire. It
was some time before he looked about him again or even
turned to his neighbours.

He looked first for his friends. Sam had begged to be
allowed to wait on his master, but had been told that for this
time he was a guest of honour. Frodo could see him now,
sitting with Pippin and Merry at the upper end of one of the
side-tables close to the dais. He could see no sign of Strider.

Next to Frodo on his right sat a dwarf of important appearance, richly dressed. His beard, very long and forked, was white, nearly as white as the snow-white cloth of his garments. He wore a silver belt, and round his neck hung a chain of silver and diamonds. Frodo stopped eating to look at him.

'Welcome and well met!' said the dwarf, turning towards him. Then he actually rose from his seat and bowed. 'Glóin at your service,' he said, and bowed still lower.

'Frodo Baggins at your service and your family's,' said Frodo correctly, rising in surprise and scattering his cushions. 'Am I right in guessing that you are *the* Glóin, one of the twelve companions of the great Thorin Oakenshield?'

'Quite right,' answered the dwarf, gathering up the cushions and courteously assisting Frodo back into his seat. 'And I do not ask, for I have already been told that you are the kinsman and adopted heir of our friend Bilbo the renowned. Allow me to congratulate you on your recovery.'

'Thank you very much,' said Frodo.

'You have had some very strange adventures, I hear,' said Glóin. 'I wonder greatly what brings *four* hobbits on so long a journey. Nothing like it has happened since Bilbo came with us. But perhaps I should not inquire too closely, since Elrond and Gandalf do not seem disposed to talk of this?'

'I think we will not speak of it, at least not yet,' said Frodo politely. He guessed that even in Elrond's house the matter of the Ring was not one for casual talk; and in any case he wished to forget his troubles for a time. 'But I am equally curious,' he added, 'to learn what brings so important a dwarf so far from the Lonely Mountain.'

Glóin looked at him. 'If you have not heard, I think we will not speak yet of that either. Master Elrond will summon us all ere long, I believe, and then we shall all hear many things. But there is much else that may be told.'

Throughout the rest of the meal they talked together, but Frodo listened more than he spoke; for the news of the Shire, apart from the Ring, seemed small and far-away and unimportant, while Glóin had much to tell of events in the northern regions of Wilderland. Frodo learned that Grimbeorn the

Old, son of Beorn, was now the lord of many sturdy men, and to their land between the Mountains and Mirkwood neither orc nor wolf dared to go.

'Indeed,' said Glóin, 'if it were not for the Beornings, the passage from Dale to Rivendell would long ago have become impossible. They are valiant men and keep open the High Pass and the Ford of. Carrock. But their tolls are high,' he added with a shake of his head; 'and like Beorn of old they are not over fond of dwarves. Still, they are trusty, and that is much in these days. Nowhere are there any men so friendly to us as the Men of Dale. They are good folk, the Bardings. The grandson of Bard the Bowman rules them, Brand son of Bain son of Bard. He is a strong king, and his realm now reaches far south and east of Esgaroth.'

'And what of your own people?' asked Frodo.

'There is much to tell, good and bad,' said Glóin; 'yet it is mostly good: we have so far been fortunate, though we do not escape the shadow of these times. If you really wish to hear of us, I will tell you tidings gladly. But stop me when you are weary! Dwarves' tongues run on when speaking of their handiwork, they say.'

And with that Glóin embarked on a long account of the doings of the Dwarf-kingdom. He was delighted to have found so polite a listener; for Frodo showed no sign of weariness and made no attempt to change the subject, though actually he soon got rather lost among the strange names of people and places that he had never heard of before. He was interested, however, to hear that Dáin was still King under the Mountain, and was now old (having passed his two hundred and fiftieth year), venerable, and fabulously rich. Of the ten companions who had survived the Battle of Five Armies seven were still with him: Dwalin, Glóin, Dori, Nori, Bifur, Bofur, and Bombur. Bombur was now so fat that he could not move himself from his couch to his chair at table, and it took six young dwarves to lift him.

'And what has become of Balin and Ori and Óin?' asked Frodo.

A shadow passed over Glóin's face. 'We do not know,' he answered. 'It is largely on account of Balin that I have come to ask the advice of those that dwell in Rivendell. But tonight let us speak of merrier things!'

Glóin began then to talk of the works of his people, telling Frodo about their great labours in Dale and under the Mountain. 'We have done well,' he said. 'But in metal-work we cannot rival our fathers, many of whose secrets are lost. We make good armour and keen swords, but we cannot again make mail or blade to match those that were made before the dragon came. Only in mining and building have we surpassed the old days. You should see the waterways of Dale, Frodo, and the fountains, and the pools! You should see the stone-paved roads of many colours! And the halls and cavernous streets under the earth with arches carved like trees; and the terraces and towers upon the Mountain's sides! Then you would see that we have not been idle.'

'I will come and see them, if ever I can,' said Frodo. 'How surprised Bilbo would have been to see all the changes in the Desolation of Smaug!'

Glóin looked at Frodo and smiled. 'You were very fond of Bilbo were you not?' he asked.

'Yes,' answered Frodo. 'I would rather see him than all the towers and palaces in the world.'

At length the feast came to an end. Elrond and Arwen rose and went down the hall, and the company followed them in due order. The doors were thrown open, and they went across a wide passage and through other doors, and came into a further hall. In it were no tables, but a bright fire was burning in a great hearth between the carven pillars upon either side.

Frodo found himself walking with Gandalf. 'This is the Hall of Fire,' said the wizard. 'Here you will hear many songs and tales – if you can keep awake. But except on high days it usually stands empty and quiet, and people come here who wish for peace, and thought. There is always a fire here, all the year round, but there is little other light.'

As Elrond entered and went towards the seat prepared for him, elvish minstrels began to make sweet music. Slowly the hall filled, and Frodo looked with delight upon the many fair faces that were gathered together; the golden firelight played upon them and shimmered in their hair. Suddenly he noticed, not far from the further end of the fire, a small dark figure seated on a stool with his back propped against a pillar. Beside him on the ground was a drinking-cup and some bread. Frodo wondered whether he was ill (if people were ever ill in Rivendell), and had been unable to come to the feast. His head seemed sunk in sleep on his breast, and a fold of his dark cloak was drawn over his face.

Elrond went forward and stood beside the silent figure. 'Awake, little master!' he said, with a smile. Then, turning to Frodo, he beckoned to him. 'Now at last the hour has come that you have wished for, Frodo,' he said. 'Here is a friend that you have long missed.'

The dark figure raised its head and uncovered its face.

'Bilbo!' cried Frodo with sudden recognition, and he sprang forward.

'Hullo, Frodo my lad!' said Bilbo. 'So you have got here at last. I hoped you would manage it. Well, well! So all this feasting is in your honour, I hear. I hope you enjoyed yourself?'

'Why weren't you there?' cried Frodo. 'And why haven't I been allowed to see you before?'

'Because you were asleep. I have seen a good deal of *you*. I have sat by your side with Sam each day. But as for the feast, I don't go in for such things much now. And I had something else to do.'

'What were you doing?'

'Why, sitting and thinking. I do a lot of that nowadays, and this is the best place to do it in, as a rule. Wake up, indeed!' he said, cocking an eye at Elrond. There was a bright twinkle in it and no sign of sleepiness that Frodo could see.

'Wake up! I was not asleep, Master Elrond. If you want to know, you have all come out from your feast too soon, and you have disturbed me – in the middle of making up a song. I was stuck over a line or two, and was thinking about them; but now I don't suppose I shall ever get them right. There will be such a deal of singing that the ideas will be driven clean out of my head. I shall have to get my friend the Dúnadan to help me. Where is he?'

Elrond laughed. 'He shall be found,' he said. 'Then you two shall go into a corner and finish your task, and we will hear it and judge it before we end our merrymaking.' Messengers were sent to find Bilbo's friend, though none knew where he was, or why he had not been present at the feast.

In the meanwhile Frodo and Bilbo sat side by side, and Sam came quickly and placed himself near them. They talked together in soft voices, oblivious of the mirth and music in the hall about them. Bilbo had not much to say of himself. When he had left Hobbiton he had wandered off aimlessly, along the Road or in the country on either side; but somehow he had steered all the time towards Rivendell.

'I got here without much adventure,' he said, 'and after a rest I went on with the dwarves to Dale: my last journey. I shan't travel again. Old Balin had gone away. Then I came back here, and here I have been. I have done this and that. I have written some more of my book. And, of course, I make up a few songs. They sing them occasionally: just to please me, I think; for, of course, they aren't really good enough for Rivendell. And I listen and I think. Time doesn't seem to pass here: it just is. A remarkable place altogether.

'I hear all kinds of news, from over the Mountains, and out of the South, but hardly anything from the Shire. I heard about the Ring, of course. Gandalf has been here often. Not that he has told me a great deal, he has become closer than ever these last few years. The Dúnadan has told me more. Fancy that ring of mine causing such a disturbance! It is a pity that Gandalf did not find out more sooner. I could have brought the thing here myself long ago without so much trouble. I have thought several times of going back to Hobbiton for it; but I am getting old, and they would not let me: Gandalf and Elrond, I mean. They seemed to think that the Enemy was looking high and low for me, and would make mincemeat of me, if he caught me tottering about in the Wild.

'And Gandalf said: "The Ring has passed on, Bilbo. It would do no good to you or to others, if you tried to meddle with it again." Odd sort of remark, just like Gandalf. But he said he was looking after you, so I let things be. I am frightfully glad to see you safe and sound.' He paused and looked at Frodo doubtfully.

'Have you got it here?' he asked in a whisper. 'I can't help feeling curious, you know, after all I've heard. I should very much like just to peep at it again.'

'Yes, I've got it,' answered Frodo, feeling a strange reluctance. 'It looks just the same as ever it did.'

'Well, I should just like to see it for a moment,' said Bilbo.

When he had dressed, Frodo found that while he slept the Ring had been hung about his neck on a new chain, light but strong. Slowly he drew it out. Bilbo put out his hand. But Frodo quickly drew back the Ring. To his distress and amazement he found that he was no longer looking at Bilbo; a shadow seemed to have fallen between them, and through it he found himself eyeing a little wrinkled creature with a hungry face and bony groping hands. He felt a desire to strike him.

The music and singing round them seemed to falter, and a silence fell. Bilbo looked quickly at Frodo's face and passed his hand across his eyes. 'I understand now,' he said. 'Put it away! I am sorry: sorry you have come in for this burden: sorry about everything. Don't adventures ever have an end? I suppose not. Someone else always has to carry on the story. Well, it can't be helped. I wonder if it's any good trying to finish my book? But don't let's worry about it now – let's have some real News! Tell me all about the Shire!'

★   ★   ★

Frodo hid the Ring away, and the shadow passed leaving hardly a shred of memory. The light and music of Rivendell was about him again. Bilbo smiled and laughed happily. Every item of news from the Shire that Frodo could tell – aided and corrected now and again by Sam – was of the greatest interest to him, from the felling of the least tree to the pranks of the smallest child in Hobbiton. They were so deep in the doings of the Four Farthings that they did not notice the arrival of a man clad in dark green cloth. For many minutes he stood looking down at them with a smile.

Suddenly Bilbo looked up. 'Ah, there you are at last, Dúnadan!' he cried.

'Strider!' said Frodo. 'You seem to have a lot of names.'

'Well, *Strider* is one that I haven't heard before, anyway,' said Bilbo. 'What do you call him that for?'

'They call me that in Bree,' said Strider laughing, 'and that is how I was introduced to him.'

'And why do you call him Dúnadan?' asked Frodo.

'*The* Dúnadan,' said Bilbo. 'He is often called that here. But I thought you knew enough Elvish at least to know *dún-adan*: Man of the West, Númenorean. But this is not the time for lessons!' He turned to Strider. 'Where have you been, my friend? Why weren't you at the feast? The Lady Arwen was there.'

Strider looked down at Bilbo gravely. 'I know,' he said. 'But often I must put mirth aside. Elladan and Elrohir have returned out of the Wild unlooked-for, and they had tidings that I wished to hear at once.'

'Well, my dear fellow,' said Bilbo, 'now you've heard the news, can't you spare me a moment? I want your help in something urgent. Elrond says this song of mine is to be finished before the end of the evening, and I am stuck. Let's go off into a corner and polish it up!'

Strider smiled. 'Come then!' he said. 'Let me hear it!'

Frodo was left to himself for a while, for Sam had fallen asleep. He was alone and felt rather forlorn, although all about him the folk of Rivendell were gathered. But those near him were silent, intent upon the music of the voices and the instruments, and they gave no heed to anything else. Frodo began to listen.

At first the beauty of the melodies and of the interwoven words in elven-tongues, even though he understood them little, held him in a spell, as soon as he began to attend to them. Almost it seemed that the words took shape, and visions of far lands and bright things that he had never yet imagined opened out before him; and the firelit hall became like a golden mist above seas of foam that sighed upon the margins of the world. Then the enchantment became more and more dreamlike, until he felt that an endless river of swelling gold and silver was flowing over him, too multitudinous for its pattern to be comprehended; it became part of the throbbing air about him, and it drenched and drowned him. Swiftly he sank under its shining weight into a deep realm of sleep.

There he wandered long in a dream of music that turned into running water, and then suddenly into a voice. It seemed to be the voice of Bilbo chanting verses. Faint at first and then clearer ran the words.

> *Eärendil was a mariner*
> *that tarried in Arvernien;*
> *he built a boat of timber felled*
> *in Nimbrethil to journey in;*
> *her sails he wove of silver fair,*
> *of silver were her lanterns made,*
> *her prow was fashioned like a swan,*
> *and light upon her banners laid.*
>
> *In panoply of ancient kings,*
> *in chainéd rings he armoured him;*
> *his shining shield was scored with runes*
> *to ward all wounds and harm from him;*
> *his bow was made of dragon-horn,*

his arrows shorn of ebony,
of silver was his habergeon,
his scabbard of chalcedony;
his sword of steel was valiant,
of adamant his helmet tall,
an eagle-plume upon his crest,
upon his breast an emerald.

Beneath the Moon and under star
he wandered far from northern strands,
bewildered on enchanted ways
beyond the days of mortal lands.
From gnashing of the Narrow Ice
where shadow lies on frozen hills,
from nether heats and burning waste
he turned in haste, and roving still
on starless waters far astray
at last he came to Night of Naught,
and passed, and never sight he saw
of shining shore nor light he sought.
The winds of wrath came driving him,
and blindly in the foam he fled
from west to east and errandless,
unheralded he homeward sped.

There flying Elwing came to him,
and flame was in the darkness lit;
more bright than light of diamond
the fire upon her carcanet.
The Silmaril she bound on him
and crowned him with the living light
and dauntless then with burning brow
he turned his prow; and in the night
from Otherworld beyond the Sea
there strong and free a storm arose,
a wind of power in Tarmenel;
by paths that seldom mortal goes

his boat it bore with biting breath
as might of death across the grey
and long-forsaken seas distressed:
from east to west he passed away.

Through Evernight he back was borne
on black and roaring waves that ran
o'er leagues unlit and foundered shores
that drowned before the Days began,
until he heard on strands of pearl
where ends the world the music long,
where ever-foaming billows roll
the yellow gold and jewels wan.
He saw the Mountain silent rise
where twilight lies upon the knees
of Valinor, and Eldamar
beheld afar beyond the seas.
A wanderer escaped from night
to haven white he came at last,
to Elvenhome the green and fair
where keen the air, where pale as glass
beneath the Hill of Ilmarin
a-glimmer in a valley sheer
the lamplit towers of Tirion
are mirrored on the Shadowmere.

He tarried there from errantry,
and melodies they taught to him,
and sages old him marvels told,
and harps of gold they brought to him.
They clothed him then in elven-white,
and seven lights before him sent,
as through the Calacirian
to hidden land forlorn he went.
He came unto the timeless halls
where shining fall the countless years,
and endless reigns the Elder King

in Ilmarin on Mountain sheer;
and words unheard were spoken then
of folk of Men and Elven-kin,
beyond the world were visions showed
forbid to those that dwell therein.

A ship then new they built for him
of mithril and of elven-glass
with shining prow; no shaven oar
nor sail she bore on silver mast:
the Silmaril as lantern light
and banner bright with living flame
to gleam thereon by Elbereth
herself was set, who thither came
and wings immortal made for him,
and laid on him undying doom,
to sail the shoreless skies and come
behind the Sun and light of Moon.

From Evereven's lofty hills
where softly silver fountains fall
his wings him bore, a wandering light,
beyond the mighty Mountain Wall.
From World's End then he turned away,
and yearned again to find afar
his home through shadows journeying,
and burning as an island star
on high above the mists he came,
a distant flame before the Sun,
a wonder ere the waking dawn
where grey the Norland waters run.

And over Middle-earth he passed
and heard at last the weeping sore
of women and of elven-maids
in Elder Days, in years of yore.
But on him mighty doom was laid,

> *till Moon should fade, an orbéd star*
> *to pass, and tarry never more*
> *on Hither Shores where mortals are;*
> *for ever still a herald on*
> *an errand that should never rest*
> *to bear his shining lamp afar,*
> *the Flammifer of Westernesse.*

The chanting ceased. Frodo opened his eyes and saw that Bilbo was seated on his stool in a circle of listeners, who were smiling and applauding.

'Now we had better have it again,' said an Elf.

Bilbo got up and bowed. 'I am flattered, Lindir,' he said. 'But it would be too tiring to repeat it all.'

'Not too tiring for you,' the Elves answered laughing. 'You know you are never tired of reciting your own verses. But really we cannot answer your question at one hearing!'

'What!' cried Bilbo. 'You can't tell which parts were mine, and which were the Dúnadan's?'

'It is not easy for us to tell the difference between two mortals,' said the Elf.

'Nonsense, Lindir,' snorted Bilbo. 'If you can't distinguish between a Man and a Hobbit, your judgement is poorer than I imagined. They're as different as peas and apples.'

'Maybe. To sheep other sheep no doubt appear different,' laughed Lindir. 'Or to shepherds. But Mortals have not been our study. We have other business.'

'I won't argue with you,' said Bilbo. 'I am sleepy after so much music and singing. I'll leave you to guess, if you want to.'

He got up and came towards Frodo. 'Well, that's over,' he said in a low voice. 'It went off better than I expected. I don't often get asked for a second hearing. What did you think of it?'

'I am not going to try and guess,' said Frodo smiling.

'You needn't,' said Bilbo. 'As a matter of fact it was all mine. Except that Aragorn insisted on my putting in a green stone. He seemed to think it important. I don't know why. Otherwise he obviously thought the whole thing rather above my head, and he said that if I had the cheek to make verses about Eärendil in the house of Elrond, it was my affair. I suppose he was right.'

'I don't know,' said Frodo. 'It seemed to me to fit somehow, though I can't explain. I was half asleep when you began, and it seemed to follow on from something that I was dreaming about. I didn't understand that it was really you speaking until near the end.'

'It *is* difficult to keep awake here, until you get used to it,' said Bilbo. 'Not that hobbits would ever acquire quite the elvish appetite for music and poetry and tales. They seem to like them as much as food, or more. They will be going on for a long time yet. What do you say to slipping off for some more quiet talk?'

'Can we?' said Frodo.

'Of course. This is merrymaking not business. Come and go as you like, as long as you don't make a noise.'

They got up and withdrew quietly into the shadows, and made for the doors. Sam they left behind, fast asleep still with a smile on his face. In spite of his delight in Bilbo's company Frodo felt a tug of regret as they passed out of the Hall of Fire. Even as they stepped over the threshold a single clear voice rose in song.

> *A Elbereth Gilthoniel,*
> *silivren penna míriel*
> *o menel aglar elenath!*
> *Na-chaered palan-díriel*
> *o galadhremmin ennorath,*
> *Fanuilos, le linnathon*
> *nef aear, si nef aearon!*

Frodo halted for a moment, looking back. Elrond was in his chair and the fire was on his face like summer-light upon

the trees. Near him sat the Lady Arwen. To his surprise
Frodo saw that Aragorn stood beside her; his dark cloak was
thrown back, and he seemed to be clad in elven-mail, and a
star shone on his breast. They spoke together, and then suddenly it seemed to Frodo that Arwen turned towards him,
and the light of her eyes fell on him from afar and pierced
his heart.

He stood still enchanted, while the sweet syllables of the
elvish song fell like clear jewels of blended word and melody.
'It is a song to Elbereth,' said Bilbo. 'They will sing that, and
other songs of the Blessed Realm, many times tonight. Come
on!'

He led Frodo back to his own little room. It opened on to
the gardens and looked south across the ravine of the
Bruinen. There they sat for some while, looking through the
window at the bright stars above the steep-climbing woods,
and talking softly. They spoke no more of the small news of
the Shire far away, nor of the dark shadows and perils that
encompassed them, but of the fair things they had seen in
the world together, of the Elves, of the stars, of trees, and
the gentle fall of the bright year in the woods.

At last there came a knock on the door. 'Begging your
pardon,' said Sam, putting in his head, 'but I was just wondering if you would be wanting anything.'

'And begging yours, Sam Gamgee,' replied Bilbo. 'I guess
you mean that it is time your master went to bed.'

'Well, sir, there is a Council early tomorrow, I hear, and
he only got up today for the first time.'

'Quite right, Sam,' laughed Bilbo. 'You can trot off and
tell Gandalf that he has gone to bed. Good night, Frodo!
Bless me, but it has been good to see you again! There are
no folk like hobbits after all for a real good talk. I am getting
very old, and I began to wonder if I should ever live to see
your chapters of our story. Good night! I'll take a walk, I
think, and look at the stars of Elbereth in the garden. Sleep
well!'

CHAPTER II

THE COUNCIL OF ELROND

Next day Frodo woke early, feeling refreshed and well. He walked along the terraces above the loud-flowing Bruinen and watched the pale, cool sun rise above the far mountains, and shine down, slanting through the thin silver mist; the dew upon the yellow leaves was glimmering, and the woven nets of gossamer twinkled on every bush. Sam walked beside him, saying nothing, but sniffing the air, and looking every now and again with wonder in his eyes at the great heights in the East. The snow was white upon their peaks.

On a seat cut in the stone beside a turn in the path they came upon Gandalf and Bilbo deep in talk. 'Hullo! Good morning!' said Bilbo. 'Feel ready for the great council?'

'I feel ready for anything,' answered Frodo. 'But most of all I should like to go walking today and explore the valley. I should like to get into those pine-woods up there.' He pointed away far up the side of Rivendell to the north.

'You may have a chance later,' said Gandalf. 'But we cannot make any plans yet. There is much to hear and decide today.'

Suddenly as they were talking a single clear bell rang out. 'That is the warning bell for the Council of Elrond,' cried Gandalf. 'Come along now! Both you and Bilbo are wanted.'

Frodo and Bilbo followed the wizard quickly along the winding path back to the house; behind them, uninvited and for the moment forgotten, trotted Sam.

Gandalf led them to the porch where Frodo had found his friends the evening before. The light of the clear autumn morning was now glowing in the valley. The noise of bubbling waters came up from the foaming river-bed. Birds were singing, and a wholesome peace lay on the land. To Frodo his dangerous flight, and the rumours of the darkness growing in the world outside, already seemed only the memories of a troubled dream; but the faces that were turned to meet them as they entered were grave.

Elrond was there, and several others were seated in silence about him. Frodo saw Glorfindel and Glóin; and in a corner alone Strider was sitting, clad in his old travel-worn clothes again. Elrond drew Frodo to a seat by his side, and presented him to the company, saying:

'Here, my friends, is the hobbit, Frodo son of Drogo. Few have ever come hither through greater peril or on an errand more urgent.'

He then pointed out and named those whom Frodo had not met before. There was a younger dwarf at Glóin's side: his son Gimli. Beside Glorfindel there were several other counsellors of Elrond's household, of whom Erestor was the chief; and with him was Galdor, an Elf from the Grey Havens who had come on an errand from Círdan the Shipwright. There was also a strange Elf clad in green and brown, Legolas, a messenger from his father, Thranduil, the King of the Elves of Northern Mirkwood. And seated a little apart was a tall man with a fair and noble face, dark-haired and grey-eyed, proud and stern of glance.

He was cloaked and booted as if for a journey on horseback; and indeed though his garments were rich, and his cloak was lined with fur, they were stained with long travel. He had a collar of silver in which a single white stone was set; his locks were shorn about his shoulders. On a baldric he wore a great horn tipped with silver that now was laid upon his knees. He gazed at Frodo and Bilbo with sudden wonder.

'Here,' said Elrond, turning to Gandalf, 'is Boromir, a man from the South. He arrived in the grey morning, and seeks for counsel. I have bidden him to be present, for here his questions will be answered.'

*   *   *

Not all that was spoken and debated in the Council need now be told. Much was said of events in the world outside, especially in the South, and in the wide lands east of the Mountains. Of these things Frodo had already heard many rumours; but the tale of Glóin was new to him, and when the dwarf spoke he listened attentively. It appeared that amid the splendour of their works of hand the hearts of the Dwarves of the Lonely Mountain were troubled.

'It is now many years ago,' said Glóin, 'that a shadow of disquiet fell upon our people. Whence it came we did not at first perceive. Words began to be whispered in secret: it was said that we were hemmed in a narrow place, and that greater wealth and splendour would be found in a wider world. Some spoke of Moria: the mighty works of our fathers that are called in our own tongue Khazad-dûm; and they declared that now at last we had the power and numbers to return.'

Glóin sighed. 'Moria! Moria! Wonder of the Northern world! Too deep we delved there, and woke the nameless fear. Long have its vast mansions lain empty since the children of Durin fled. But now we spoke of it again with longing, and yet with dread; for no dwarf has dared to pass the doors of Khazad-dûm for many lives of kings, save Thrór only, and he perished. At last, however, Balin listened to the whispers, and resolved to go; and though Dáin did not give leave willingly, he took with him Ori and Óin and many of our folk, and they went away south.

'That was nigh on thirty years ago. For a while we had news and it seemed good: messages reported that Moria had been entered and a great work begun there. Then there was silence, and no word has ever come from Moria since.

'Then about a year ago a messenger came to Dáin, but not from Moria – from Mordor: a horseman in the night, who called Dáin to his gate. The Lord Sauron the Great, so he said, wished for our friendship. Rings he would give for it, such as he gave of old. And he asked urgently concerning *hobbits*, of what kind they were, and where they dwelt. "For

Sauron knows," said he, "that one of these was known to you on a time."

'At this we were greatly troubled, and we gave no answer. And then his fell voice was lowered, and he would have sweetened it if he could. "As a small token only of your friendship Sauron asks this," he said: "that you should find this thief," such was his word, "and get from him, willing or no, a little ring, the least of rings, that once he stole. It is but a trifle that Sauron fancies, and an earnest of your good will. Find it, and three rings that the Dwarf-sires possessed of old shall be returned to you, and the realm of Moria shall be yours for ever. Find only news of the thief, whether he still lives and where, and you shall have great reward and lasting friendship from the Lord. Refuse, and things will not seem so well. Do you refuse?"

'At that his breath came like the hiss of snakes, and all who stood by shuddered, but Dáin said: "I say neither yea nor nay. I must consider this message and what it means under its fair cloak."

' "Consider well, but not too long," said he.

' "The time of my thought is my own to spend," answered Dáin.

' "For the present," said he, and rode into the darkness.

'Heavy have the hearts of our chieftains been since that night. We needed not the fell voice of the messenger to warn us that his words held both menace and deceit; for we knew already that the power that has re-entered Mordor has not changed, and ever it betrayed us of old. Twice the messenger has returned, and has gone unanswered. The third and last time, so he says, is soon to come, before the ending of the year.

'And so I have been sent at last by Dáin to warn Bilbo that he is sought by the Enemy, and to learn, if may be, why he desires this ring, this least of rings. Also we crave the advice of Elrond. For the Shadow grows and draws nearer. We discover that messengers have come also to King Brand in Dale, and that he is afraid. We fear that he may yield.

Already war is gathering on his eastern borders. If we make no answer, the Enemy may move Men of his rule to assail King Brand, and Dáin also.'

'You have done well to come,' said Elrond. 'You will hear today all that you need in order to understand the purposes of the Enemy. There is naught that you can do, other than to resist, with hope or without it. But you do not stand alone. You will learn that your trouble is but part of the trouble of all the western world. The Ring! What shall we do with the Ring, the least of rings, the trifle that Sauron fancies? That is the doom that we must deem.

'That is the purpose for which you are called hither. Called, I say, though I have not called you to me, strangers from distant lands. You have come and are here met, in this very nick of time, by chance as it may seem. Yet it is not so. Believe rather that it is so ordered that we, who sit here, and none others, must now find counsel for the peril of the world.

'Now, therefore, things shall be openly spoken that have been hidden from all but a few until this day. And first, so that all may understand what is the peril, the Tale of the Ring shall be told from the beginning even to this present. And I will begin that tale, though others shall end it.'

Then all listened while Elrond in his clear voice spoke of Sauron and the Rings of Power, and their forging in the Second Age of the world long ago. A part of his tale was known to some there, but the full tale to none, and many eyes were turned to Elrond in fear and wonder as he told of the Elven-smiths of Eregion and their friendship with Moria, and their eagerness for knowledge, by which Sauron ensnared them. For in that time he was not yet evil to behold, and they received his aid and grew mighty in craft, whereas he learned all their secrets, and betrayed them, and forged secretly in the Mountain of Fire the One Ring to be their master. But Celebrimbor was aware of him, and hid the Three which he had made; and there was war, and the land was laid waste, and the gate of Moria was shut.

Then through all the years that followed he traced the
Ring; but since that history is elsewhere recounted, even as
Elrond himself set it down in his books of lore, it is not here
recalled. For it is a long tale, full of deeds great and terrible,
and briefly though Elrond spoke, the sun rode up the sky,
and the morning was passing ere he ceased.

Of Númenor he spoke, its glory and its fall, and the return
of the Kings of Men to Middle-earth out of the deeps of the
Sea, borne upon the wings of storm. Then Elendil the Tall
and his mighty sons, Isildur and Anárion, became great lords;
and the North-realm they made in Arnor, and the South-
realm in Gondor above the mouths of Anduin. But Sauron
of Mordor assailed them, and they made the Last Alliance
of Elves and Men, and the hosts of Gil-galad and Elendil
were mustered in Arnor.

Thereupon Elrond paused a while and sighed. 'I remember
well the splendour of their banners,' he said. 'It recalled to
me the glory of the Elder Days and the hosts of Beleriand,
so many great princes and captains were assembled. And yet
not so many, nor so fair, as when Thangorodrim was broken,
and the Elves deemed that evil was ended for ever, and it
was not so.'

'You remember?' said Frodo, speaking his thought aloud
in his astonishment. 'But I thought,' he stammered as Elrond
turned towards him, 'I thought that the fall of Gil-galad was
a long age ago.'

'So it was indeed,' answered Elrond gravely. 'But my
memory reaches back even to the Elder Days. Eärendil was
my sire, who was born in Gondolin before its fall; and my
mother was Elwing, daughter of Dior, son of Lúthien of
Doriath. I have seen three ages in the West of the world, and
many defeats, and many fruitless victories.

'I was the herald of Gil-galad and marched with his host.
I was at the Battle of Dagorlad before the Black Gate of
Mordor, where we had the mastery: for the Spear of Gil-galad
and the Sword of Elendil, Aiglos and Narsil, none could
withstand. I beheld the last combat on the slopes of Orodruin,

where Gil-galad died, and Elendil fell, and Narsil broke beneath him; but Sauron himself was overthrown, and Isildur cut the Ring from his hand with the hilt-shard of his father's sword, and took it for his own.'

At this the stranger, Boromir, broke in. 'So that is what became of the Ring!' he cried. 'If ever such a tale was told in the South, it has long been forgotten. I have heard of the Great Ring of him that we do not name; but we believed that it perished from the world in the ruin of his first realm. Isildur took it! That is tidings indeed.'

'Alas! yes,' said Elrond. 'Isildur took it, as should not have been. It should have been cast then into Orodruin's fire nigh at hand where it was made. But few marked what Isildur did. He alone stood by his father in that last mortal contest; and by Gil-galad only Círdan stood, and I. But Isildur would not listen to our counsel.

'"This I will have as weregild for my father, and my brother," he said; and therefore whether we would or no, he took it to treasure it. But soon he was betrayed by it to his death; and so it is named in the North Isildur's Bane. Yet death maybe was better than what else might have befallen him.

'Only to the North did these tidings come, and only to a few. Small wonder it is that you have not heard them, Boromir. From the ruin of the Gladden Fields, where Isildur perished, three men only came ever back over the mountains after long wandering. One of these was Ohtar, the esquire of Isildur, who bore the shards of the sword of Elendil; and he brought them to Valandil, the heir of Isildur, who being but a child had remained here in Rivendell. But Narsil was broken and its light extinguished, and it has not yet been forged again.

'Fruitless did I call the victory of the Last Alliance? Not wholly so, yet it did not achieve its end. Sauron was diminished, but not destroyed. His Ring was lost but not unmade. The Dark Tower was broken, but its foundations were not removed; for they were made with the power of the Ring, and while it remains they will endure. Many Elves and many mighty Men, and many of their friends, had perished in the war. Anárion was slain, and Isildur was slain; and Gil-galad and Elendil were no more. Never again shall there be any such league of Elves and Men; for Men multiply and the Firstborn decrease, and the two kindreds are estranged. And ever since that day the race of Númenor has decayed, and the span of their years has lessened.

'In the North after the war and the slaughter of the Gladden Fields the Men of Westernesse were diminished, and their city of Annúminas beside Lake Evendim fell into ruin; and the heirs of Valandil removed and dwelt at Fornost on the high North Downs, and that now too is desolate. Men call it Deadmen's Dike, and they fear to tread there. For the folk of Arnor dwindled, and their foes devoured them, and their lordship passed, leaving only green mounds in the grassy hills.

'In the South the realm of Gondor long endured; and for a while its splendour grew, recalling somewhat of the might of Númenor, ere it fell. High towers that people built, and strong places, and havens of many ships; and the winged crown of the Kings of Men was held in awe by folk of many tongues. Their chief city was Osgiliath, Citadel of the Stars, through the midst of which the River flowed. And Minas Ithil they built, Tower of the Rising Moon, eastward upon a shoulder of the Mountains of Shadow; and westward at the feet of the White Mountains Minas Anor they made, Tower of the Setting Sun. There in the courts of the King grew a white tree, from the seed of that tree which Isildur brought over the deep waters, and the seed of that tree before came from Eressëa, and before that out of the Uttermost West in the Day before days when the world was young.

'But in the wearing of the swift years of Middle-earth the line of Meneldil son of Anárion failed, and the Tree withered, and the blood of the Númenoreans became mingled with that of lesser men. Then the watch upon the walls of Mordor slept, and dark things crept back to Gorgoroth. And on a time evil things came forth, and they took Minas Ithil and abode in it, and they made it into a place of dread; and it is called Minas Morgul, the Tower of Sorcery. Then Minas Anor was named anew Minas Tirith, the Tower of Guard; and these two cities were ever at war, but Osgiliath which lay between was deserted and in its ruins shadows walked.

'So it has been for many lives of men. But the Lords of Minas Tirith still fight on, defying our enemies, keeping the passage of the River from Argonath to the Sea. And now that part of the tale that I shall tell is drawn to its close. For in the days of Isildur the Ruling Ring passed out of all knowledge, and the Three were released from its dominion. But now in this latter day they are in peril once more, for to our sorrow the One has been found. Others shall speak of its finding, for in that I played small part.'

He ceased, but at once Boromir stood up, tall and proud, before them. 'Give me leave, Master Elrond,' said he, 'first to say more of Gondor, for verily from the land of Gondor I am come. And it would be well for all to know what passes there. For few, I deem, know of our deeds, and therefore guess little of their peril, if we should fail at last.

'Believe not that in the land of Gondor the blood of Númenor is spent, nor all its pride and dignity forgotten. By our valour the wild folk of the East are still restrained, and the terror of Morgul kept at bay; and thus alone are peace and freedom maintained in the lands behind us, bulwark of the West. But if the passages of the River should be won, what then?

'Yet that hour, maybe, is not now far away. The Nameless Enemy has arisen again. Smoke rises once more from Orodruin that we call Mount Doom. The power of the Black Land grows and we are hard beset. When the Enemy returned our folk were driven from Ithilien, our fair domain east of the River, though we kept a foothold there and strength of arms. But this very year, in the days of June, sudden war came upon us out of Mordor, and we were swept away. We were outnumbered, for Mordor has allied itself with the Easterlings and the cruel Haradrim; but it was not by numbers that we were defeated. A power was there that we have not felt before.

'Some said that it could be seen, like a great black horseman, a dark shadow under the moon. Wherever he came a madness filled our foes, but fear fell on our boldest, so that horse and man gave way and fled. Only a remnant of our eastern force came back, destroying the last bridge that still stood amid the ruins of Osgiliath.

'I was in the company that held the bridge, until it was cast down behind us. Four only were saved by swimming: my brother and myself and two others. But still we fight on, holding all the west shores of Anduin; and those who shelter behind us give us praise, if ever they hear our name: much praise but little help. Only from Rohan now will any men ride to us when we call.

'In this evil hour I have come on an errand over many dangerous leagues to Elrond: a hundred and ten days I have journeyed all alone. But I do not seek allies in war. The might of Elrond is in wisdom not in weapons, it is said. I come to ask for counsel and the unravelling of hard words. For on the eve of the sudden assault a dream came to my brother in a troubled sleep; and afterwards a like dream came oft to him again, and once to me.

'In that dream I thought the eastern sky grew dark and there was a growing thunder, but in the West a pale light lingered, and out of it I heard a voice, remote but clear, crying:

> Seek for the Sword that was broken:
> > In Imladris it dwells;
> There shall be counsels taken
> > Stronger than Morgul-spells.
> There shall be shown a token
> > That Doom is near at hand,
> For Isildur's Bane shall waken,
> > And the Halfling forth shall stand.

Of these words we could understand little, and we spoke to our father, Denethor, Lord of Minas Tirith, wise in the lore of Gondor. This only would he say, that Imladris was of old the name among the Elves of a far northern dale, where Elrond the Halfelven dwelt, greatest of lore-masters. Therefore my brother, seeing how desperate was our need, was eager to heed the dream and seek for Imladris; but since the way was full of doubt and danger, I took the journey upon myself. Loth was my father to give me leave, and long have I wandered by roads forgotten, seeking the house of Elrond, of which many had heard, but few knew where it lay.'

'And here in the house of Elrond more shall be made clear to you,' said Aragorn, standing up. He cast his sword upon the table that stood before Elrond, and the blade was in two pieces. 'Here is the Sword that was Broken!' he said.

'And who are you, and what have you to do with Minas Tirith?' asked Boromir, looking in wonder at the lean face of the Ranger and his weather-stained cloak.

'He is Aragorn son of Arathorn,' said Elrond; 'and he is descended through many fathers from Isildur Elendil's son of Minas Ithil. He is the Chief of the Dúnedain in the North, and few are now left of that folk.'

'Then it belongs to you, and not to me at all!' cried Frodo in amazement, springing to his feet, as if he expected the Ring to be demanded at once.

'It does not belong to either of us,' said Aragorn; 'but it has been ordained that you should hold it for a while.'

'Bring out the Ring, Frodo!' said Gandalf solemnly. 'The time has come. Hold it up, and then Boromir will understand the remainder of his riddle.'

There was a hush, and all turned their eyes on Frodo. He was shaken by a sudden shame and fear; and he felt a great reluctance to reveal the Ring, and a loathing of its touch. He wished he was far away. The Ring gleamed and flickered as he held it up before them in his trembling hand.

'Behold Isildur's Bane!' said Elrond.

Boromir's eyes glinted as he gazed at the golden thing. 'The Halfling!' he muttered. 'Is then the doom of Minas Tirith come at last? But why then should we seek a broken sword?'

'The words were not *the doom of Minas Tirith*,' said Aragorn. 'But doom and great deeds are indeed at hand. For the Sword that was Broken is the Sword of Elendil that broke beneath him when he fell. It has been treasured by his heirs when all other heirlooms were lost; for it was spoken of old among us that it should be made again when the Ring, Isildur's Bane, was found. Now you have seen the sword that you have sought, what would you ask? Do you wish for the House of Elendil to return to the Land of Gondor?'

'I was not sent to beg any boon, but to seek only the meaning of a riddle,' answered Boromir proudly. 'Yet we are hard pressed, and the Sword of Elendil would be a help beyond our hope – if such a thing could indeed return out of the shadows of the past.' He looked again at Aragorn, and doubt was in his eyes.

Frodo felt Bilbo stir impatiently at his side. Evidently he was annoyed on his friend's behalf. Standing suddenly up he burst out:

> *All that is gold does not glitter,*
> *Not all those who wander are lost;*
> *The old that is strong does not wither,*
> *Deep roots are not reached by the frost.*
> *From the ashes a fire shall be woken,*
> *A light from the shadows shall spring;*
> *Renewed shall be blade that was broken:*
> *The crownless again shall be king.*

'Not very good perhaps, but to the point – if you need more beyond the word of Elrond. If that was worth a journey of

a hundred and ten days to hear, you had best listen to it.'
He sat down with a snort.

'I made that up myself,' he whispered to Frodo, 'for the
Dúnadan, a long time ago when he first told me about himself. I almost wish that my adventures were not over, and
that I could go with him when his day comes.'

Aragorn smiled at him; then he turned to Boromir again.
'For my part I forgive your doubt,' he said. 'Little do I
resemble the figures of Elendil and Isildur as they stand
carven in their majesty in the halls of Denethor. I am but the
heir of Isildur, not Isildur himself. I have had a hard life and
a long; and the leagues that lie between here and Gondor are
a small part in the count of my journeys. I have crossed many
mountains and many rivers, and trodden many plains, even
into the far countries of Rhûn and Harad where the stars are
strange.

'But my home, such as I have, is in the North. For here
the heirs of Valandil have ever dwelt in long line unbroken
from father unto son for many generations. Our days have
darkened, and we have dwindled; but ever the Sword has
passed to a new keeper. And this I will say to you, Boromir,
ere I end. Lonely men are we, Rangers of the wild, hunters
– but hunters ever of the servants of the Enemy; for they are
found in many places, not in Mordor only.

'If Gondor, Boromir, has been a stalwart tower, we have
played another part. Many evil things there are that your
strong walls and bright swords do not stay. You know little
of the lands beyond your bounds. Peace and freedom, do
you say? The North would have known them little but for
us. Fear would have destroyed them. But when dark things
come from the houseless hills, or creep from sunless woods,
they fly from us. What roads would any dare to tread, what
safety would there be in quiet lands, or in the homes of simple
men at night, if the Dúnedain were asleep, or were all gone
into the grave?

'And yet less thanks have we than you. Travellers scowl
at us, and countrymen give us scornful names. "Strider" I

am to one fat man who lives within a day's march of foes that would freeze his heart, or lay his little town in ruin, if he were not guarded ceaselessly. Yet we would not have it otherwise. If simple folk are free from care and fear, simple they will be, and we must be secret to keep them so. That has been the task of my kindred, while the years have lengthened and the grass has grown.

'But now the world is changing once again. A new hour comes. Isildur's Bane is found. Battle is at hand. The Sword shall be reforged. I will come to Minas Tirith.'

'Isildur's Bane is found, you say,' said Boromir. 'I have seen a bright ring in the Halfling's hand; but Isildur perished ere this age of the world began, they say. How do the Wise know that this ring is his? And how has it passed down the years, until it is brought hither by so strange a messenger?'

'That shall be told,' said Elrond.

'But not yet, I beg, Master!' said Bilbo. 'Already the Sun is climbing to noon, and I feel the need of something to strengthen me.'

'I had not named you,' said Elrond smiling. 'But I do so now. Come! Tell us your tale. And if you have not yet cast your story into verse, you may tell it in plain words. The briefer, the sooner shall you be refreshed.'

'Very well,' said Bilbo. 'I will do as you bid. But I will now tell the true story, and if some here have heard me tell it otherwise' – he looked sidelong at Glóin – 'I ask them to forget it and forgive me. I only wished to claim the treasure as my very own in those days, and to be rid of the name of thief that was put on me. But perhaps I understand things a little better now. Anyway, this is what happened.'

To some there Bilbo's tale was wholly new, and they listened with amazement while the old hobbit, actually not at all displeased, recounted his adventure with Gollum, at full length. He did not omit a single riddle. He would have given also an account of his party and disappearance from the Shire, if he had been allowed; but Elrond raised his hand.

'Well told, my friend,' he said, 'but that is enough at this time. For the moment it suffices to know that the Ring passed to Frodo, your heir. Let him now speak!'

Then, less willingly than Bilbo, Frodo told of all his dealings with the Ring from the day that it passed into his keeping. Every step of his journey from Hobbiton to the Ford of Bruinen was questioned and considered, and everything that he could recall concerning the Black Riders was examined. At last he sat down again.

'Not bad,' Bilbo said to him. 'You would have made a good story of it, if they hadn't kept on interrupting. I tried to make a few notes, but we shall have to go over it all again together some time, if I am to write it up. There are whole chapters of stuff before you ever got here!'

'Yes, it made quite a long tale,' answered Frodo. 'But the story still does not seem complete to me. I still want to know a good deal, especially about Gandalf.'

Galdor of the Havens, who sat near by, overheard him. 'You speak for me also,' he cried, and turning to Elrond he said: 'The Wise may have good reason to believe that the halfling's trove is indeed the Great Ring of long debate, unlikely though that may seem to those who know less. But may we not hear the proofs? And I would ask this also. What of Saruman? He is learned in the lore of the Rings, yet he is not among us. What is his counsel – if he knows the things that we have heard?'

'The questions that you ask, Galdor, are bound together,' said Elrond. 'I had not overlooked them, and they shall be answered. But these things it is the part of Gandalf to make clear; and I call upon him last, for it is the place of honour, and in all this matter he has been the chief.'

'Some, Galdor,' said Gandalf, 'would think the tidings of Glóin, and the pursuit of Frodo, proof enough that the halfling's trove is a thing of great worth to the Enemy. Yet it is a ring. What then? The Nine the Nazgûl keep. The Seven are taken or destroyed.' At this Glóin stirred, but did not speak. 'The Three we know of. What then is this one that he desires so much?

'There is indeed a wide waste of time between the River and the Mountain, between the loss and the finding. But the gap in the knowledge of the Wise has been filled at last. Yet too slowly. For the Enemy has been close behind, closer even than I feared. And well is it that not until this year, this very summer, as it seems, did he learn the full truth.

'Some here will remember that many years ago I myself dared to pass the doors of the Necromancer in Dol Guldur, and secretly explored his ways, and found thus that our fears were true: he was none other than Sauron, our Enemy of old, at length taking shape and power again. Some, too, will remember also that Saruman dissuaded us from open deeds against him, and for long we watched him only. Yet at last, as his shadow grew, Saruman yielded, and the Council put forth its strength and drove the evil out of Mirkwood – and that was in the very year of the finding of this Ring: a strange chance, if chance it was.

'But we were too late, as Elrond foresaw. Sauron also had watched us, and had long prepared against our stroke, governing Mordor from afar through Minas Morgul, where his Nine servants dwelt, until all was ready. Then he gave way before us, but only feigned to flee, and soon after came to the Dark Tower and openly declared himself. Then for the last time the Council met; for now we learned that he was seeking ever more eagerly for the One. We feared then that he had some news of it that we knew nothing of. But Saruman said nay, and repeated what he had said to us before: that the One would never again be found in Middle-earth.

' "At the worst," said he, "our Enemy knows that we have it not, and that it still is lost. But what was lost may yet be found, he thinks. Fear not! His hope will cheat him. Have I not earnestly studied this matter? Into Anduin the Great it fell; and long ago, while Sauron slept, it was rolled down the River to the Sea. There let it lie until the End." '

*   *   *

Gandalf fell silent, gazing eastward from the porch to the far peaks of the Misty Mountains, at whose great roots the peril of the world had so long lain hidden. He sighed.

'There I was at fault,' he said. 'I was lulled by the words of Saruman the Wise; but I should have sought for the truth sooner, and our peril would now be less.'

'We were all at fault,' said Elrond, 'and but for your vigilance the Darkness, maybe, would already be upon us. But say on!'

'From the first my heart misgave me, against all reason that I knew,' said Gandalf, 'and I desired to know how this thing came to Gollum, and how long he had possessed it. So I set a watch for him, guessing that he would ere long come forth from his darkness to seek for his treasure. He came, but he escaped and was not found. And then alas! I let the matter rest, watching and waiting only, as we have too often done.

'Time passed with many cares, until my doubts were awakened again to sudden fear. Whence came the hobbit's ring? What, if my fear was true, should be done with it? Those things I must decide. But I spoke yet of my dread to none, knowing the peril of an untimely whisper, if it went astray. In all the long wars with the Dark Tower treason has ever been our greatest foe.

'That was seventeen years ago. Soon I became aware that spies of many sorts, even beasts and birds, were gathered round the Shire, and my fear grew. I called for the help of the Dúnedain, and their watch was doubled; and I opened my heart to Aragorn, the heir of Isildur.'

'And I,' said Aragorn, 'counselled that we should hunt for Gollum, too late though it may seem. And since it seemed fit that Isildur's heir should labour to repair Isildur's fault, I went with Gandalf on the long and hopeless search.'

Then Gandalf told how they had explored the whole length of Wilderland, down even to the Mountains of Shadow and the fences of Mordor. 'There we had rumour of him, and we guess that he dwelt there long in the dark hills; but we never found him, and at last I despaired. And then in my despair I thought again of a test that might make the finding of Gollum unneeded. The ring itself might tell if it were the One. The memory of words at the Council came back to me: words of Saruman, half-heeded at the time. I heard them now clearly in my heart.

' "The Nine, the Seven, and the Three," he said, "had each their proper gem. Not so the One. It was round and unadorned, as it were one of the lesser rings; but its maker set marks upon it that the skilled, maybe, could still see and read."

'What those marks were he had not said. Who now would know? The maker. And Saruman? But great though his lore may be, it must have a source. What hand save Sauron's ever held this thing, ere it was lost? The hand of Isildur alone.

'With that thought, I forsook the chase, and passed swiftly to Gondor. In former days the members of my order had been well received there, but Saruman most of all. Often he had been for long the guest of the Lords of the City. Less welcome did the Lord Denethor show me then than of old, and grudgingly he permitted me to search among his hoarded scrolls and books.

' "If indeed you look only, as you say, for records of ancient days, and the beginnings of the City, read on!" he said. "For to me what was is less dark than what is to come, and that is my care. But unless you have more skill even than Saruman, who has studied here long, you will find naught that is not well known to me, who am master of the lore of this City."

'So said Denethor. And yet there lie in his hoards many records that few now can read, even of the lore-masters, for their scripts and tongues have become dark to later men. And Boromir, there lies in Minas Tirith still, unread, I guess, by any save Saruman and myself since the kings failed, a scroll that Isildur made himself. For Isildur did not march away straight from the war in Mordor, as some have told the tale.'

'Some in the North, maybe,' Boromir broke in. 'All know in Gondor that he went first to Minas Anor and dwelt a while with his nephew Meneldil, instructing him, before he committed to him the rule of the South Kingdom. In that time he planted there the last sapling of the White Tree in memory of his brother.'

'But in that time also he made this scroll,' said Gandalf; 'and that is not remembered in Gondor, it would seem. For this scroll concerns the Ring, and thus wrote Isildur therein:

> The Great Ring shall go now to be an heirloom of the North Kingdom; but records of it shall be left in Gondor, where also dwell the heirs of Elendil, lest a time come when the memory of these great matters shall grow dim.

'And after these words Isildur described the Ring, such as he found it.

> It was hot when I first took it, hot as a glede, and my hand was scorched, so that I doubt if ever again I shall be free of the pain of it. Yet even as I write it is cooled, and it seemeth to shrink, though it loseth neither its beauty nor its shape. Already the writing upon it, which at first was as clear as red flame, fadeth and is now only barely to be read. It is fashioned in an elven-script of Eregion, for they have no letters in Mordor for such subtle work; but the language is unknown to me. I deem it to be a tongue of the Black Land, since it is foul and uncouth. What evil it saith I do not know; but I trace here a copy of it, lest it fade beyond recall. The Ring misseth, maybe, the heat of Sauron's hand, which was black and yet burned like fire, and so Gil-galad was destroyed; and maybe were the gold made hot again, the writing would be refreshed. But for my part I will risk no hurt to this thing: of all the works of Sauron the only fair. It is precious to me, though I buy it with great pain.

'When I read these words, my quest was ended. For the traced writing was indeed as Isildur guessed, in the tongue of Mordor and the servants of the Tower. And what was said therein was already known. For in the day that Sauron first put on the One, Celebrimbor, maker of the Three, was aware of him, and from afar he heard him speak these words, and so his evil purposes were revealed.

'At once I took my leave of Denethor, but even as I went northwards, messages came to me out of Lórien that Aragorn had passed that way, and that he had found the creature called Gollum. Therefore I went first to meet him and hear his tale. Into what deadly perils he had gone alone I dared not guess.'

'There is little need to tell of them,' said Aragorn. 'If a man must needs walk in sight of the Black Gate, or tread the deadly flowers of Morgul Vale, then perils he will have. I, too, despaired at last, and I began my homeward journey. And then, by fortune, I came suddenly on what I sought: the marks of soft feet beside a muddy pool. But now the trail was fresh and swift, and it led not to Mordor but away. Along the skirts of the Dead Marshes I followed it, and then I had him. Lurking by a stagnant mere, peering in the water as the dark eve fell, I caught him, Gollum. He was covered with green slime. He will never love me, I fear; for he bit me, and I was not gentle. Nothing more did I ever get from his mouth than the marks of his teeth. I deemed it the worst part of all my journey, the road back, watching him day and night, making him walk before me with a halter on his neck, gagged, until he was tamed by lack of drink and food, driving him ever towards Mirkwood. I brought him there at last and gave him to the Elves, for we had agreed that this should be done; and I was glad to be rid of his company, for he stank. For my part I hope never to look upon him again; but Gandalf came and endured long speech with him.'

'Yes, long and weary,' said Gandalf, 'but not without profit. For one thing, the tale he told of his loss agreed with that which Bilbo has now told openly for the first time; but that mattered little, since I had already guessed it. But I learned then first that Gollum's ring came out of the Great River nigh to the Gladden Fields. And I learned also that he had possessed it long. Many lives of his small kind. The power of the ring had lengthened his years far beyond their span; but that power only the Great Rings wield.

'And if that is not proof enough, Galdor, there is the other test that I spoke of. Upon this very ring which you have here seen held aloft, round and unadorned, the letters that Isildur reported may still be read, if one has the strength of will to set the golden thing in the fire a while. That I have done, and this I have read:

Ash nazg durbatulûk, ash nazg gimbatul, ash nazg thrakatulûk agh burzum-ishi krimpatul.'

The change in the wizard's voice was astounding. Suddenly it became menacing, powerful, harsh as stone. A shadow seemed to pass over the high sun, and the porch for a moment grew dark. All trembled, and the Elves stopped their ears.

'Never before has any voice dared to utter words of that tongue in Imladris, Gandalf the Grey,' said Elrond, as the shadow passed and the company breathed once more.

'And let us hope that none will ever speak it here again,' answered Gandalf. 'Nonetheless I do not ask your pardon, Master Elrond. For if that tongue is not soon to be heard in every corner of the West, then let all put doubt aside that this thing is indeed what the Wise have declared: the treasure of the Enemy, fraught with all his malice; and in it lies a great part of his strength of old. Out of the Black Years come the words that the Smiths of Eregion heard, and knew that they had been betrayed:

One Ring to rule them all, One Ring to find them, One Ring to bring them all and in the Darkness bind them.

'Know also, my friends, that I learned more yet from Gollum. He was loth to speak and his tale was unclear, but it is beyond all doubt that he went to Mordor, and there all that he knew was forced from him. Thus the Enemy knows now that the One is found, that it was long in the Shire; and since his servants have pursued it almost to our door, he soon will know, already he may know, even as I speak, that we have it here.'

All sat silent for a while, until at length Boromir spoke. 'He is a small thing, you say, this Gollum? Small, but great in mischief. What became of him? To what doom did you put him?'

'He is in prison, but no worse,' said Aragorn. 'He had suffered much. There is no doubt that he was tormented, and the fear of Sauron lies black on his heart. Still I for one am glad that he is safely kept by the watchful Elves of Mirkwood. His malice is great and gives him a strength hardly to be believed in one so lean and withered. He could work much mischief still, if he were free. And I do not doubt that he was allowed to leave Mordor on some evil errand.'

'Alas! alas!' cried Legolas, and in his fair elvish face there was great distress. 'The tidings that I was sent to bring must now be told. They are not good, but only here have I learned how evil they may seem to this company. Sméagol, who is now called Gollum, has escaped.'

'Escaped?' cried Aragorn. 'That is ill news indeed. We shall all rue it bitterly, I fear. How came the folk of Thranduil to fail in their trust?'

'Not through lack of watchfulness,' said Legolas; 'but perhaps through over-kindliness. And we fear that the prisoner had aid from others, and that more is known of our doings than we could wish. We guarded this creature day and night, at Gandalf's bidding, much though we wearied of the task. But Gandalf bade us hope still for his cure, and we had not the heart to keep him ever in dungeons under the earth, where he would fall back into his old black thoughts.'

'You were less tender to me,' said Glóin with a flash of his eyes, as old memories were stirred of his imprisonment in the deep places of the Elven-king's halls.

'Now come!' said Gandalf. 'Pray do not interrupt, my good Glóin. That was a regrettable misunderstanding, long set right. If all the grievances that stand between Elves and Dwarves are to be brought up here, we may as well abandon this Council.'

Glóin rose and bowed, and Legolas continued. 'In the days of fair weather we led Gollum through the woods; and there was a high tree standing alone far from the others which he liked to climb. Often we let him mount up to the highest branches, until he felt the free wind; but we set a guard at the tree's foot. One day he refused to come down, and the guards had no mind to climb after him: he had learned the trick of clinging to boughs with his feet as well as with his hands; so they sat by the tree far into the night.

'It was that very night of summer, yet moonless and star-less, that Orcs came on us at unawares. We drove them off after some time; they were many and fierce, but they came from over the mountains, and were unused to the woods. When the battle was over, we found that Gollum was gone, and his guards were slain or taken. It then seemed plain to us that the attack had been made for his rescue, and that he knew of it beforehand. How that was contrived we cannot guess; but Gollum is cunning, and the spies of the Enemy are many. The dark things that were driven out in the year of the Dragon's fall have returned in greater numbers, and Mirkwood is again an evil place, save where our realm is maintained.

'We have failed to recapture Gollum. We came on his trail among those of many Orcs, and it plunged deep into the Forest, going south. But ere long it escaped our skill, and we dared not continue the hunt; for we were drawing nigh to Dol Guldur, and that is still a very evil place; we do not go that way.'

'Well, well, he is gone,' said Gandalf. 'We have no

time to seek for him again. He must do what he will. But he may play a part yet that neither he nor Sauron have foreseen.

'And now I will answer Galdor's other questions. What of Saruman? What are his counsels to us in this need? This tale I must tell in full, for only Elrond has heard it yet, and that in brief; but it will bear on all that we must resolve. It is the last chapter in the Tale of the Ring, so far as it has yet gone.

'At the end of June I was in the Shire, but a cloud of anxiety was on my mind, and I rode to the southern borders of the little land; for I had a foreboding of some danger, still hidden from me but drawing near. There messages reached me telling me of war and defeat in Gondor, and when I heard of the Black Shadow a chill smote my heart. But I found nothing save a few fugitives from the South; yet it seemed to me that on them sat a fear of which they would not speak. I turned then east and north and journeyed along the Greenway; and not far from Bree I came upon a traveller sitting on a bank beside the road with his grazing horse beside him. It was Radagast the Brown, who at one time dwelt at Rhosgobel, near the borders of Mirkwood. He is one of my order, but I had not seen him for many a year.

'"Gandalf!" he cried. "I was seeking you. But I am a stranger in these parts. All I knew was that you might be found in a wild region with the uncouth name of Shire."

'"Your information was correct," I said. "But do not put it that way, if you meet any of the inhabitants. You are near the borders of the Shire now. And what do you want with me? It must be pressing. You were never a traveller, unless driven by great need."

'"I have an urgent errand," he said. "My news is evil." Then he looked about him, as if the hedges might have ears. "Nazgûl," he whispered. "The Nine are abroad again. They have crossed the River secretly and are moving westward. They have taken the guise of riders in black."

'I knew then what I had dreaded without knowing it.

' "The Enemy must have some great need or purpose," said Radagast; "but what it is that makes him look to these distant and desolate parts, I cannot guess."

' "What do you mean?" said I.

' "I have been told that wherever they go the Riders ask for news of a land called Shire."

' "*The* Shire," I said; but my heart sank. For even the Wise might fear to withstand the Nine, when they are gathered together under their fell chieftain. A great king and sorcerer he was of old, and now he wields a deadly fear. "Who told you, and who sent you?" I asked.

' "Saruman the White," answered Radagast. "And he told me to say that if you feel the need, he will help; but you must seek his aid at once, or it will be too late."

'And that message brought me hope. For Saruman the White is the greatest of my order. Radagast is, of course, a worthy Wizard, a master of shapes and changes of hue; and he has much lore of herbs and beasts, and birds are especially his friends. But Saruman has long studied the arts of the Enemy himself, and thus we have often been able to forestall him. It was by the devices of Saruman that we drove him from Dol Guldur. It might be that he had found some weapons that would drive back the Nine.

' "I will go to Saruman," I said.

' "Then you must go *now*," said Radagast; "for I have wasted time in looking for you, and the days are running short. I was told to find you before Midsummer, and that is now here. Even if you set out from this spot, you will hardly reach him before the Nine discover the land that they seek. I myself shall turn back at once." And with that he mounted and would have ridden straight off.

' "Stay a moment!" I said. "We shall need your help, and the help of all things that will give it. Send out messages to all the beasts and birds that are your friends. Tell them to bring news of anything that bears on this matter to Saruman and Gandalf. Let messages be sent to Orthanc."

'"I will do that," he said, and rode off as if the Nine were after him.

'I could not follow him then and there. I had ridden very far already that day, and I was as weary as my horse; and I needed to consider matters. I stayed the night in Bree, and decided that I had no time to return to the Shire. Never did I make a greater mistake!

'However, I wrote a message to Frodo, and trusted to my friend the innkeeper to send it to him. I rode away at dawn; and I came at long last to the dwelling of Saruman. That is far south in Isengard, in the end of the Misty Mountains, not far from the Gap of Rohan. And Boromir will tell you that that is a great open vale that lies between the Misty Mountains and the northmost foothills of Ered Nimrais, the White Mountains of his home. But Isengard is a circle of sheer rocks that enclose a valley as with a wall, and in the midst of that valley is a tower of stone called Orthanc. It was not made by Saruman, but by the Men of Númenor long ago; and it is very tall and has many secrets; yet it looks not to be a work of craft. It cannot be reached save by passing the circle of Isengard; and in that circle there is only one gate.

'Late one evening I came to the gate, like a great arch in the wall of rock; and it was strongly guarded. But the keepers of the gate were on the watch for me and told me that Saruman awaited me. I rode under the arch, and the gate closed silently behind me, and suddenly I was afraid, though I knew no reason for it.

'But I rode to the foot of Orthanc, and came to the stair of Saruman; and there he met me and led me up to his high chamber. He wore a ring on his finger.

'"So you have come, Gandalf," he said to me gravely; but in his eyes there seemed to be a white light, as if a cold laughter was in his heart.

'"Yes, I have come," I said. "I have come for your aid, Saruman the White." And that title seemed to anger him.

'"Have you indeed, Gandalf the *Grey*!" he scoffed. "For

aid? It has seldom been heard of that Gandalf the Grey sought for aid, one so cunning and so wise, wandering about the lands, and concerning himself in every business, whether it belongs to him or not."

'I looked at him and wondered. "But if I am not deceived," said I, "things are now moving which will require the union of all our strength."

' "That may be so," he said, "but the thought is late in coming to you. How long, I wonder, have you concealed from me, the head of the Council, a matter of greatest import? What brings you now from your lurking-place in the Shire?"

' "The Nine have come forth again," I answered. "They have crossed the River. So Radagast said to me."

' "Radagast the Brown!" laughed Saruman, and he no longer concealed his scorn. "Radagast the Bird-tamer! Radagast the Simple! Radagast the Fool! Yet he had just the wit to play the part that I set him. For you have come, and that was all the purpose of my message. And here you will stay, Gandalf the Grey, and rest from journeys. For I am Saruman the Wise, Saruman Ring-maker, Saruman of Many Colours!"

'I looked then and saw that his robes, which had seemed white, were not so, but were woven of all colours, and if he moved they shimmered and changed hue so that the eye was bewildered.

' "I liked white better," I said.

' "White!" he sneered. "It serves as a beginning. White cloth may be dyed. The white page can be overwritten; and the white light can be broken."

' "In which case it is no longer white," said I. "And he that breaks a thing to find out what it is has left the path of wisdom."

' "You need not speak to me as to one of the fools that you take for friends," said he. "I have not brought you hither to be instructed by you, but to give you a choice."

'He drew himself up then and began to declaim, as if he were making a speech long rehearsed. "The Elder Days are gone. The Middle Days are passing. The Younger Days are beginning. The time of the Elves is over, but our time is at hand: the world of Men, which we must rule. But we must have power, power to order all things as we will, for that good which only the Wise can see.

' "And listen, Gandalf, my old friend and helper!" he said, coming near and speaking now in a softer voice. "I said *we*, for *we* it may be, if you will join with me. A new Power is rising. Against it the old allies and policies will not avail us at all. There is no hope left in Elves or dying Númenor. This then is one choice before you, before us. We may join with that Power. It would be wise, Gandalf. There is hope that way. Its victory is at hand; and there will be rich reward for those that aided it. As the Power grows, its proved friends will also grow; and the Wise, such as you and I, may with patience come at last to direct its courses, to control it. We can bide our time, we can keep our thoughts in our hearts, deploring maybe evils done by the way, but approving the high and ultimate purpose: Knowledge, Rule, Order; all the things that we have so far striven in vain to accomplish, hindered rather than helped by our weak or idle friends. There need not be, there would not be, any real change in our designs, only in our means."

' "Saruman," I said, "I have heard speeches of this kind before, but only in the mouths of emissaries sent from Mordor to deceive the ignorant. I cannot think that you brought me so far only to weary my ears."

'He looked at me sidelong, and paused a while considering. "Well, I see that this wise course does not commend itself to you," he said. "Not yet? Not if some better way can be contrived?"

'He came and laid his long hand on my arm. "And why not, Gandalf?" he whispered. "Why not? The Ruling Ring? If we could command that, then the Power would pass to *us*. That is in truth why I brought you here. For I have many eyes in my service, and I believe that you know where this precious thing now lies. Is it not so? Or why do the Nine ask for the Shire, and what is your business there?" As he said this a lust which he could not conceal shone suddenly in his eyes.

'"Saruman," I said, standing away from him, "only one hand at a time can wield the One, and you know that well, so do not trouble to say *we*! But I would not give it, nay, I would not give even news of it to you, now that I learn your mind. You were head of the Council, but you have unmasked yourself at last. Well, the choices are, it seems, to submit to Sauron, or to yourself. I will take neither. Have you others to offer?"

'He was cold now and perilous. "Yes," he said. "I did not expect you to show wisdom, even in your own behalf; but I gave you the chance of aiding me willingly, and so saving yourself much trouble and pain. The third choice is to stay here, until the end."

'"Until what end?"

'"Until you reveal to me where the One may be found. I may find means to persuade you. Or until it is found in your despite, and the Ruler has time to turn to lighter matters: to devise, say, a fitting reward for the hindrance and insolence of Gandalf the Grey."

'"That may not prove to be one of the lighter matters," said I. He laughed at me, for my words were empty, and he knew it.

'They took me and they set me alone on the pinnacle of Orthanc, in the place where Saruman was accustomed to watch the stars. There is no descent save by a narrow stair of many thousand steps, and the valley below seems far away. I looked on it and saw that, whereas it had once been green and fair, it was now filled with pits and forges. Wolves and orcs were housed in Isengard, for Saruman was mustering a great force on his own account, in rivalry of Sauron and not in his service yet. Over all his works a dark smoke hung and wrapped itself about the sides of Orthanc. I stood alone on an island in the clouds; and I had no chance of escape, and my days were bitter. I was pierced with cold, and I had but little room in which to pace to and fro, brooding on the coming of the Riders to the North.

'That the Nine had indeed arisen I felt assured, apart from the words of Saruman which might be lies. Long ere I came to Isengard I had heard tidings by the way that could not be mistaken. Fear was ever in my heart for my friends in the Shire; but still I had some hope. I hoped that Frodo had set forth at once, as my letter had urged, and that he had reached Rivendell before the deadly pursuit began. And both my fear and my hope proved ill-founded. For my hope was founded on a fat man in Bree; and my fear was founded on the cunning of Sauron. But fat men who sell ale have many calls to answer; and the power of Sauron is still less than fear makes it. But in the circle of Isengard, trapped and alone, it was not easy to think that the hunters before whom all have fled or fallen would falter in the Shire far away.'

'I saw you!' cried Frodo. 'You were walking backwards and forwards. The moon shone in your hair.'

Gandalf paused astonished and looked at him. 'It was only a dream,' said Frodo, 'but it suddenly came back to me. I had quite forgotten it. It came some time ago; after I left the Shire, I think.'

'Then it was late in coming,' said Gandalf, 'as you will see. I was in an evil plight. And those who know me will agree that I have seldom been in such need, and do not bear such misfortune well. Gandalf the Grey caught like a fly in a spider's treacherous web! Yet even the most subtle spiders may leave a weak thread.

'At first I feared, as Saruman no doubt intended, that Radagast had also fallen. Yet I had caught no hint of anything wrong in his voice or in his eye at our meeting. If I had, I should never have gone to Isengard, or I should have gone more warily. So Saruman guessed, and he had concealed his mind and deceived his messenger. It would have been useless in any case to try and win over the honest Radagast to treachery. He sought me in good faith, and so persuaded me.

'That was the undoing of Saruman's plot. For Radagast knew no reason why he should not do as I asked; and he rode away towards Mirkwood where he had many friends of old. And the Eagles of the Mountains went far and wide, and they saw many things: the gathering of wolves and the mustering of Orcs; and the Nine Riders going hither and thither in the lands; and they heard news of the escape of Gollum. And they sent a messenger to bring these tidings to me.

'So it was that when summer waned, there came a night of moon, and Gwaihir the Windlord, swiftest of the Great Eagles, came unlooked-for to Orthanc; and he found me standing on the pinnacle. Then I spoke to him and he bore me away, before Saruman was aware. I was far from Isengard, ere the wolves and orcs issued from the gate to pursue me.

'"How far can you bear me?" I said to Gwaihir.

'"Many leagues," said he, "but not to the ends of the earth. I was sent to bear tidings not burdens."

'"Then I must have a steed on land," I said, "and a steed surpassingly swift, for I have never had such need of haste before."

'"Then I will bear you to Edoras, where the Lord of Rohan sits in his halls," he said; "for that is not very far off." And I was glad, for in the Riddermark of Rohan the Rohirrim, the Horse-lords, dwell, and there are no horses like those that are bred in that great vale between the Misty Mountains and the White.

'"Are the Men of Rohan still to be trusted, do you think?" I said to Gwaihir, for the treason of Saruman had shaken my faith.

'"They pay a tribute of horses," he answered, "and send many yearly to Mordor, or so it is said; but they are not yet under the yoke. But if Saruman has become evil, as you say, then their doom cannot be long delayed."

'He set me down in the land of Rohan ere dawn; and now I have lengthened my tale over long. The rest must be more

brief. In Rohan I found evil already at work: the lies of
Saruman; and the king of the land would not listen to my
warnings. He bade me take a horse and be gone; and I chose
one much to my liking, but little to his. I took the best horse
in his land, and I have never seen the like of him.'

'Then he must be a noble beast indeed,' said Aragorn;
'and it grieves me more than many tidings that might seem
worse to learn that Sauron levies such tribute. It was not so
when last I was in that land.'

'Nor is it now, I will swear,' said Boromir. 'It is a lie that
comes from the Enemy. I know the Men of Rohan, true and
valiant, our allies, dwelling still in the lands that we gave them
long ago.'

'The shadow of Mordor lies on distant lands,' answered
Aragorn. 'Saruman has fallen under it. Rohan is beset. Who
knows what you will find there, if ever you return?'

'Not this at least,' said Boromir, 'that they will buy their
lives with horses. They love their horses next to their kin.
And not without reason, for the horses of the Riddermark
come from the fields of the North, far from the Shadow, and
their race, as that of their masters, is descended from the free
days of old.'

'True indeed!' said Gandalf. 'And there is one among them
that might have been foaled in the morning of the world.
The horses of the Nine cannot vie with him; tireless, swift
as the flowing wind. Shadowfax they called him. By day his
coat glistens like silver; and by night it is like a shade, and
he passes unseen. Light is his footfall! Never before had any
man mounted him, but I took him and I tamed him, and so
speedily he bore me that I reached the Shire when Frodo
was on the Barrow-downs, though I set out from Rohan only
when he set out from Hobbiton.

'But fear grew in me as I rode. Ever as I came north I
heard tidings of the Riders, and though I gained on them
day by day, they were ever before me. They had divided
their forces, I learned: some remained on the eastern borders,
not far from the Greenway, and some invaded the Shire from

the south. I came to Hobbiton and Frodo had gone; but I had words with old Gamgee. Many words and few to the point. He had much to say about the shortcomings of the new owners of Bag End.

' "I can't abide changes," said he, "not at my time of life, and least of all changes for the worst." "Changes for the worst," he repeated many times.

' "Worst is a bad word," I said to him, "and I hope you do not live to see it." But amidst his talk I gathered at last that Frodo had left Hobbiton less than a week before, and that a black horseman had come to the Hill the same evening. Then I rode on in fear. I came to Buckland and found it in uproar, as busy as a hive of ants that has been stirred with a stick. I came to the house at Crickhollow, and it was broken open and empty; but on the threshold there lay a cloak that had been Frodo's. Then for a while hope left me, and I did not wait to gather news, or I might have been comforted; but I rode on the trail of the Riders. It was hard to follow, for it went many ways, and I was at a loss. But it seemed to me that one or two had ridden towards Bree; and that way I went, for I thought of words that might be said to the innkeeper.

' "Butterbur they call him," thought I. "If this delay was his fault, I will melt all the butter in him. I will roast the old fool over a slow fire." He expected no less, and when he saw my face he fell down flat and began to melt on the spot.'

'What did you do to him?' cried Frodo in alarm. 'He was really very kind to us and did all that he could.'

Gandalf laughed. 'Don't be afraid!' he said. 'I did not bite, and I barked very little. So overjoyed was I by the news that I got out of him, when he stopped quaking, that I embraced the old fellow. How it happened I could not then guess, but I learned that you had been in Bree the night before, and had gone off that morning with Strider.

' "Strider!" I cried, shouting for joy.

' "Yes, sir, I am afraid so, sir," said Butterbur, mistaking me. "He got at them, in spite of all that I could do, and they took up with him. They behaved very queer all the time they were here: wilful, you might say."

' "Ass! Fool! Thrice worthy and beloved Barliman!" said I. "It's the best news I have had since midsummer: it's worth a gold piece at the least. May your beer be laid under an enchantment of surpassing excellence for seven years!" said I. "Now I can take a night's rest, the first since I have forgotten when."

'So I stayed there that night, wondering much what had become of the Riders; for only of two had there yet been any news in Bree, it seemed. But in the night we heard more. Five at least came from the west, and they threw down the gates and passed through Bree like a howling wind; and the Bree-folk are still shivering and expecting the end of the world. I got up before dawn and went after them.

'I do not know, but it seems clear to me that this is what happened. Their Captain remained in secret away south of Bree, while two rode ahead through the village, and four more invaded the Shire. But when these were foiled in Bree and at Crickhollow, they returned to their Captain with tidings, and so left the Road unguarded for a while, except by their spies. The Captain then sent some eastward straight across country, and he himself with the rest rode along the Road in great wrath.

'I galloped to Weathertop like a gale, and I reached it before sundown on my second day from Bree – and they were there before me. They drew away from me, for they felt the coming of my anger and they dared not face it while the Sun was in the sky. But they closed round at night, and I was besieged on the hill-top, in the old ring of Amon Sûl. I was hard put to it indeed: such light and flame cannot have been seen on Weathertop since the war-beacons of old.

'At sunrise I escaped and fled towards the north. I could not hope to do more. It was impossible to find you, Frodo, in the wilderness, and it would have been folly to try with all the Nine at my heels. So I had to trust to Aragorn. But I hoped to draw some of them off, and yet reach Rivendell ahead of you and send out help. Four Riders did indeed follow me, but they turned back after a while and made for the Ford, it seems. That helped a little, for there were only five, not nine, when your camp was attacked.

'I reached here at last by a long hard road, up the Hoarwell and through the Ettenmoors, and down from the north. It took me nearly fourteen days from Weathertop, for I could not ride among the rocks of the troll-fells, and Shadowfax departed. I sent him back to his master; but a great friendship has grown between us, and if I have need he will come at my call. But so it was that I came to Rivendell only three days before the Ring, and news of its peril had already been brought here – which proved well indeed.

'And that, Frodo, is the end of my account. May Elrond and the others forgive the length of it. But such a thing has not happened before, that Gandalf broke tryst and did not come when he promised. An account to the Ring-bearer of so strange an event was required, I think.

'Well, the Tale is now told, from first to last. Here we all are, and here is the Ring. But we have not yet come any nearer to our purpose. What shall we do with it?'

There was a silence. At last Elrond spoke again.

'This is grievous news concerning Saruman,' he said; 'for we trusted him and he is deep in all our counsels. It is perilous to study too deeply the arts of the Enemy, for good or for ill. But such falls and betrayals, alas, have happened before. Of the tales that we have heard this day the tale of Frodo was most strange to me. I have known few hobbits, save Bilbo here; and it seems to me that he is perhaps not so alone and singular as I had thought him. The world has changed much since I last was on the westward roads.

'The Barrow-wights we know by many names; and of the Old Forest many tales have been told: all that now remains is but an outlier of its northern march. Time was when a squirrel could go from tree to tree from what is now the Shire to Dunland west of Isengard. In those lands I journeyed once, and many things wild and strange I knew. But I had forgotten Bombadil, if indeed this is still the same that walked the woods and hills long ago, and even then was older than the old. That was not then his name. Iarwain Ben-adar we called him, oldest and fatherless. But many another name he has since been given by other folk: Forn by the Dwarves, Orald by Northern Men, and other names beside. He is a strange creature, but maybe I should have summoned him to our Council.'

'He would not have come,' said Gandalf.

'Could we not still send messages to him and obtain his help?' asked Erestor. 'It seems that he has a power even over the Ring.'

'No, I should not put it so,' said Gandalf. 'Say rather that the Ring has no power over him. He is his own master. But he cannot alter the Ring itself, nor break its power over others. And now he is withdrawn into a little land, within bounds that he has set, though none can see them, waiting perhaps for a change of days, and he will not step beyond them.'

'But within those bounds nothing seems to dismay him,' said Erestor. 'Would he not take the Ring and keep it there, for ever harmless?'

'No,' said Gandalf, 'not willingly. He might do so, if all the free folk of the world begged him, but he would not understand the need. And if he were given the Ring, he would soon forget it, or most likely throw it away. Such things have no hold on his mind. He would be a most unsafe guardian; and that alone is answer enough.'

'But in any case,' said Glorfindel, 'to send the Ring to him would only postpone the day of evil. He is far away. We could not now take it back to him, unguessed, unmarked by any spy. And even if we could, soon or late the Lord of the Rings would learn of its hiding place and would bend all his power towards it. Could that power be defied by Bombadil alone? I think not. I think that in the end, if all else is conquered, Bombadil will fall, Last as he was First; and then Night will come.'

'I know little of Iarwain save the name,' said Galdor; 'but Glorfindel, I think, is right. Power to defy our Enemy is not in him, unless such power is in the earth itself. And yet we see that Sauron can torture and destroy the very hills. What power still remains lies with us, here in Imladris, or with Círdan at the Havens, or in Lórien. But have they the strength, have we here the strength to withstand the Enemy, the coming of Sauron at the last, when all else is overthrown?'

'I have not the strength,' said Elrond; 'neither have they.'

'Then if the Ring cannot be kept from him for ever by strength,' said Glorfindel, 'two things only remain for us to attempt: to send it over the Sea, or to destroy it.'

'But Gandalf has revealed to us that we cannot destroy it by any craft that we here possess,' said Elrond. 'And they who dwell beyond the Sea would not receive it: for good or ill it belongs to Middle-earth; it is for us who still dwell here to deal with it.'

'Then,' said Glorfindel, 'let us cast it into the deeps, and so make the lies of Saruman come true. For it is clear now that even at the Council his feet were already on a crooked path. He knew that the Ring was not lost for ever, but wished us to think so; for he began to lust for it for himself. Yet oft in lies truth is hidden: in the Sea it would be safe.'

'Not safe for ever,' said Gandalf. 'There are many things in the deep waters; and seas and lands may change. And it is not our part here to take thought only for a season, or for a few lives of Men, or for a passing age of the world. We should seek a final end of this menace, even if we do not hope to make one.'

'And that we shall not find on the roads to the Sea,' said Galdor. 'If the return to Iarwain be thought too dangerous, then flight to the Sea is now fraught with gravest peril. My heart tells me that Sauron will expect us to take the western way, when he learns what has befallen. He soon will. The Nine have been unhorsed indeed but that is but a respite, ere they find new steeds and swifter. Only the waning might of Gondor stands now between him and a march in power along the coasts into the North; and if he comes, assailing the White Towers and the Havens, hereafter the Elves may have no escape from the lengthening shadows of Middle-earth.'

'Long yet will that march be delayed,' said Boromir. 'Gondor wanes, you say. But Gondor stands, and even the end of its strength is still very strong.'

'And yet its vigilance can no longer keep back the Nine,' said Galdor. 'And other roads he may find that Gondor does not guard.'

'Then,' said Erestor, 'there are but two courses, as Glorfindel already has declared: to hide the Ring for ever; or to unmake it. But both are beyond our power. Who will read this riddle for us?'

'None here can do so,' said Elrond gravely. 'At least none can foretell what will come to pass, if we take this road or that. But it seems to me now clear which is the road that we must take. The westward road seems easiest. Therefore it must be shunned. It will be watched. Too often the Elves have fled that way. Now at this last we must take a hard road, a road unforeseen. There lies our hope, if hope it be. To walk into peril – to Mordor. We must send the Ring to the Fire.'

Silence fell again. Frodo, even in that fair house, looking out upon a sunlit valley filled with the noise of clear waters, felt a dead darkness in his heart. Boromir stirred, and Frodo looked at him. He was fingering his great horn and frowning. At length he spoke.

'I do not understand all this,' he said. 'Saruman is a traitor, but did he not have a glimpse of wisdom? Why do you speak ever of hiding and destroying? Why should we not think that the Great Ring has come into our hands to serve us in the very hour of need? Wielding it the Free Lords of the Free may surely defeat the Enemy. That is what he most fears, I deem.

'The Men of Gondor are valiant, and they will never submit; but they may be beaten down. Valour needs first strength, and then a weapon. Let the Ring be your weapon, if it has such power as you say. Take it and go forth to victory!'

'Alas, no,' said Elrond. 'We cannot use the Ruling Ring. That we now know too well. It belongs to Sauron and was made by him alone, and is altogether evil. Its strength, Boromir, is too great for anyone to wield at will, save only those who have already a great power of their own. But for them it holds an even deadlier peril. The very desire of it corrupts the heart. Consider Saruman. If any of the Wise should with this Ring overthrow the Lord of Mordor, using his own arts, he would then set himself on Sauron's throne, and yet another Dark Lord would appear. And that is another reason why the Ring should be destroyed: as long as it is in the world it will be a danger even to the Wise. For nothing is evil in the beginning. Even Sauron was not so. I fear to take the Ring to hide it. I will not take the Ring to wield it.'

'Nor I,' said Gandalf.

Boromir looked at them doubtfully, but he bowed his head. 'So be it,' he said. 'Then in Gondor we must trust to such weapons as we have. And at the least, while the Wise ones guard this Ring, we will fight on. Mayhap the Sword-that-was-Broken may still stem the tide – if the hand that wields it has inherited not an heirloom only, but the sinews of the Kings of Men.'

'Who can tell?' said Aragorn. 'But we will put it to the test one day.'

'May the day not be too long delayed,' said Boromir. 'For though I do not ask for aid, we need it. It would comfort us to know that others fought also with all the means that they have.'

'Then be comforted,' said Elrond. 'For there are other powers and realms that you know not, and they are hidden from you. Anduin the Great flows past many shores, ere it comes to Argonath and the Gates of Gondor.'

'Still it might be well for all,' said Glóin the Dwarf, 'if all these strengths were joined, and the powers of each were used in league. Other rings there may be, less treacherous, that might be used in our need. The Seven are lost to us – if Balin has not found the ring of Thrór, which was the last; naught has been heard of it since Thrór perished in Moria. Indeed I may now reveal that it was partly in hope to find that ring that Balin went away.'

'Balin will find no ring in Moria,' said Gandalf. 'Thrór gave it to Thráin his son, but not Thráin to Thorin. It was taken with torment from Thráin in the dungeons of Dol Guldur. I came too late.'

'Ah, alas!' cried Glóin. 'When will the day come of our revenge? But still there are the Three. What of the Three Rings of the Elves? Very mighty Rings, it is said. Do not the Elf-lords keep them? Yet they too were made by the Dark Lord long ago. Are they idle? I see Elf-lords here. Will they not say?'

The Elves returned no answer. 'Did you not hear me, Glóin?' said Elrond. 'The Three were not made by Sauron, nor did he ever touch them. But of them it is not permitted to speak. So much only in this hour of doubt I may now say. They are not idle. But they were not made as weapons of war or conquest: that is not their power. Those who made them did not desire strength or domination or hoarded wealth, but understanding, making, and healing, to preserve all things unstained. These things the Elves of Middle-earth have in some measure gained, though with sorrow. But all that has been wrought by those who wield the Three will turn to their undoing, and their minds and hearts will become revealed to Sauron, if he regains the One. It would be better if the Three had never been. That is his purpose.'

'But what then would happen, if the Ruling Ring were destroyed, as you counsel?' asked Glóin.

'We know not for certain,' answered Elrond sadly. 'Some hope that the Three Rings, which Sauron has never touched, would then become free, and their rulers might heal the hurts of the world that he has wrought. But maybe when the One has gone, the Three will fail, and many fair things will fade and be forgotten. That is my belief.'

'Yet all the Elves are willing to endure this chance,' said Glorfindel, 'if by it the power of Sauron may be broken, and the fear of his dominion be taken away for ever.'

'Thus we return once more to the destroying of the Ring,' said Erestor, 'and yet we come no nearer. What strength have we for the finding of the Fire in which it was made? That is the path of despair. Of folly I would say, if the long wisdom of Elrond did not forbid me.'

'Despair, or folly?' said Gandalf. 'It is not despair, for despair is only for those who see the end beyond all doubt. We do not. It is wisdom to recognize necessity, when all other courses have been weighed, though as folly it may appear to those who cling to false hope. Well, let folly be our cloak, a veil before the eyes of the Enemy! For he is very wise, and weighs all things to a nicety in the scales of his malice. But the only measure that he knows is desire, desire for power; and so he judges all hearts. Into his heart the thought will not enter that any will refuse it, that having the Ring we may seek to destroy it. If we seek this, we shall put him out of reckoning.'

'At least for a while,' said Elrond. 'The road must be trod, but it will be very hard. And neither strength nor wisdom will carry us far upon it. This quest may be attempted by the weak with as much hope as the strong. Yet such is oft the course of deeds that move the wheels of the world: small hands do them because they must, while the eyes of the great are elsewhere.'

* * *

'Very well, very well, Master Elrond!' said Bilbo suddenly.
'Say no more! It is plain enough what you are pointing at.
Bilbo the silly hobbit started this affair, and Bilbo had better
finish it, or himself. I was very comfortable here, and getting
on with my book. If you want to know, I am just writing an
ending for it. I had thought of putting: *and he lived happily
ever afterwards to the end of his days.* It is a good ending, and
none the worse for having been used before. Now I shall
have to alter that: it does not look like coming true; and
anyway there will evidently have to be several more chapters,
if I live to write them. It is a frightful nuisance. When ought
I to start?'

Boromir looked in surprise at Bilbo, but the laughter died
on his lips when he saw that all the others regarded the old
hobbit with grave respect. Only Glóin smiled, but his smile
came from old memories.

'Of course, my dear Bilbo,' said Gandalf. 'If you had really
started this affair, you might be expected to finish it. But you
know well enough now that *starting* is too great a claim for
any, and that only a small part is played in great deeds by
any hero. You need not bow! Though the word was meant,
and we do not doubt that under jest you are making a valiant
offer. But one beyond your strength, Bilbo. You cannot take
this thing back. It has passed on. If you need my advice any
longer, I should say that your part is ended, unless as a
recorder. Finish your book, and leave the ending unaltered!
There is still hope for it. But get ready to write a sequel,
when they come back.'

Bilbo laughed. 'I have never known you give me pleasant
advice before,' he said. 'As all your unpleasant advice has
been good, I wonder if this advice is not bad. Still, I don't
suppose I have the strength or luck left to deal with the Ring.
It has grown, and I have not. But tell me: what do you mean
by *they*?'

'The messengers who are sent with the Ring.'

'Exactly! And who are they to be? That seems to me what
this Council has to decide, and all that it has to decide.

Elves may thrive on speech alone, and Dwarves endure great weariness; but I am only an old hobbit, and I miss my meal at noon. Can't you think of some names now? Or put it off till after dinner?'

No one answered. The noon-bell rang. Still no one spoke. Frodo glanced at all the faces, but they were not turned to him. All the Council sat with downcast eyes, as if in deep thought. A great dread fell on him, as if he was awaiting the pronouncement of some doom that he had long foreseen and vainly hoped might after all never be spoken. An overwhelming longing to rest and remain at peace by Bilbo's side in Rivendell filled all his heart. At last with an effort he spoke, and wondered to hear his own words, as if some other will was using his small voice.

'I will take the Ring,' he said, 'though I do not know the way.'

Elrond raised his eyes and looked at him, and Frodo felt his heart pierced by the sudden keenness of the glance. 'If I understand aright all that I have heard,' he said, 'I think that this task is appointed for you, Frodo; and that if you do not find a way, no one will. This is the hour of the Shire-folk, when they arise from their quiet fields to shake the towers and counsels of the Great. Who of all the Wise could have foreseen it? Or, if they are wise, why should they expect to know it, until the hour has struck?

'But it is a heavy burden. So heavy that none could lay it on another. I do not lay it on you. But if you take it freely, I will say that your choice is right; and though all the mighty elf-friends of old, Hador, and Húrin, and Túrin, and Beren himself were assembled together, your seat should be among them.'

'But you won't send him off alone surely, Master?' cried Sam, unable to contain himself any longer, and jumping up from the corner where he had been quietly sitting on the floor.

'No indeed!' said Elrond, turning towards him with a smile. 'You at least shall go with him. It is hardly possible to separate you from him, even when he is summoned to a secret council and you are not.'

Sam sat down, blushing and muttering. 'A nice pickle we have landed ourselves in, Mr. Frodo!' he said, shaking his head.

CHAPTER III

THE RING GOES SOUTH

Later that day the hobbits held a meeting of their own in Bilbo's room. Merry and Pippin were indignant when they heard that Sam had crept into the Council, and had been chosen as Frodo's companion.

'It's most unfair,' said Pippin. 'Instead of throwing him out, and clapping him in chains, Elrond goes and *rewards* him for his cheek!'

'Rewards!' said Frodo. 'I can't imagine a more severe punishment. You are not thinking what you are saying: condemned to go on this hopeless journey, a reward? Yesterday I dreamed that my task was done, and I could rest here, a long while, perhaps for good.'

'I don't wonder,' said Merry, 'and I wish you could. But we are envying Sam, not you. If you have to go, then it will be a punishment for any of us to be left behind, even in Rivendell. We have come a long way with you and been through some stiff times. We want to go on.'

'That's what I meant,' said Pippin. 'We hobbits ought to stick together, and we will. I shall go, unless they chain me up. There must be someone with intelligence in the party.'

'Then you certainly will not be chosen, Peregrin Took!' said Gandalf, looking in through the window, which was near the ground. 'But you are all worrying yourselves unnecessarily. Nothing is decided yet.'

'Nothing decided!' cried Pippin. 'Then what were you all doing? You were shut up for hours.'

'Talking,' said Bilbo. 'There was a deal of talk, and everyone had an eye-opener. Even old Gandalf. I think Legolas's bit of news about Gollum caught even him on the hop, though he passed it off.'

'You were wrong,' said Gandalf. 'You were inattentive. I had already heard of it from Gwaihir. If you want to know, the only real eye-openers, as you put it, were you and Frodo; and I was the only one that was not surprised.'

'Well, anyway,' said Bilbo, 'nothing was decided beyond choosing poor Frodo and Sam. I was afraid all the time that it might come to that, if I was let off. But if you ask me, Elrond will send out a fair number, when the reports come in. Have they started yet, Gandalf?'

'Yes,' said the wizard. 'Some of the scouts have been sent out already. More will go tomorrow. Elrond is sending Elves, and they will get in touch with the Rangers, and maybe with Thranduil's folk in Mirkwood. And Aragorn has gone with Elrond's sons. We shall have to scour the lands all round for many long leagues before any move is made. So cheer up, Frodo! You will probably make quite a long stay here.'

'Ah!' said Sam gloomily. 'We'll just wait long enough for winter to come.'

'That can't be helped,' said Bilbo. 'It's your fault partly, Frodo my lad: insisting on waiting for my birthday. A funny way of honouring it, I can't help thinking. *Not* the day I should have chosen for letting the S.-B.s into Bag End. But there it is: you can't wait now till spring; and you can't go till the reports come back.

> *When winter first begins to bite*
> *and stones crack in the frosty night,*
> *when pools are black and trees are bare,*
> *'tis evil in the Wild to fare.*

But that I am afraid will be just your luck.'

'I am afraid it will,' said Gandalf. 'We can't start until we have found out about the Riders.'

'I thought they were all destroyed in the flood,' said Merry.

'You cannot destroy Ringwraiths like that,' said Gandalf. 'The power of their master is in them, and they stand or fall by him. We hope that they were all unhorsed and unmasked, and so made for a while less dangerous; but we must find out for certain. In the meantime you should try and forget your troubles, Frodo. I do not know if I can do anything to help you; but I will whisper this in your ears. Someone said that intelligence would be needed in the party. He was right. I think I shall come with you.'

So great was Frodo's delight at this announcement that Gandalf left the window-sill, where he had been sitting, and took off his hat and bowed. 'I only said *I think I shall come*. Do not count on anything yet. In this matter Elrond will have much to say, and your friend the Strider. Which reminds me, I want to see Elrond. I must be off.'

'How long do you think I shall have here?' said Frodo to Bilbo when Gandalf had gone.

'Oh, I don't know. I can't count days in Rivendell,' said Bilbo. 'But quite long, I should think. We can have many a good talk. What about helping me with my book, and making a start on the next? Have you thought of an ending?'

'Yes, several, and all are dark and unpleasant,' said Frodo.

'Oh, that won't do!' said Bilbo. 'Books ought to have good endings. How would this do: *and they all settled down and lived together happily ever after?*'

'It will do well, if it ever comes to that,' said Frodo.

'Ah!' said Sam. 'And where will they live? That's what I often wonder.'

For a while the hobbits continued to talk and think of the past journey and of the perils that lay ahead; but such was the virtue of the land of Rivendell that soon all fear and anxiety was lifted from their minds. The future, good or ill, was not forgotten, but ceased to have any power over the present. Health and hope grew strong in them, and they were content with each good day as it came, taking pleasure in every meal, and in every word and song.

So the days slipped away, as each morning dawned bright and fair, and each evening followed cool and clear. But autumn was waning fast; slowly the golden light faded to pale silver, and the lingering leaves fell from the naked trees. A wind began to blow chill from the Misty Mountains to the east. The Hunter's Moon waxed round in the night sky, and put to flight all the lesser stars. But low in the South one star shone red. Every night, as the Moon waned again, it shone brighter and brighter. Frodo could see it from his window, deep in the heavens, burning like a watchful eye that glared above the trees on the brink of the valley.

The hobbits had been nearly two months in the House of Elrond, and November had gone by with the last shreds of autumn, and December was passing, when the scouts began to return. Some had gone north beyond the springs of the Hoarwell into the Ettenmoors; and others had gone west, and with the help of Aragorn and the Rangers had searched the lands far down the Greyflood, as far as Tharbad, where the old North Road crossed the river by a ruined town. Many had gone east and south; and some of these had crossed the Mountains and entered Mirkwood, while others had climbed the pass at the source of the Gladden River, and had come down into Wilderland and over the Gladden Fields and so at length had reached the old home of Radagast at Rhosgobel. Radagast was not there; and they had returned over the high pass that was called the Dimrill Stair. The sons of Elrond, Elladan and Elrohir, were the last to return; they had made a great journey, passing down the Silverlode into a strange country, but of their errand they would not speak to any save to Elrond.

In no region had the messengers discovered any signs or tidings of the Riders or other servants of the Enemy. Even from the Eagles of the Misty Mountains they had learned no fresh news. Nothing had been seen or heard of Gollum; but the wild wolves were still gathering, and were hunting again far up the Great River. Three of the black horses had been found at once drowned in the flooded Ford. On the rocks of the rapids below it searchers discovered the bodies of five more, and also a long black cloak, slashed and tattered. Of the Black Riders no other trace was to be seen, and nowhere was their presence to be felt. It seemed that they had vanished from the North.

'Eight out of the Nine are accounted for at least,' said Gandalf. 'It is rash to be too sure, yet I think that we may hope now that the Ringwraiths were scattered, and have been obliged to return as best they could to their Master in Mordor, empty and shapeless.

'If that is so, it will be some time before they can begin the hunt again. Of course the Enemy has other servants, but they will have to journey all the way to the borders of Rivendell before they can pick up our trail. And if we are careful that will be hard to find. But we must delay no longer.'

Elrond summoned the hobbits to him. He looked gravely at Frodo. 'The time has come,' he said. 'If the Ring is to set out, it must go soon. But those who go with it must not count on their errand being aided by war or force. They must pass into the domain of the Enemy far from aid. Do you still hold to your word, Frodo, that you will be the Ring-bearer?'

'I do,' said Frodo. 'I will go with Sam.'

'Then I cannot help you much, not even with counsel,' said Elrond. 'I can foresee very little of your road; and how your task is to be achieved I do not know. The Shadow has crept now to the feet of the Mountains, and draws nigh even to the borders of the Greyflood; and under the Shadow all is dark to me. You will meet many foes, some open, and some disguised; and you may find friends upon your way when you least look for it. I will send out messages, such as I can contrive, to those whom I know in the wide world; but so perilous are the lands now become that some may well miscarry, or come no quicker than you yourself.

'And I will choose you companions to go with you, as far as they will or fortune allows. The number must be few, since your hope is in speed and secrecy. Had I a host of Elves in armour of the Elder Days, it would avail little, save to arouse the power of Mordor.

'The Company of the Ring shall be Nine; and the Nine Walkers shall be set against the Nine Riders that are evil. With you and your faithful servant, Gandalf will go; for this shall be his great task, and maybe the end of his labours.

'For the rest, they shall represent the other Free Peoples of the World: Elves, Dwarves, and Men. Legolas shall be for the Elves; and Gimli son of Glóin for the Dwarves. They are willing to go at least to the passes of the Mountains, and maybe beyond. For men you shall have Aragorn son of Arathorn, for the Ring of Isildur concerns him closely.'

'Strider!' cried Frodo.

'Yes,' he said with a smile. 'I ask leave once again to be your companion, Frodo.'

'I would have begged you to come,' said Frodo, 'only I thought you were going to Minas Tirith with Boromir.'

'I am,' said Aragorn. 'And the Sword-that-was-Broken shall be re-forged ere I set out to war. But your road and our road lie together for many hundreds of miles. Therefore Boromir will also be in the Company. He is a valiant man.'

'There remain two more to be found,' said Elrond. 'These I will consider. Of my household I may find some that it seems good to me to send.'

'But that will leave no place for us!' cried Pippin in dismay. 'We don't want to be left behind. We want to go with Frodo.'

'That is because you do not understand and cannot imagine what lies ahead,' said Elrond.

'Neither does Frodo,' said Gandalf, unexpectedly supporting Pippin. 'Nor do any of us see clearly. It is true that if these hobbits understood the danger, they would not dare to go. But they would still wish to go, or wish that they dared, and be shamed and unhappy. I think, Elrond, that in this matter it would be well to trust rather to their friendship than to great wisdom. Even if you chose for us an elf-lord, such as Glorfindel, he could not storm the Dark Tower, nor open the road to the Fire by the power that is in him.'

'You speak gravely,' said Elrond, 'but I am in doubt. The

Shire, I forebode, is not free now from peril; and these two I had thought to send back there as messengers, to do what they could, according to the fashion of their country, to warn the people of their danger. In any case, I judge that the younger of these two, Peregrin Took, should remain. My heart is against his going.'

'Then, Master Elrond, you will have to lock me in prison, or send me home tied in a sack,' said Pippin. 'For otherwise I shall follow the Company.'

'Let it be so then. You shall go,' said Elrond, and he sighed. 'Now the tale of Nine is filled. In seven days the Company must depart.'

The Sword of Elendil was forged anew by Elvish smiths, and on its blade was traced a device of seven stars set between the crescent Moon and the rayed Sun, and about them was written many runes; for Aragorn son of Arathorn was going to war upon the marches of Mordor. Very bright was that sword when it was made whole again; the light of the sun shone redly in it, and the light of the moon shone cold, and its edge was hard and keen. And Aragorn gave it a new name and called it Andúril, Flame of the West.

Aragorn and Gandalf walked together or sat speaking of their road and the perils they would meet; and they pondered the storied and figured maps and books of lore that were in the house of Elrond. Sometimes Frodo was with them; but he was content to lean on their guidance, and he spent as much time as he could with Bilbo.

In those last days the hobbits sat together in the evening in the Hall of Fire, and there among many tales they heard told in full the lay of Beren and Lúthien and the winning of the Great Jewel; but in the day, while Merry and Pippin were out and about, Frodo and Sam were to be found with Bilbo in his own small room. Then Bilbo would read passages from his book (which still seemed very incomplete), or scraps of his verses, or would take notes of Frodo's adventures.

On the morning of the last day Frodo was alone with Bilbo,

and the old hobbit pulled out from under his bed a wooden box. He lifted the lid and fumbled inside.

'Here is your sword,' he said. 'But it was broken, you know. I took it to keep it safe but I've forgotten to ask if the smiths could mend it. No time now. So I thought, perhaps, you would care to have this, don't you know?'

He took from the box a small sword in an old shabby leathern scabbard. Then he drew it, and its polished and well-tended blade glittered suddenly, cold and bright. 'This is Sting,' he said, and thrust it with little effort deep into a wooden beam. 'Take it, if you like. I shan't want it again, I expect.'

Frodo accepted it gratefully.

'Also there is this!' said Bilbo, bringing out a parcel which seemed to be rather heavy for its size. He unwound several folds of old cloth, and held up a small shirt of mail. It was close-woven of many rings, as supple almost as linen, cold as ice, and harder than steel. It shone like moonlit silver, and was studded with white gems. With it was a belt of pearl and crystal.

'It's a pretty thing, isn't it?' said Bilbo, moving it in the light. 'And useful. It is my dwarf-mail that Thorin gave me. I got it back from Michel Delving before I started, and packed it with my luggage. I brought all the mementoes of my Journey away with me, except the Ring. But I did not expect to use this, and I don't need it now, except to look at sometimes. You hardly feel any weight when you put it on.'

'I should look – well, I don't think I should look right in it,' said Frodo.

'Just what I said myself,' said Bilbo. 'But never mind about looks. You can wear it under your outer clothes. Come on! You must share this secret with me. Don't tell anybody else! But I should feel happier if I knew you were wearing it. I have a fancy it would turn even the knives of the Black Riders,' he ended in a low voice.

'Very well, I will take it,' said Frodo. Bilbo put it on him, and fastened Sting upon the glittering belt; and then Frodo put over the top his old weather-stained breeches, tunic, and jacket.

'Just a plain hobbit you look,' said Bilbo. 'But there is more about you now than appears on the surface. Good luck to you!' He turned away and looked out of the window, trying to hum a tune.

'I cannot thank you as I should, Bilbo, for this, and for all your past kindnesses,' said Frodo.

'Don't try!' said the old hobbit, turning round and slapping him on the back. 'Ow!' he cried. 'You are too hard now to slap! But there you are: Hobbits must stick together, and especially Bagginses. All I ask in return is: take as much care of yourself as you can, and bring back all the news you can, and any old songs and tales you can come by. I'll do my best to finish my book before you return. I should like to write the second book, if I am spared.' He broke off and turned to the window again, singing softly.

> I sit beside the fire and think
>   of all that I have seen,
> of meadow-flowers and butterflies
>   in summers that have been;
>
> Of yellow leaves and gossamer
>   in autumns that there were,
> with morning mist and silver sun
>   and wind upon my hair.
>
> I sit beside the fire and think
>   of how the world will be
> when winter comes without a spring
>   that I shall ever see.
>
> For still there are so many things
>   that I have never seen:
> in every wood in every spring
>   there is a different green.

I sit beside the fire and think
of people long ago,
and people who will see a world
that I shall never know.

But all the while I sit and think
of times there were before,
I listen for returning feet
and voices at the door.

It was a cold grey day near the end of December. The East Wind was streaming through the bare branches of the trees, and seething in the dark pines on the hills. Ragged clouds were hurrying overhead, dark and low. As the cheerless shadows of the early evening began to fall the Company made ready to set out. They were to start at dusk, for Elrond counselled them to journey under cover of night as often as they could, until they were far from Rivendell.

'You should fear the many eyes of the servants of Sauron,' he said. 'I do not doubt that news of the discomfiture of the Riders has already reached him, and he will be filled with wrath. Soon now his spies on foot and wing will be abroad in the northern lands. Even of the sky above you must beware as you go on your way.'

The Company took little gear of war, for their hope was in secrecy not in battle. Aragorn had Andúril but no other weapon, and he went forth clad only in rusty green and brown, as a Ranger of the wilderness. Boromir had a long sword, in fashion like Andúril but of less lineage, and he bore also a shield and his war-horn.

'Loud and clear it sounds in the valleys of the hills,' he said, 'and then let all the foes of Gondor flee!' Putting it to his lips he blew a blast, and the echoes leapt from rock to rock, and all that heard that voice in Rivendell sprang to their feet.

'Slow should you be to wind that horn again, Boromir,'

said Elrond, 'until you stand once more on the borders of your land, and dire need is on you.'

'Maybe,' said Boromir. 'But always I have let my horn cry at setting forth, and though thereafter we may walk in the shadows, I will not go forth as a thief in the night.'

Gimli the dwarf alone wore openly a short shirt of steel-rings, for dwarves make light of burdens; and in his belt was a broad-bladed axe. Legolas had a bow and a quiver, and at his belt a long white knife. The younger hobbits wore the swords that they had taken from the barrow; but Frodo took only Sting; and his mail-coat, as Bilbo wished, remained hidden. Gandalf bore his staff, but girt at his side was the elven-sword Glamdring, the mate of Orcrist that lay now upon the breast of Thorin under the Lonely Mountain.

All were well furnished by Elrond with thick warm clothes, and they had jackets and cloaks lined with fur. Spare food and clothes and blankets and other needs were laden on a pony, none other than the poor beast that they had brought from Bree.

The stay in Rivendell had worked a great wonder of change on him: he was glossy and seemed to have the vigour of youth. It was Sam who had insisted on choosing him, declaring that Bill (as he called him) would pine, if he did not come.

'That animal can nearly talk,' he said, 'and would talk, if he stayed here much longer. He gave me a look as plain as Mr. Pippin could speak it: if you don't let me go with you, Sam, I'll follow on my own.' So Bill was going as the beast of burden, yet he was the only member of the Company that did not seem depressed.

Their farewells had been said in the great hall by the fire, and they were only waiting now for Gandalf, who had not yet come out of the house. A gleam of firelight came from the open doors, and soft lights were glowing in many windows. Bilbo huddled in a cloak stood silent on the door-step beside Frodo. Aragorn sat with his head bowed to his knees; only Elrond knew fully what this hour meant to him.

The others could be seen as grey shapes in the darkness.

Sam was standing by the pony, sucking his teeth, and staring moodily into the gloom where the river roared stonily below; his desire for adventure was at its lowest ebb.

'Bill, my lad,' he said, 'you oughtn't to have took up with us. You could have stayed here and et the best hay till the new grass comes.' Bill swished his tail and said nothing.

Sam eased the pack on his shoulders, and went over anxiously in his mind all the things that he had stowed in it, wondering if he had forgotten anything: his chief treasure, his cooking gear; and the little box of salt that he always carried and refilled when he could; a good supply of pipe-weed (but not near enough, I'll warrant); flint and tinder; woollen hose; linen; various small belongings of his master's that Frodo had forgotten and Sam had stowed to bring them out in triumph when they were called for. He went through them all.

'Rope!' he muttered. 'No rope! And only last night you said to yourself: "Sam, what about a bit of rope? You'll want it, if you haven't got it." Well, I'll want it. I can't get it now.'

At that moment Elrond came out with Gandalf, and he called the Company to him. 'This is my last word,' he said in a low voice. 'The Ring-bearer is setting out on the Quest of Mount Doom. On him alone is any charge laid: neither to cast away the Ring, nor to deliver it to any servant of the Enemy nor indeed to let any handle it, save members of the Company and the Council, and only then in gravest need. The others go with him as free companions, to help him on his way. You may tarry, or come back, or turn aside into other paths, as chance allows. The further you go, the less easy will it be to withdraw; yet no oath or bond is laid on you to go further than you will. For you do not yet know the strength of your hearts, and you cannot foresee what each may meet upon the road.'

'Faithless is he that says farewell when the road darkens,' said Gimli.

'Maybe,' said Elrond, 'but let him not vow to walk in the dark, who has not seen the nightfall.'

'Yet sworn word may strengthen quaking heart,' said Gimli.

'Or break it,' said Elrond. 'Look not too far ahead! But go now with good hearts! Farewell, and may the blessing of Elves and Men and all Free Folk go with you. May the stars shine upon your faces!'

'Good . . . good luck!' cried Bilbo, stuttering with the cold. 'I don't suppose you will be able to keep a diary, Frodo my lad, but I shall expect a full account when you get back. And don't be too long! Farewell!'

Many others of Elrond's household stood in the shadows and watched them go, bidding them farewell with soft voices. There was no laughter, and no song or music. At last they turned away and faded silently into the dusk.

They crossed the bridge and wound slowly up the long steep paths that led out of the cloven vale of Rivendell; and they came at length to the high moor where the wind hissed through the heather. Then with one glance at the Last Homely House twinkling below them they strode away far into the night.

At the Ford of Bruinen they left the Road and turning southwards went on by narrow paths among the folded lands. Their purpose was to hold this course west of the Mountains for many miles and days. The country was much rougher and more barren than in the green vale of the Great River in Wilderland on the other side of the range, and their going would be slow; but they hoped in this way to escape the notice of unfriendly eyes. The spies of Sauron had hitherto seldom been seen in this empty country, and the paths were little known except to the people of Rivendell.

Gandalf walked in front, and with him went Aragorn, who knew this land even in the dark. The others were in file behind, and Legolas whose eyes were keen was the rearguard.

The first part of their journey was hard and dreary, and Frodo remembered little of it, save the wind. For many sunless days an icy blast came from the Mountains in the east, and no garment seemed able to keep out its searching fingers. Though the Company was well clad, they seldom felt warm, either moving or at rest. They slept uneasily during the middle of the day, in some hollow of the land, or hidden under the tangled thorn-bushes that grew in thickets in many places. In the late afternoon they were roused by the watch, and took their chief meal: cold and cheerless as a rule, for they could seldom risk the lighting of a fire. In the evening they went on again, always as nearly southward as they could find a way.

At first it seemed to the hobbits that although they walked and stumbled until they were weary, they were creeping forward like snails, and getting nowhere. Each day the land looked much the same as it had the day before. Yet steadily the mountains were drawing nearer. South of Rivendell they rose ever higher, and bent westwards; and about the feet of the main range there was tumbled an ever wider land of bleak hills, and deep valleys filled with turbulent waters. Paths were few and winding, and led them often only to the edge of some sheer fall, or down into treacherous swamps.

They had been a fortnight on the way when the weather changed. The wind suddenly fell and then veered round to the south. The swift-flowing clouds lifted and melted away, and the sun came out, pale and bright. There came a cold clear dawn at the end of a long stumbling night-march. The travellers reached a low ridge crowned with ancient holly-trees whose grey-green trunks seemed to have been built out of the very stone of the hills. Their dark leaves shone and their berries glowed red in the light of the rising sun.

Away in the south Frodo could see the dim shapes of lofty mountains that seemed now to stand across the path that the Company was taking. At the left of this high range rose three peaks; the tallest and nearest stood up like a tooth tipped with snow; its great, bare, northern precipice was still largely in the shadow, but where the sunlight slanted upon it, it glowed red.

Gandalf stood at Frodo's side and looked out under his hand. 'We have done well,' he said. 'We have reached the borders of the country that Men call Hollin; many Elves lived here in happier days, when Eregion was its name. Five-and-forty leagues as the crow flies we have come, though many long miles further our feet have walked. The land and the weather will be milder now, but perhaps all the more dangerous.'

'Dangerous or not, a real sunrise is mighty welcome,' said Frodo, throwing back his hood and letting the morning light fall on his face.

'But the mountains are ahead of us,' said Pippin. 'We must have turned eastwards in the night.'

'No,' said Gandalf. 'But you see further ahead in the clear light. Beyond those peaks the range bends round south-west. There are many maps in Elrond's house, but I suppose you never thought to look at them?'

'Yes I did, sometimes,' said Pippin, 'but I don't remember them. Frodo has a better head for that sort of thing.'

'I need no map,' said Gimli, who had come up with Legolas, and was gazing out before him with a strange light in his deep eyes. 'There is the land where our fathers worked of old, and we have wrought the image of those mountains into many works of metal and of stone, and into many songs and tales. They stand tall in our dreams: Baraz, Zirak, Shathûr.

'Only once before have I seen them from afar in waking life, but I know them and their names, for under them lies Khazad-dûm, the Dwarrowdelf, that is now called the Black Pit, Moria in the Elvish tongue. Yonder stands Barazinbar, the Redhorn, cruel Caradhras; and beyond him are Silvertine and Cloudyhead: Celebdil the White, and Fanuidhol the Grey, that we call Zirakzigil and Bundushathûr.

'There the Misty Mountains divide, and between their

arms lies the deep-shadowed valley which we cannot forget: Azanulbizar, the Dimrill Dale, which the Elves call Nanduhirion.'

'It is for the Dimrill Dale that we are making,' said Gandalf. 'If we climb the pass that is called the Redhorn Gate, under the far side of Caradhras, we shall come down by the Dimrill Stair into the deep vale of the Dwarves. There lies the Mirrormere, and there the River Silverlode rises in its icy springs.'

'Dark is the water of Kheled-zâram,' said Gimli, 'and cold are the springs of Kibil-nâla. My heart trembles at the thought that I may see them soon.'

'May you have joy of the sight, my good dwarf!' said Gandalf. 'But whatever you may do, we at least cannot stay in that valley. We must go down the Silverlode into the secret woods, and so to the Great River, and then——'

He paused.

'Yes, and where then?' asked Merry.

'To the end of the journey – in the end,' said Gandalf. 'We cannot look too far ahead. Let us be glad that the first stage is safely over. I think we will rest here, not only today but tonight as well. There is a wholesome air about Hollin. Much evil must befall a country before it wholly forgets the Elves, if once they dwelt there.'

'That is true,' said Legolas. 'But the Elves of this land were of a race strange to us of the silvan folk, and the trees and the grass do not now remember them. Only I hear the stones lament them: *deep they delved us, fair they wrought us, high they builded us; but they are gone*. They are gone. They sought the Havens long ago.'

That morning they lit a fire in a deep hollow shrouded by great bushes of holly, and their supper-breakfast was merrier than it had been since they set out. They did not hurry to bed afterwards, for they expected to have all the night to sleep in, and they did not mean to go on again until the evening of the next day. Only Aragorn was silent and restless.

After a while he left the Company and wandered on to the ridge; there he stood in the shadow of a tree, looking out southwards and westwards, with his head posed as if he was listening. Then he returned to the brink of the dell and looked down at the others laughing and talking.

'What is the matter, Strider?' Merry called up. 'What are you looking for? Do you miss the East Wind?'

'No indeed,' he answered. 'But I miss something. I have been in the country of Hollin in many seasons. No folk dwell here now, but many other creatures live here at all times, especially birds. Yet now all things but you are silent. I can feel it. There is no sound for miles about us, and your voices seem to make the ground echo. I do not understand it.'

Gandalf looked up with sudden interest. 'But what do you guess is the reason?' he asked. 'Is there more in it than surprise at seeing four hobbits, not to mention the rest of us, where people are so seldom seen or heard?'

'I hope that is it,' answered Aragorn. 'But I have a sense of watchfulness, and of fear, that I have never had here before.'

'Then we must be more careful,' said Gandalf. 'If you bring a Ranger with you, it is well to pay attention to him, especially if the Ranger is Aragorn. We must stop talking aloud, rest quietly, and set the watch.'

It was Sam's turn that day to take the first watch, but Aragorn joined him. The others fell asleep. Then the silence grew until even Sam felt it. The breathing of the sleepers could be plainly heard. The swish of the pony's tail and the occasional movements of his feet became loud noises. Sam could hear his own joints creaking, if he stirred. Dead silence was around him, and over all hung a clear blue sky, as the Sun rode up from the East. Away in the South a dark patch appeared, and grew, and drove north like flying smoke in the wind.

'What's that, Strider? It don't look like a cloud,' said Sam in a whisper to Aragorn. He made no answer, he was gazing intently at the sky; but before long Sam could see for himself what was approaching. Flocks of birds, flying at great speed, were wheeling and circling, and traversing all the land as if they were searching for something; and they were steadily drawing nearer.

'Lie flat and still!' hissed Aragorn, pulling Sam down into the shade of a holly-bush; for a whole regiment of birds had broken away suddenly from the main host, and came, flying low, straight towards the ridge. Sam thought they were a kind of crow of large size. As they passed overhead, in so dense a throng that their shadow followed them darkly over the ground below, one harsh croak was heard.

Not until they had dwindled into the distance, north and west, and the sky was again clear would Aragorn rise. Then he sprang up and went and wakened Gandalf.

'Regiments of black crows are flying over all the land between the Mountains and the Greyflood,' he said, 'and they have passed over Hollin. They are not natives here; they are *crebain* out of Fangorn and Dunland. I do not know what they are about: possibly there is some trouble away south from which they are fleeing; but I think they are spying out the land. I have also glimpsed many hawks flying high up in the sky. I think we ought to move again this evening. Hollin is no longer wholesome for us: it is being watched.'

'And in that case so is the Redhorn Gate,' said Gandalf; 'and how we can get over that without being seen, I cannot imagine. But we will think of that when we must. As for moving as soon as it is dark, I am afraid that you are right.'

'Luckily our fire made little smoke, and had burned low before the *crebain* came,' said Aragorn. 'It must be put out and not lit again.'

'Well if that isn't a plague and a nuisance!' said Pippin. The news: no fire, and a move again by night, had been broken to him, as soon as he woke in the late afternoon. 'All because of a pack of crows! I had looked forward to a real good meal tonight: something hot.'

'Well, you can go on looking forward,' said Gandalf.

'There may be many unexpected feasts ahead for you. For myself I should like a pipe to smoke in comfort, and warmer feet. However, we are certain of one thing at any rate: it will get warmer as we get south.'

'Too warm, I shouldn't wonder,' muttered Sam to Frodo. 'But I'm beginning to think it's time we got a sight of that Fiery Mountain, and saw the end of the Road, so to speak. I thought at first that this here Redhorn, or whatever its name is, might be it, till Gimli spoke his piece. A fair jaw-cracker dwarf-language must be!' Maps conveyed nothing to Sam's mind, and all distances in these strange lands seemed so vast that he was quite out of his reckoning.

All that day the Company remained in hiding. The dark birds passed over now and again; but as the westering Sun grew red they disappeared southwards. At dusk the Company set out, and turning now half east they steered their course towards Caradhras, which far away still glowed faintly red in the last light of the vanished Sun. One by one white stars sprang forth as the sky faded.

Guided by Aragorn they struck a good path. It looked to Frodo like the remains of an ancient road, that had once been broad and well planned, from Hollin to the mountain-pass. The Moon, now at the full, rose over the mountains, and cast a pale light in which the shadows of stones were black. Many of them looked to have been worked by hands, though now they lay tumbled and ruinous in a bleak, barren land.

It was the cold chill hour before the first stir of dawn, and the moon was low. Frodo looked up at the sky. Suddenly he saw or felt a shadow pass over the high stars, as if for a moment they faded and then flashed out again. He shivered.

'Did you see anything pass over?' he whispered to Gandalf, who was just ahead.

'No, but I felt it, whatever it was,' he answered. 'It may be nothing, only a wisp of thin cloud.'

'It was moving fast then,' muttered Aragorn, 'and not with the wind.'

★   ★   ★

Nothing further happened that night. The next morning dawned even brighter than before. But the air was chill again; already the wind was turning back towards the east. For two more nights they marched on, climbing steadily but ever more slowly as their road wound up into the hills, and the mountains towered up, nearer and nearer. On the third morning Caradhras rose before them, a mighty peak, tipped with snow like silver, but with sheer naked sides, dull red as if stained with blood.

There was a black look in the sky, and the sun was wan. The wind had gone now round to the north-east. Gandalf snuffed the air and looked back.

'Winter deepens behind us,' he said quietly to Aragorn. 'The heights away north are whiter than they were; snow is lying far down their shoulders. Tonight we shall be on our way high up towards the Redhorn Gate. We may well be seen by watchers on that narrow path, and waylaid by some evil; but the weather may prove a more deadly enemy than any. What do you think of your course now, Aragorn?'

Frodo overheard these words, and understood that Gandalf and Aragorn were continuing some debate that had begun long before. He listened anxiously.

'I think no good of our course from beginning to end, as you know well, Gandalf,' answered Aragorn. 'And perils known and unknown will grow as we go on. But we must go on; and it is no good our delaying the passage of the mountains. Further south there are no passes, till one comes to the Gap of Rohan. I do not trust that way since your news of Saruman. Who knows which side now the marshals of the Horse-lords serve?'

'Who knows indeed!' said Gandalf. 'But there is another way, and not by the pass of Caradhras: the dark and secret way that we have spoken of.'

'But let us not speak of it again! Not yet. Say nothing to the others, I beg, not until it is plain that there is no other way.'

'We must decide before we go further,' answered Gandalf.

'Then let us weigh the matter in our minds, while the others rest and sleep,' said Aragorn.

In the late afternoon, while the others were finishing their breakfast, Gandalf and Aragorn went aside together and stood looking at Caradhras. Its sides were now dark and sullen, and its head was in grey cloud. Frodo watched them, wondering which way the debate would go. When they returned to the Company Gandalf spoke, and then he knew that it had been decided to face the weather and the high pass. He was relieved. He could not guess what was the other dark and secret way, but the very mention of it had seemed to fill Aragorn with dismay, and Frodo was glad that it had been abandoned.

'From signs that we have seen lately,' said Gandalf, 'I fear that the Redhorn Gate may be watched; and also I have doubts of the weather that is coming up behind. Snow may come. We must go with all the speed that we can. Even so it will take us more than two marches before we reach the top of the pass. Dark will come early this evening. We must leave as soon as you can get ready.'

'I will add a word of advice, if I may,' said Boromir. 'I was born under the shadow of the White Mountains and know something of journeys in the high places. We shall meet bitter cold, if no worse, before we come down on the other side. It will not help us to keep so secret that we are frozen to death. When we leave here, where there are still a few trees and bushes, each of us should carry a faggot of wood, as large as he can bear.'

'And Bill could take a bit more, couldn't you, lad?' said Sam. The pony looked at him mournfully.

'Very well,' said Gandalf. 'But we must not use the wood – not unless it is a choice between fire and death.'

The Company set out again, with good speed at first; but soon their way became steep and difficult. The twisting and climbing road had in many places almost disappeared, and was blocked with many fallen stones. The night grew deadly dark under great clouds. A bitter wind swirled among the rocks. By midnight they had climbed to the knees of the great mountains. The narrow path now wound under a sheer wall of cliffs to the left, above which the grim flanks of Caradhras towered up invisible in the gloom; on the right was a gulf of darkness where the land fell suddenly into a deep ravine.

Laboriously they climbed a sharp slope and halted for a moment at the top. Frodo felt a soft touch on his face. He put out his arm and saw the dim white flakes of snow settling on his sleeve.

They went on. But before long the snow was falling fast, filling all the air, and swirling into Frodo's eyes. The dark bent shapes of Gandalf and Aragorn only a pace or two ahead could hardly be seen.

'I don't like this at all,' panted Sam just behind. 'Snow's all right on a fine morning, but I like to be in bed while it's falling. I wish this lot would go off to Hobbiton! Folk might welcome it there.' Except on the high moors of the North-farthing a heavy fall was rare in the Shire, and was regarded as a pleasant event and a chance for fun. No living hobbit (save Bilbo) could remember the Fell Winter of 1311, when white wolves invaded the Shire over the frozen Brandywine.

Gandalf halted. Snow was thick on his hood and shoulders; it was already ankle-deep about his boots.

'This is what I feared,' he said. 'What do you say now, Aragorn?'

'That I feared it too,' Aragorn answered, 'but less than other things. I knew the risk of snow, though it seldom falls heavily so far south, save high up in the mountains. But we are not high yet; we are still far down, where the paths are usually open all the winter.'

'I wonder if this is a contrivance of the Enemy,' said Boromir. 'They say in my land that he can govern the storms in the Mountains of Shadow that stand upon the borders of Mordor. He has strange powers and many allies.'

'His arm has grown long indeed,' said Gimli, 'if he can

draw snow down from the North to trouble us here three hundred leagues away.'

'His arm has grown long,' said Gandalf.

While they were halted, the wind died down, and the snow slackened until it almost ceased. They tramped on again. But they had not gone more than a furlong when the storm returned with fresh fury. The wind whistled and the snow became a blinding blizzard. Soon even Boromir found it hard to keep going. The hobbits, bent nearly double, toiled along behind the taller folk, but it was plain that they could not go much further, if the snow continued. Frodo's feet felt like lead. Pippin was dragging behind. Even Gimli, as stout as any dwarf could be, was grumbling as he trudged.

The Company halted suddenly, as if they had come to an agreement without any words being spoken. They heard eerie noises in the darkness round them. It may have been only a trick of the wind in the cracks and gullies of the rocky wall, but the sounds were those of shrill cries, and wild howls of laughter. Stones began to fall from the mountain-side, whistling over their heads, or crashing on the path beside them. Every now and again they heard a dull rumble, as a great boulder rolled down from hidden heights above.

'We cannot go further tonight,' said Boromir. 'Let those call it the wind who will; there are fell voices on the air; and these stones are aimed at us.'

'I do call it the wind,' said Aragorn. 'But that does not make what you say untrue. There are many evil and unfriendly things in the world that have little love for those that go on two legs, and yet are not in league with Sauron, but have purposes of their own. Some have been in this world longer than he.'

'Caradhras was called the Cruel, and had an ill name,' said Gimli, 'long years ago, when rumour of Sauron had not been heard in these lands.'

'It matters little who is the enemy, if we cannot beat off his attack,' said Gandalf.

'But what can we do?' cried Pippin miserably. He was leaning on Merry and Frodo, and he was shivering.

'Either stop where we are, or go back,' said Gandalf. 'It is no good going on. Only a little higher, if I remember rightly, this path leaves the cliff and runs into a wide shallow trough at the bottom of a long hard slope. We should have no shelter there from snow, or stones – or anything else.'

'And it is no good going back while the storm holds,' said Aragorn. 'We have passed no place on the way up that offered more shelter than this cliff-wall we are under now.'

'Shelter!' muttered Sam. 'If this is shelter, then one wall and no roof make a house.'

The Company now gathered together as close to the cliff as they could. It faced southwards, and near the bottom it leaned out a little, so that they hoped it would give them some protection from the northerly wind and from the falling stones. But eddying blasts swirled round them from every side, and the snow flowed down in ever denser clouds.

They huddled together with their backs to the wall. Bill the pony stood patiently but dejectedly in front of the hobbits, and screened them a little; but before long the drifting snow was above his hocks, and it went on mounting. If they had had no larger companions the hobbits would soon have been entirely buried.

A great sleepiness came over Frodo; he felt himself sinking fast into a warm and hazy dream. He thought a fire was heating his toes, and out of the shadows on the other side of the hearth he heard Bilbo's voice speaking. *I don't think much of your diary*, he said. *Snowstorms on January the twelfth: there was no need to come back to report that!*

But I wanted rest and sleep, Bilbo, Frodo answered with an effort, when he felt himself shaken, and he came back painfully to wakefulness. Boromir had lifted him off the ground out of a nest of snow.

'This will be the death of the halflings, Gandalf,' said Boromir. 'It is useless to sit here until the snow goes over our heads. We must do something to save ourselves.'

'Give them this,' said Gandalf, searching in his pack and drawing out a leathern flask. 'Just a mouthful each – for all of us. It is very precious. It is *miruvor*, the cordial of Imladris. Elrond gave it to me at our parting. Pass it round!'

As soon as Frodo had swallowed a little of the warm and fragrant liquor he felt a new strength of heart, and the heavy drowsiness left his limbs. The others also revived and found fresh hope and vigour. But the snow did not relent. It whirled about them thicker than ever, and the wind blew louder.

'What do you say to fire?' asked Boromir suddenly. 'The choice seems near now between fire and death, Gandalf. Doubtless we shall be hidden from all unfriendly eyes when the snow has covered us, but that will not help us.'

'You may make a fire, if you can,' answered Gandalf. 'If there are any watchers that can endure this storm, then they can see us, fire or no.'

But though they had brought wood and kindlings by the advice of Boromir, it passed the skill of Elf or even Dwarf to strike a flame that would hold amid the swirling wind or catch in the wet fuel. At last reluctantly Gandalf himself took a hand. Picking up a faggot he held it aloft for a moment, and then with a word of command, *naur an edraith ammen!* he thrust the end of his staff into the midst of it. At once a great spout of green and blue flame sprang out, and the wood flared and sputtered.

'If there are any to see, then I at least am revealed to them,' he said. 'I have written *Gandalf is here* in signs that all can read from Rivendell to the mouths of Anduin.'

But the Company cared no longer for watchers or unfriendly eyes. Their hearts were rejoiced to see the light of the fire. The wood burned merrily; and though all round it the snow hissed, and pools of slush crept under their feet, they warmed their hands gladly at the blaze. There they stood, stooping in a circle round the little dancing and blowing flames. A red light was on their tired and anxious faces; behind them the night was like a black wall.

But the wood was burning fast, and the snow still fell.

The fire burned low, and the last faggot was thrown on.

'The night is getting old,' said Aragorn. 'The dawn is not far off.'

'If any dawn can pierce these clouds,' said Gimli.

Boromir stepped out of the circle and stared up into the blackness. 'The snow is growing less,' he said, 'and the wind is quieter.'

Frodo gazed wearily at the flakes still falling out of the dark to be revealed white for a moment in the light of the dying fire; but for a long time he could see no sign of their slackening. Then suddenly, as sleep was beginning to creep over him again, he was aware that the wind had indeed fallen, and the flakes were becoming larger and fewer. Very slowly a dim light began to grow. At last the snow stopped altogether.

As the light grew stronger it showed a silent shrouded world. Below their refuge were white humps and domes and shapeless deeps beneath which the path that they had trodden was altogether lost; but the heights above were hidden in great clouds still heavy with the threat of snow.

Gimli looked up and shook his head. 'Caradhras has not forgiven us,' he said. 'He has more snow yet to fling at us, if we go on. The sooner we go back and down the better.'

To this all agreed, but their retreat was now difficult. It might well prove impossible. Only a few paces from the ashes of their fire the snow lay many feet deep, higher than the heads of the hobbits; in places it had been scooped and piled by the wind into great drifts against the cliff.

'If Gandalf would go before us with a bright flame, he might melt a path for you,' said Legolas. The storm had troubled him little, and he alone of the Company remained still light of heart.

'If Elves could fly over mountains, they might fetch the Sun

to save us,' answered Gandalf. 'But I must have something to
work on. I cannot burn snow.'

'Well,' said Boromir, 'when heads are at a loss bodies must
serve, as we say in my country. The strongest of us must
seek a way. See! Though all is now snow-clad, our path, as
we came up, turned about that shoulder of rock down yonder.
It was there that the snow first began to burden us. If we
could reach that point, maybe it would prove easier beyond.
It is no more than a furlong off, I guess.'

'Then let us force a path thither, you and I!' said Aragorn.

Aragorn was the tallest of the Company, but Boromir, little
less in height, was broader and heavier in build. He led the
way, and Aragorn followed him. Slowly they moved off, and
were soon toiling heavily. In places the snow was breast-high,
and often Boromir seemed to be swimming or burrowing
with his great arms rather than walking.

Legolas watched them for a while with a smile upon his
lips, and then he turned to the others. 'The strongest must
seek a way, say you? But I say: let a ploughman plough, but
choose an otter for swimming, and for running light over
grass and leaf, or over snow – an Elf.'

With that he sprang forth nimbly, and then Frodo noticed
as if for the first time, though he had long known it, that the
Elf had no boots, but wore only light shoes, as he always did,
and his feet made little imprint in the snow.

'Farewell!' he said to Gandalf. 'I go to find the Sun!' Then
swift as a runner over firm sand he shot away, and quickly
overtaking the toiling men, with a wave of his hand he passed
them, and sped into the distance, and vanished round the
rocky turn.

The others waited huddled together, watching until Boromir and Aragorn dwindled into black specks in the whiteness.
At length they too passed from sight. The time dragged on.
The clouds lowered, and now a few flakes of snow came
curling down again.

An hour, maybe, went by, though it seemed far longer,

and then at last they saw Legolas coming back. At the same time Boromir and Aragorn reappeared round the bend far behind him and came labouring up the slope.

'Well,' cried Legolas as he ran up, 'I have not brought the Sun. She is walking in the blue fields of the South, and a little wreath of snow on this Redhorn hillock troubles her not at all. But I have brought back a gleam of good hope for those who are doomed to go on feet. There is the greatest wind-drift of all just beyond the turn, and there our Strong Men were almost buried. They despaired, until I returned and told them that the drift was little wider than a wall. And on the other side the snow suddenly grows less, while further down it is no more than a white coverlet to cool a hobbit's toes.'

'Ah, it is as I said,' growled Gimli. 'It was no ordinary storm. It is the ill will of Caradhras. He does not love Elves and Dwarves, and that drift was laid to cut off our escape.'

'But happily your Caradhras has forgotten that you have Men with you,' said Boromir, who came up at that moment. 'And doughty Men too, if I may say it; though lesser men with spades might have served you better. Still, we have thrust a lane through the drift; and for that all here may be grateful who cannot run as light as Elves.'

'But how are we to get down there, even if you have cut through the drift?' said Pippin, voicing the thought of all the hobbits.

'Have hope!' said Boromir. 'I am weary, but I still have some strength left, and Aragorn too. We will bear the little folk. The others no doubt will make shift to tread the path behind us. Come, Master Peregrin! I will begin with you.'

He lifted up the hobbit. 'Cling to my back! I shall need my arms,' he said and strode forward. Aragorn with Merry came behind. Pippin marvelled at his strength, seeing the passage that he had already forced with no other tool than his great limbs. Even now, burdened as he was, he was widening the track for those who followed, thrusting the snow aside as he went.

They came at length to the great drift. It was flung across the mountain-path like a sheer and sudden wall, and its crest, sharp as if shaped with knives, reared up more than twice the height of Boromir; but through the middle a passage had been beaten, rising and falling like a bridge. On the far side Merry and Pippin were set down, and there they waited with Legolas for the rest of the Company to arrive.

After a while Boromir returned carrying Sam. Behind in the narrow but now well-trodden track came Gandalf, leading Bill with Gimli perched among the baggage. Last came Aragorn carrying Frodo. They passed through the lane; but hardly had Frodo touched the ground when with a deep rumble there rolled down a fall of stones and slithering snow. The spray of it half blinded the Company as they crouched against the cliff, and when the air cleared again they saw that the path was blocked behind them.

'Enough, enough!' cried Gimli. 'We are departing as quickly as we may!' And indeed with that last stroke the malice of the mountain seemed to be expended, as if Caradhras was satisfied that the invaders had been beaten off and would not dare to return. The threat of snow lifted; the clouds began to break and the light grew broader.

As Legolas had reported, they found that the snow became steadily more shallow as they went down, so that even the hobbits could trudge along. Soon they all stood once more on the flat shelf at the head of the steep slope where they had felt the first flakes of snow the night before.

The morning was now far advanced. From the high place they looked back westwards over the lower lands. Far away in the tumble of country that lay at the foot of the mountain was the dell from which they had started to climb the pass.

Frodo's legs ached. He was chilled to the bone and hungry; and his head was dizzy as he thought of the long and painful march downhill. Black specks swam before his eyes. He rubbed them, but the black specks remained. In the distance below him, but still high above the lower foothills, dark dots were circling in the air.

'The birds again!' said Aragorn, pointing down.

'That cannot be helped now,' said Gandalf. 'Whether they are good or evil, or have nothing to do with us at all, we must go down at once. Not even on the knees of Caradhras will we wait for another night-fall!'

A cold wind flowed down behind them, as they turned their backs on the Redhorn Gate, and stumbled wearily down the slope. Caradhras had defeated them.

CHAPTER IV

A JOURNEY IN THE DARK

It was evening, and the grey light was again waning fast,
when they halted for the night. They were very weary. The
mountains were veiled in deepening dusk, and the wind was
cold. Gandalf spared them one more mouthful each of the
miruvor of Rivendell. When they had eaten some food he
called a council.

'We cannot, of course, go on again tonight,' he said. 'The
attack on the Redhorn Gate has tired us out, and we must
rest here for a while.'

'And then where are we to go?' asked Frodo.

'We still have our journey and our errand before us,'
answered Gandalf. 'We have no choice but to go on, or to
return to Rivendell.'

Pippin's face brightened visibly at the mere mention of
return to Rivendell; Merry and Sam looked up hopefully. But
Aragorn and Boromir made no sign. Frodo looked troubled.

'I wish I was back there,' he said. 'But how can I return
without shame – unless there is indeed no other way, and we
are already defeated?'

'You are right, Frodo,' said Gandalf: 'to go back is to admit
defeat, and face worse defeat to come. If we go back now,
then the Ring must remain there: we shall not be able to set
out again. Then sooner or later Rivendell will be besieged,
and after a brief and bitter time it will be destroyed. The
Ringwraiths are deadly enemies, but they are only shadows
yet of the power and terror they would possess if the Ruling
Ring was on their master's hand again.'

'Then we must go on, if there is a way,' said Frodo with
a sigh. Sam sank back into gloom.

'There is a way that we may attempt,' said Gandalf. 'I

thought from the beginning, when first I considered this journey, that we should try it. But it is not a pleasant way, and I have not spoken of it to the Company before. Aragorn was against it, until the pass over the mountains had at least been tried.'

'If it is a worse road than the Redhorn Gate, then it must be evil indeed,' said Merry. 'But you had better tell us about it, and let us know the worst at once.'

'The road that I speak of leads to the Mines of Moria,' said Gandalf. Only Gimli lifted up his head; a smouldering fire was in his eyes. On all the others a dread fell at the mention of that name. Even to the hobbits it was a legend of vague fear.

'The road may lead to Moria, but how can we hope that it will lead through Moria?' said Aragorn darkly.

'It is a name of ill omen,' said Boromir. 'Nor do I see the need to go there. If we cannot cross the mountains, let us journey southwards, until we come to the Gap of Rohan, where men are friendly to my people, taking the road that I followed on my way hither. Or we might pass by and cross the Isen into Langstrand and Lebennin, and so come to Gondor from the regions nigh to the sea.'

'Things have changed since you came north, Boromir,' answered Gandalf. 'Did you not hear what I told you of Saruman? With him I may have business of my own ere all is over. But the Ring must not come near Isengard, if that can by any means be prevented. The Gap of Rohan is closed to us while we go with the Bearer.

'As for the longer road: we cannot afford the time. We might spend a year in such a journey, and we should pass through many lands that are empty and harbourless. Yet they would not be safe. The watchful eyes both of Saruman and of the Enemy are on them. When you came north, Boromir, you were in the Enemy's eyes only one stray wanderer from the South and a matter of small concern to him: his mind was busy with the pursuit of the Ring. But you return now as a member of the Ring's Company, and you are in peril as long as you remain with us. The danger will increase with every league that we go south under the naked sky.

'Since our open attempt on the mountain-pass our plight has become more desperate, I fear. I see now little hope, if we do not soon vanish from sight for a while, and cover our trail. Therefore I advise that we should go neither over the mountains, nor round them, but under them. That is a road at any rate that the Enemy will least expect us to take.'

'We do not know what he expects,' said Boromir. 'He may watch all roads, likely and unlikely. In that case to enter Moria would be to walk into a trap, hardly better than knocking at the gates of the Dark Tower itself. The name of Moria is black.'

'You speak of what you do not know, when you liken Moria to the stronghold of Sauron,' answered Gandalf. 'I alone of you have ever been in the dungeons of the Dark Lord, and only in his older and lesser dwelling in Dol Guldur. Those who pass the gates of Barad-dûr do not return. But I would not lead you into Moria if there were no hope of coming out again. If there are Orcs there, it may prove ill for us, that is true. But most of the Orcs of the Misty Mountains were scattered or destroyed in the Battle of Five Armies. The Eagles report that Orcs are gathering again from afar; but there is a hope that Moria is still free.

'There is even a chance that Dwarves are there, and that in some deep hall of his fathers, Balin son of Fundin may be found. However it may prove, one must tread the path that need chooses!'

'I will tread the path with you, Gandalf!' said Gimli. 'I will go and look on the halls of Durin, whatever may wait there – if you can find the doors that are shut.'

'Good, Gimli!' said Gandalf. 'You encourage me. We will seek the hidden doors together. And we will come through. In the ruins of the Dwarves, a dwarf's head will be less easy to bewilder than Elves or Men or Hobbits. Yet it will not be the first time that I have been to Moria. I sought there long for Thráin son of Thrór after he was lost. I passed through, and I came out again alive!'

'I too once passed the Dimrill Gate,' said Aragorn quietly; 'but though I also came out again, the memory is very evil. I do not wish to enter Moria a second time.'

'And I don't wish to enter it even once,' said Pippin.

'Nor me,' muttered Sam.

'Of course not!' said Gandalf. 'Who would? But the question is: who will follow me, if I lead you there?'

'I will,' said Gimli eagerly.

'I will,' said Aragorn heavily. 'You followed my lead almost to disaster in the snow, and have said no word of blame. I will follow your lead now – if this last warning does not move you. It is not of the Ring, nor of us others that I am thinking now, but of you, Gandalf. And I say to you: if you pass the doors of Moria, beware!'

'I will *not* go,' said Boromir; 'not unless the vote of the whole company is against me. What do Legolas and the little folk say? The Ring-bearer's voice surely should be heard?'

'I do not wish to go to Moria,' said Legolas.

The hobbits said nothing. Sam looked at Frodo. At last Frodo spoke. 'I do not wish to go,' he said; 'but neither do I wish to refuse the advice of Gandalf. I beg that there should be no vote, until we have slept on it. Gandalf will get votes easier in the light of the morning than in this cold gloom. How the wind howls!'

At these words all fell into silent thought. They heard the wind hissing among the rocks and trees, and there was a howling and wailing round them in the empty spaces of the night.

Suddenly Aragorn leapt to his feet. 'How the wind howls!' he cried. 'It is howling with wolf-voices. The Wargs have come west of the Mountains!'

'Need we wait until morning then?' said Gandalf. 'It is as I said. The hunt is up! Even if we live to see the dawn, who now will wish to journey south by night with the wild wolves on his trail?'

'How far is Moria?' asked Boromir.

'There was a door south-west of Caradhras, some fifteen miles as the crow flies, and maybe twenty as the wolf runs,' answered Gandalf grimly.

'Then let us start as soon as it is light tomorrow, if we can,' said Boromir. 'The wolf that one hears is worse than the orc that one fears.'

'True!' said Aragorn, loosening his sword in its sheath. 'But where the warg howls, there also the orc prowls.'

'I wish I had taken Elrond's advice,' muttered Pippin to Sam. 'I am no good after all. There is not enough of the breed of Bandobras the Bullroarer in me: these howls freeze my blood. I don't ever remember feeling so wretched.'

'My heart's right down in my toes, Mr. Pippin,' said Sam. 'But we aren't etten yet, and there are some stout folk here with us. Whatever may be in store for old Gandalf, I'll wager it isn't a wolf's belly.'

For their defence in the night the Company climbed to the top of the small hill under which they had been sheltering. It was crowned with a knot of old and twisted trees, about which lay a broken circle of boulder-stones. In the midst of this they lit a fire, for there was no hope that darkness and silence would keep their trail from discovery by the hunting packs.

Round the fire they sat, and those that were not on guard dozed uneasily. Poor Bill the pony trembled and sweated where he stood. The howling of the wolves was now all round them, sometimes nearer and sometimes further off. In the dead of night many shining eyes were seen peering over the brow of the hill. Some advanced almost to the ring of stones. At a gap in the circle a great dark wolf-shape could be seen halted, gazing at them. A shuddering howl broke from him, as if he were a captain summoning his pack to the assault.

Gandalf stood up and strode forward, holding his staff

aloft. 'Listen, Hound of Sauron!' he cried. 'Gandalf is here. Fly, if you value your foul skin! I will shrivel you from tail to snout, if you come within this ring.'

The wolf snarled and sprang towards them with a great leap. At that moment there was a sharp twang. Legolas had loosed his bow. There was a hideous yell, and the leaping shape thudded to the ground; the elvish arrow had pierced its throat. The watching eyes were suddenly extinguished. Gandalf and Aragorn strode forward, but the hill was deserted; the hunting packs had fled. All about them the darkness grew silent, and no cry came on the sighing wind.

The night was old, and westward the waning moon was setting, gleaming fitfully through the breaking clouds. Suddenly Frodo started from sleep. Without warning a storm of howls broke out fierce and wild all about the camp. A great host of Wargs had gathered silently and was now attacking them from every side at once.

'Fling fuel on the fire!' cried Gandalf to the hobbits. 'Draw your blades, and stand back to back!'

In the leaping light, as the fresh wood blazed up, Frodo saw many grey shapes spring over the ring of stones. More and more followed. Through the throat of one huge leader Aragorn passed his sword with a thrust; with a great sweep Boromir hewed the head off another. Beside them Gimli stood with his stout legs apart, wielding his dwarf-axe. The bow of Legolas was singing.

In the wavering firelight Gandalf seemed suddenly to grow: he rose up, a great menacing shape like the monument of some ancient king of stone set upon a hill. Stooping like a cloud, he lifted a burning branch and strode to meet the wolves. They gave back before him. High in the air he tossed the blazing brand. It flared with a sudden white radiance like lightning; and his voice rolled like thunder.

'*Naur an edraith ammen! Naur dan i ngaurhoth!*' he cried.

There was a roar and a crackle, and the tree above him

burst into a leaf and bloom of blinding flame. The fire leapt
from tree-top to tree-top. The whole hill was crowned with
dazzling light. The swords and knives of the defenders shone
and flickered. The last arrow of Legolas kindled in the air
as it flew, and plunged burning into the heart of a great
wolf-chieftain. All the others fled.

Slowly the fire died till nothing was left but falling ash and
sparks; a bitter smoke curled above the burned tree-stumps,
and blew darkly from the hill, as the first light of dawn came
dimly in the sky. Their enemies were routed and did not
return.

'What did I tell you, Mr. Pippin?' said Sam, sheathing his
sword. 'Wolves won't get him. That was an eye-opener, and
no mistake! Nearly singed the hair off my head!'

When the full light of the morning came no signs of the
wolves were to be found, and they looked in vain for
the bodies of the dead. No trace of the fight remained but
the charred trees and the arrows of Legolas lying on the
hill-top. All were undamaged save one of which only the
point was left.

'It is as I feared,' said Gandalf. 'These were no ordinary
wolves hunting for food in the wilderness. Let us eat quickly
and go!'

That day the weather changed again, almost as if it was at
the command of some power that had no longer any use for
snow, since they had retreated from the pass, a power that
wished now to have a clear light in which things that moved
in the wild could be seen from far away. The wind had been
turning through north to north-west during the night, and
now it failed. The clouds vanished southwards and the
sky was opened, high and blue. As they stood upon the hill-
side, ready to depart, a pale sunlight gleamed over the
mountain-tops.

'We must reach the doors before sunset,' said Gandalf, 'or
I fear we shall not reach them at all. It is not far, but our
path may be winding, for here Aragorn cannot guide us; he

has seldom walked in this country, and only once have I been under the west wall of Moria, and that was long ago.

'There it lies,' he said, pointing away south-eastwards to where the mountains' sides fell sheer into the shadows at their feet. In the distance could be dimly seen a line of bare cliffs, and in their midst, taller than the rest, one great grey wall. 'When we left the pass I led you southwards, and not back to our starting point, as some of you may have noticed. It is well that I did so, for now we have several miles less to cross, and haste is needed. Let us go!'

'I do not know which to hope,' said Boromir grimly: 'that Gandalf will find what he seeks, or that coming to the cliff we shall find the gates lost for ever. All choices seem ill, and to be caught between wolves and the wall the likeliest chance. Lead on!'

Gimli now walked ahead by the wizard's side, so eager was he to come to Moria. Together they led the Company back towards the mountains. The only road of old to Moria from the west had lain along the course of a stream, the Sirannon, that ran out from the feet of the cliffs near where the doors had stood. But either Gandalf was astray, or else the land had changed in recent years; for he did not strike the stream where he looked to find it, only a few miles southwards from their start.

The morning was passing towards noon, and still the Company wandered and scrambled in a barren country of red stones. Nowhere could they see any gleam of water or hear any sound of it. All was bleak and dry. Their hearts sank. They saw no living thing, and not a bird was in the sky; but what the night would bring, if it caught them in that lost land, none of them cared to think.

Suddenly Gimli, who had pressed on ahead, called back to them. He was standing on a knoll and pointing to the right. Hurrying up they saw below them a deep and narrow channel. It was empty and silent, and hardly a trickle of water flowed among the brown and red-stained stones of its bed;

but on the near side there was a path, much broken and decayed, that wound its way among the ruined walls and paving-stones of an ancient highroad.

'Ah! Here it is at last!' said Gandalf. 'This is where the stream ran: Sirannon, the Gate-stream, they used to call it. But what has happened to the water, I cannot guess; it used to be swift and noisy. Come! We must hurry on. We are late.'

The Company were footsore and tired; but they trudged doggedly along the rough and winding track for many miles. The sun turned from the noon and began to go west. After a brief halt and a hasty meal they went on again. Before them the mountains frowned, but their path lay in a deep trough of land and they could see only the higher shoulders and the far eastward peaks.

At length they came to a sharp bend. There the road, which had been veering southwards between the brink of the channel and a steep fall of the land to the left, turned and went due east again. Rounding the corner they saw before them a low cliff, some five fathoms high, with a broken and jagged top. Over it a trickling water dripped, through a wide cleft that seemed to have been carved out by a fall that had once been strong and full.

'Indeed things have changed!' said Gandalf. 'But there is no mistaking the place. There is all that remains of the Stair Falls. If I remember right, there was a flight of steps cut in the rock at their side, but the main road wound away left and climbed with several loops up to the level ground at the top. There used to be a shallow valley beyond the falls right up to the Walls of Moria, and the Sirannon flowed through it with the road beside it. Let us go and see what things are like now!'

They found the stone steps without difficulty, and Gimli sprang swiftly up them, followed by Gandalf and Frodo. When they reached the top they saw that they could go no further that way, and the reason for the drying up of the

Gate-stream was revealed. Behind them the sinking Sun filled the cool western sky with glimmering gold. Before them stretched a dark still lake. Neither sky nor sunset was reflected on its sullen surface. The Sirannon had been dammed and had filled all the valley. Beyond the ominous water were reared vast cliffs, their stern faces pallid in the fading light: final and impassable. No sign of gate or entrance, not a fissure or crack could Frodo see in the frowning stone.

'There are the Walls of Moria,' said Gandalf, pointing across the water. 'And there the Gate stood once upon a time, the Elven Door at the end of the road from Hollin by which we have come. But this way is blocked. None of the Company, I guess, will wish to swim this gloomy water at the end of the day. It has an unwholesome look.'

'We must find a way round the northern edge,' said Gimli. 'The first thing for the Company to do is to climb up by the main path and see where that will lead us. Even if there were no lake, we could not get our baggage-pony up this stair.'

'But in any case we cannot take the poor beast into the Mines,' said Gandalf. 'The road under the mountains is a dark road, and there are places narrow and steep which he cannot tread, even if we can.'

'Poor old Bill!' said Frodo. 'I had not thought of that. And poor Sam! I wonder what he will say?'

'I am sorry,' said Gandalf. 'Poor Bill has been a useful companion, and it goes to my heart to turn him adrift now. I would have travelled lighter and brought no animal, least of all this one that Sam is fond of, if I had had my way. I feared all along that we should be obliged to take this road.'

The day was drawing to its end, and cold stars were glinting in the sky high above the sunset, when the Company, with all the speed they could, climbed up the slopes and reached the side of the lake. In breadth it looked to be no more than two or three furlongs at the widest point. How far it stretched away southward they could not see in the failing light; but its northern end was no more than half a mile from where they stood, and between the stony ridges that enclosed the valley and the water's edge there was a rim of open ground. They hurried forward, for they had still a mile or two to go before they could reach the point on the far shore that Gandalf was making for; and then he had still to find the doors.

When they came to the northernmost corner of the lake they found a narrow creek that barred their way. It was green and stagnant, thrust out like a slimy arm towards the enclosing hills. Gimli strode forward undeterred, and found that the water was shallow, no more than ankle-deep at the edge. Behind him they walked in file, threading their way with care, for under the weedy pools were sliding and greasy stones, and footing was treacherous. Frodo shuddered with disgust at the touch of the dark unclean water on his feet.

As Sam, the last of the Company, led Bill up on to the dry ground on the far side, there came a soft sound: a swish, followed by a plop, as if a fish had disturbed the still surface of the water. Turning quickly they saw ripples, black-edged with shadow in the waning light: great rings were widening outwards from a point far out in the lake. There was a bubbling noise, and then silence. The dusk deepened, and the last gleams of the sunset were veiled in cloud.

Gandalf now pressed on at a great pace, and the others followed as quickly as they could. They reached the strip of dry land between the lake and the cliffs: it was narrow, often hardly a dozen yards across, and encumbered with fallen rock and stones; but they found a way, hugging the cliff, and keeping as far from the dark water as they might. A mile southwards along the shore they came upon holly trees. Stumps and dead boughs were rotting in the shallows, the remains it seemed of old thickets, or of a hedge that had once lined the road across the drowned valley. But close under the cliff there stood, still strong and living, two tall trees, larger than any trees of holly that Frodo had ever seen or imagined. Their great roots spread from the wall to the water. Under the looming cliffs they had looked like mere bushes, when seen far off from the top of the Stair; but now they towered overhead, stiff, dark, and silent, throwing deep night-shadows about their feet, standing like sentinel pillars at the end of the road.

'Well, here we are at last!' said Gandalf. 'Here the Elven-way from Hollin ended. Holly was the token of the people of that land, and they planted it here to mark the end of their domain; for the West-door was made chiefly for their use in their traffic with the Lords of Moria. Those were happier days, when there was still close friendship at times between folk of different race, even between Dwarves and Elves.'

'It was not the fault of the Dwarves that the friendship waned,' said Gimli.

'I have not heard that it was the fault of the Elves,' said Legolas.

'I have heard both,' said Gandalf; 'and I will not give judgement now. But I beg you two, Legolas and Gimli, at least to be friends, and to help me. I need you both. The doors are shut and hidden, and the sooner we find them the better. Night is at hand!'

Turning to the others he said: 'While I am searching, will you each make ready to enter the Mines? For here I fear we must say farewell to our good beast of burden. You must lay aside much of the stuff that we brought against bitter weather: you will not need it inside, nor, I hope, when we come through and journey on down into the South. Instead each of us must take a share of what the pony carried, especially the food and the water-skins.'

'But you can't leave poor old Bill behind in this forsaken place, Mr. Gandalf!' cried Sam, angry and distressed. 'I won't have it, and that's flat. After he has come so far and all!'

'I am sorry, Sam,' said the wizard. 'But when the Door opens I do not think you will be able to drag your Bill inside, into the long dark of Moria. You will have to choose between Bill and your master.'

'He'd follow Mr. Frodo into a dragon's den, if I led him,' protested Sam. 'It'd be nothing short of murder to turn him loose with all these wolves about.'

'It will be short of murder, I hope,' said Gandalf. He laid his hand on the pony's head, and spoke in a low voice. 'Go with words of guard and guiding on you,' he said. 'You are a wise beast, and have learned much in Rivendell. Make your ways to places where you can find grass, and so come in time to Elrond's house, or wherever you wish to go.

'There, Sam! He will have quite as much chance of escaping wolves and getting home as we have.'

Sam stood sullenly by the pony and returned no answer. Bill, seeming to understand well what was going on, nuzzled up to him, putting his nose to Sam's ear. Sam burst into tears, and fumbled with the straps, unlading all the pony's packs and throwing them on the ground. The others sorted out the goods, making a pile of all that could be left behind, and dividing up the rest.

When this was done they turned to watch Gandalf. He appeared to have done nothing. He was standing between the two trees gazing at the blank wall of the cliff, as if he would bore a hole into it with his eyes. Gimli was wandering about, tapping the stone here and there with his axe. Legolas was pressed against the rock, as if listening.

'Well, here we are and all ready,' said Merry; 'but where are the Doors? I can't see any sign of them.'

'Dwarf-doors are not made to be seen when shut,' said Gimli. 'They are invisible, and their own masters cannot find them or open them, if their secret is forgotten.'

'But this Door was not made to be a secret known only to Dwarves,' said Gandalf, coming suddenly to life and turning round. 'Unless things are altogether changed, eyes that know what to look for may discover the signs.'

He walked forward to the wall. Right between the shadow of the trees there was a smooth space, and over this he passed his hands to and fro, muttering words under his breath. Then he stepped back.

'Look!' he said. 'Can you see anything now?'

The Moon now shone upon the grey face of the rock; but they could see nothing else for a while. Then slowly on the surface, where the wizard's hands had passed, faint lines appeared, like slender veins of silver running in the stone. At first they were no more than pale gossamer-threads, so fine that they only twinkled fitfully where the Moon caught them, but steadily they grew broader and clearer, until their design could be guessed.

At the top, as high as Gandalf could reach, was an arch of interlacing letters in an Elvish character. Below, though the threads were in places blurred or broken, the outline could be seen of an anvil and a hammer surmounted by a crown with seven stars. Beneath these again were two trees, each bearing crescent moons. More clearly than all else there shone forth in the middle of the door a single star with many rays.

'There are the emblems of Durin!' cried Gimli.

'And there is the Tree of the High Elves!' said Legolas.

'And the Star of the House of Fëanor,' said Gandalf. 'They are wrought of *ithildin* that mirrors only starlight and moonlight, and sleeps until it is touched by one who speaks words now long forgotten in Middle-earth. It is long since I heard them, and I thought deeply before I could recall them to my mind.'

'What does the writing say?' asked Frodo, who was trying to decipher the inscription on the arch. 'I thought I knew the elf-letters, but I cannot read these.'

'The words are in the elven-tongue of the West of Middle-earth in the Elder Days,' answered Gandalf. 'But they do not say anything of importance to us. They say only: *The Doors of Durin, Lord of Moria. Speak, friend, and enter.* And underneath small and faint is written: *I, Narvi, made them. Celebrimbor of Hollin drew these signs.*'

'What does it mean by *speak, friend, and enter?*' asked Merry.

'That is plain enough,' said Gimli. 'If you are a friend,

speak the password, and the doors will open, and you can enter.'

'Yes,' said Gandalf, 'these doors are probably governed by words. Some dwarf-gates will open only at special times, or for particular persons; and some have locks and keys that are still needed when all necessary times and words are known. These doors have no key. In the days of Durin they were not secret. They usually stood open and doorwards sat here. But if they were shut, any who knew the opening word could speak it and pass in. At least so it is recorded, is it not, Gimli?'

'It is,' said the dwarf. 'But what the word was is not remembered. Narvi and his craft and all his kindred have vanished from the earth.'

'But do not *you* know the word, Gandalf?' asked Boromir in surprise.

'No!' said the wizard.

The others looked dismayed; only Aragorn, who knew Gandalf well, remained silent and unmoved.

'Then what was the use of bringing us to this accursed spot?' cried Boromir, glancing back with a shudder at the dark water. 'You told us that you had once passed through the Mines. How could that be, if you did not know how to enter?'

'The answer to your first question, Boromir,' said the wizard, 'is that I do not know the word – yet. But we shall soon see. And,' he added, with a glint in his eyes under their bristling brows, 'you may ask what is the use of my deeds when they are proved useless. As for your other question: do you doubt my tale? Or have you no wits left? I did not enter this way. I came from the East.

'If you wish to know, I will tell you that these doors open outwards. From the inside you may thrust them open with your hands. From the outside nothing will move them save the spell of command. They cannot be forced inwards.'

'What are you going to do then?' asked Pippin, undaunted by the wizard's bristling brows.

Here is written in the Fëanorian characters according to the mode of Beleriand: Ennyn Durin Aran Moria: pedo mellon a minno. Im Narvi hain echant: Celebrimbor o Eregion teithant i thiw hin.

'Knock on the doors with your head, Peregrin Took,' said Gandalf. 'But if that does not shatter them, and I am allowed a little peace from foolish questions, I will seek for the opening words.

'I once knew every spell in all the tongues of Elves or Men or Orcs, that was ever used for such a purpose. I can still remember ten score of them without searching in my mind. But only a few trials, I think, will be needed; and I shall not have to call on Gimli for words of the secret dwarf-tongue that they teach to none. The opening words were Elvish, like the writing on the arch: that seems certain.'

He stepped up to the rock again, and lightly touched with his staff the silver star in the middle beneath the sign of the anvil.

> *Annon edhellen, edro hi ammen!*
> *Fennas nogothrim, lasto beth lammen!*

he said in a commanding voice. The silver lines faded, but the blank grey stone did not stir.

Many times he repeated these words in different order, or varied them. Then he tried other spells, one after another, speaking now faster and louder, now soft and slow. Then he spoke many single words of Elvish speech. Nothing happened. The cliff towered into the night, the countless stars were kindled, the wind blew cold, and the doors stood fast.

Again Gandalf approached the wall, and lifting up his arms he spoke in tones of command and rising wrath. *Edro, edro!* he cried, and struck the rock with his staff. *Open, open!* he shouted, and followed it with the same command in every language that had ever been spoken in the West of Middle-earth. Then he threw his staff on the ground, and sat down in silence.

At that moment from far off the wind bore to their listening ears the howling of wolves. Bill the pony started in fear, and Sam sprang to his side and whispered softly to him.

'Do not let him run away!' said Boromir. 'It seems that we shall need him still, if the wolves do not find us. How I hate this foul pool!' He stooped and picking up a large stone he cast it far into the dark water.

The stone vanished with a soft slap; but at the same instant there was a swish and a bubble. Great rippling rings formed on the surface out beyond where the stone had fallen, and they moved slowly towards the foot of the cliff.

'Why did you do that, Boromir?' said Frodo. 'I hate this place, too, and I am afraid. I don't know of what: not of wolves, or the dark behind the doors, but of something else. I am afraid of the pool. Don't disturb it!'

'I wish we could get away!' said Merry.

'Why doesn't Gandalf do something quick?' said Pippin.

Gandalf took no notice of them. He sat with his head bowed, either in despair or in anxious thought. The mournful howling of the wolves was heard again. The ripples on the water grew and came closer; some were already lapping on the shore.

With a suddenness that startled them all the wizard sprang to his feet. He was laughing! 'I have it!' he cried. 'Of course, of course! Absurdly simple, like most riddles when you see the answer.'

Picking up his staff he stood before the rock and said in a clear voice: *Mellon!*

The star shone out briefly and faded again. Then silently a great doorway was outlined, though not a crack or joint had been visible before. Slowly it divided in the middle and swung outwards inch by inch, until both doors lay back against the wall. Through the opening a shadowy stair could be seen climbing steeply up; but beyond the lower steps the darkness was deeper than the night. The Company stared in wonder.

'I was wrong after all,' said Gandalf, 'and Gimli too. Merry, of all people, was on the right track. The opening word was inscribed on the archway all the time! The translation should have been: *Say "Friend" and enter.* I had only to speak the

Elvish word for *friend* and the doors opened. Quite simple. Too simple for a learned lore-master in these suspicious days. Those were happier times. Now let us go!'

He strode forward and set his foot on the lowest step. But at that moment several things happened. Frodo felt something seize him by the ankle, and he fell with a cry. Bill the pony gave a wild neigh of fear, and turned tail and dashed away along the lakeside into the darkness. Sam leaped after him, and then hearing Frodo's cry he ran back again, weeping and cursing. The others swung round and saw the waters of the lake seething, as if a host of snakes were swimming up from the southern end.

Out from the water a long sinuous tentacle had crawled; it was pale-green and luminous and wet. Its fingered end had hold of Frodo's foot, and was dragging him into the water. Sam on his knees was now slashing at it with a knife.

The arm let go of Frodo, and Sam pulled him away, crying out for help. Twenty other arms came rippling out. The dark water boiled, and there was a hideous stench.

'Into the gateway! Up the stairs! Quick!' shouted Gandalf leaping back. Rousing them from the horror that seemed to have rooted all but Sam to the ground where they stood, he drove them forward.

They were just in time. Sam and Frodo were only a few steps up, and Gandalf had just begun to climb, when the groping tentacles writhed across the narrow shore and fingered the cliff-wall and the doors. One came wriggling over the threshold, glistening in the starlight. Gandalf turned and paused. If he was considering what word would close the gate again from within, there was no need. Many coiling arms seized the doors on either side, and with horrible strength, swung them round. With a shattering echo they slammed, and all light was lost. A noise of rending and crashing came dully through the ponderous stone.

Sam, clinging to Frodo's arm, collapsed on a step in the black darkness. 'Poor old Bill!' he said in a choking voice.

'Poor old Bill! Wolves and snakes! But the snakes were too much for him. I had to choose, Mr. Frodo. I had to come with you.'

They heard Gandalf go back down the steps and thrust his staff against the doors. There was a quiver in the stone and the stairs trembled, but the doors did not open.

'Well, well!' said the wizard. 'The passage is blocked behind us now, and there is only one way out – on the other side of the mountains. I fear from the sounds that boulders have been piled up, and the trees uprooted and thrown across the gate. I am sorry; for the trees were beautiful, and had stood so long.'

'I felt that something horrible was near from the moment that my foot first touched the water,' said Frodo. 'What was the thing, or were there many of them?'

'I do not know,' answered Gandalf; 'but the arms were all guided by one purpose. Something has crept, or has been driven out of dark waters under the mountains. There are older and fouler things than Orcs in the deep places of the world.' He did not speak aloud his thought that whatever it was that dwelt in the lake, it had seized on Frodo first among all the Company.

Boromir muttered under his breath, but the echoing stone magnified the sound to a hoarse whisper that all could hear: 'In the deep places of the world! And thither we are going against my wish. Who will lead us now in this deadly dark?'

'I will,' said Gandalf, 'and Gimli shall walk with me. Follow my staff!'

As the wizard passed on ahead up the great steps, he held his staff aloft, and from its tip there came a faint radiance. The wide stairway was sound and undamaged. Two hundred steps they counted, broad and shallow; and at the top they found an arched passage with a level floor leading on into the dark.

'Let us sit and rest and have something to eat, here on the

landing, since we can't find a dining-room!' said Frodo. He
had begun to shake off the terror of the clutching arm, and
suddenly he felt extremely hungry.

The proposal was welcomed by all; and they sat down on
the upper steps, dim figures in the gloom. After they had
eaten, Gandalf gave them each a third sip of the *miruvor* of
Rivendell.

'It will not last much longer, I am afraid,' he said; 'but I
think we need it after that horror at the gate. And unless we
have great luck, we shall need all that is left before we see
the other side! Go carefully with the water, too! There are
many streams and wells in the Mines, but they should not
be touched. We may not have a chance of filling our skins
and bottles till we come down into Dimrill Dale.'

'How long is that going to take us?' asked Frodo.

'I cannot say,' answered Gandalf. 'It depends on many
chances. But going straight, without mishap or losing our
way, we shall take three or four marches, I expect. It cannot
be less than forty miles from West-door to East-gate in a
direct line, and the road may wind much.'

After only a brief rest they started on their way again. All
were eager to get the journey over as quickly as possible, and
were willing, tired as they were, to go on marching still for
several hours. Gandalf walked in front as before. In his left
hand he held up his glimmering staff, the light of which just
showed the ground before his feet; in his right he held his
sword Glamdring. Behind him came Gimli, his eyes glinting
in the dim light as he turned his head from side to side.
Behind the dwarf walked Frodo, and he had drawn the short
sword, Sting. No gleam came from the blades of Sting or of
Glamdring; and that was some comfort, for being the work
of Elvish smiths in the Elder Days these swords shone with
a cold light, if any Orcs were near at hand. Behind Frodo
went Sam, and after him Legolas, and the young hobbits,
and Boromir. In the dark at the rear, grim and silent, walked
Aragorn.

The passage twisted round a few turns, and then began to descend. It went steadily down for a long while before it became level once again. The air grew hot and stifling, but it was not foul, and at times they felt currents of cooler air upon their faces, issuing from half-guessed openings in the walls. There were many of these. In the pale ray of the wizard's staff, Frodo caught glimpses of stairs and arches, and of other passages and tunnels, sloping up, or running steeply down, or opening blankly dark on either side. It was bewildering beyond hope of remembering.

Gimli aided Gandalf very little, except by his stout courage. At least he was not, as were most of the others, troubled by the mere darkness in itself. Often the wizard consulted him at points where the choice of way was doubtful; but it was always Gandalf who had the final word. The Mines of Moria were vast and intricate beyond the imagination of Gimli, Glóin's son, dwarf of the mountain-race though he was. To Gandalf the far-off memories of a journey long before were now of little help, but even in the gloom and despite all windings of the road he knew whither he wished to go, and he did not falter, as long as there was a path that led towards his goal.

'Do not be afraid!' said Aragorn. There was a pause longer than usual, and Gandalf and Gimli were whispering together; the others were crowded behind, waiting anxiously. 'Do not be afraid! I have been with him on many a journey, if never on one so dark; and there are tales of Rivendell of greater deeds of his than any that I have seen. He will not go astray – if there is any path to find. He has led us in here against our fears, but he will lead us out again, at whatever cost to himself. He is surer of finding the way home in a blind night than the cats of Queen Berúthiel.'

It was well for the Company that they had such a guide. They had no fuel nor any means of making torches; in the desperate scramble at the doors many things had been left behind. But without any light they would soon have come to grief. There were not only many roads to choose from, there were also in many places holes and pitfalls, and dark wells beside the path in which their passing feet echoed. There were fissures and chasms in the walls and floor, and every now and then a crack would open right before their feet. The widest was more than seven feet across, and it was long before Pippin could summon enough courage to leap over the dreadful gap. The noise of churning water came up from far below, as if some great mill-wheel was turning in the depths.

'Rope!' muttered Sam. 'I knew I'd want it, if I hadn't got it!'

As these dangers became more frequent their march became slower. Already they seemed to have been tramping on, on, endlessly to the mountains' roots. They were more than weary, and yet there seemed no comfort in the thought of halting anywhere. Frodo's spirits had risen for a while after his escape, and after food and a draught of the cordial; but now a deep uneasiness, growing to dread, crept over him again. Though he had been healed in Rivendell of the knife-stroke, that grim wound had not been without effect. His senses were sharper and more aware of things that could not be seen. One sign of change that he soon had noticed was that he could see more in the dark than any of his companions, save perhaps Gandalf. And he was in any case the bearer of the Ring: it hung upon its chain against his breast, and at whiles it seemed a heavy weight. He felt the certainty of evil ahead and of evil following; but he said nothing. He gripped tighter on the hilt of his sword and went on doggedly.

The Company behind him spoke seldom, and then only in hurried whispers. There was no sound but the sound of their own feet; the dull stump of Gimli's dwarf-boots; the heavy tread of Boromir; the light step of Legolas; the soft, scarce-heard patter of hobbit-feet; and in the rear the slow firm footfalls of Aragorn with his long stride. When they halted for a moment they heard nothing at all, unless it were

occasionally a faint trickle and drip of unseen water. Yet
Frodo began to hear, or to imagine that he heard, something
else: like the faint fall of soft bare feet. It was never loud
enough, or near enough, for him to feel certain that he heard
it; but once it had started it never stopped, while the Company was moving. But it was not an echo, for when they
halted it pattered on for a little all by itself, and then grew
still.

It was after nightfall when they had entered the Mines.
They had been going for several hours with only brief halts,
when Gandalf came to his first serious check. Before him
stood a wide dark arch opening into three passages: all led
in the same general direction, eastwards; but the left-hand
passage plunged down, while the right-hand climbed up, and
the middle way seemed to run on, smooth and level but very
narrow.

'I have no memory of this place at all!' said Gandalf, standing uncertainly under the arch. He held up his staff in the
hope of finding some marks or inscription that might help
his choice; but nothing of the kind was to be seen. 'I am too
weary to decide,' he said, shaking his head. 'And I expect
that you are all as weary as I am, or wearier. We had better
halt here for what is left of the night. You know what I mean!
In here it is ever dark; but outside the late Moon is riding
westward and the middle-night has passed.'

'Poor old Bill!' said Sam. 'I wonder where he is. I hope
those wolves haven't got him yet.'

To the left of the great arch they found a stone door: it
was half closed, but swung back easily to a gentle thrust.
Beyond there seemed to lie a wide chamber cut in the rock.

'Steady! Steady!' cried Gandalf as Merry and Pippin
pushed forward, glad to find a place where they could rest
with at least more feeling of shelter than in the open passage.
'Steady! You do not know what is inside yet. I will go first.'

He went in cautiously, and the others filed behind. 'There!'
he said, pointing with his staff to the middle of the floor.

Before his feet they saw a large round hole like the mouth of a well. Broken and rusty chains lay at the edge and trailed down into the black pit. Fragments of stone lay near.

'One of you might have fallen in and still be wondering when you were going to strike the bottom,' said Aragorn to Merry. 'Let the guide go first while you have one.'

'This seems to have been a guardroom, made for the watching of the three passages,' said Gimli. 'That hole was plainly a well for the guards' use, covered with a stone lid. But the lid is broken, and we must all take care in the dark.'

Pippin felt curiously attracted by the well. While the others were unrolling blankets and making beds against the walls of the chamber, as far as possible from the hole in the floor, he crept to the edge and peered over. A chill air seemed to strike his face, rising from invisible depths. Moved by a sudden impulse he groped for a loose stone, and let it drop. He felt his heart beat many times before there was any sound. Then far below, as if the stone had fallen into deep water in some cavernous place, there came a *plunk*, very distant, but magnified and repeated in the hollow shaft.

'What's that?' cried Gandalf. He was relieved when Pippin confessed what he had done; but he was angry, and Pippin could see his eye glinting. 'Fool of a Took!' he growled. 'This is a serious journey, not a hobbit walking-party. Throw yourself in next time, and then you will be no further nuisance. Now be quiet!'

Nothing more was heard for several minutes; but then there came out of the depths faint knocks: *tom-tap, tap-tom*. They stopped, and when the echoes had died away, they were repeated: *tap-tom, tom-tap, tap-tap, tom*. They sounded disquietingly like signals of some sort; but after a while the knocking died away and was not heard again.

'That was the sound of a hammer, or I have never heard one,' said Gimli.

'Yes,' said Gandalf, 'and I do not like it. It may have nothing to do with Peregrin's foolish stone; but probably something has been disturbed that would have been better left quiet. Pray, do nothing of the kind again! Let us hope we shall get some rest without further trouble. You, Pippin, can go on the first watch, as a reward,' he growled, as he rolled himself in a blanket.

Pippin sat miserably by the door in the pitch dark; but he kept on turning round, fearing that some unknown thing would crawl up out of the well. He wished he could cover the hole, if only with a blanket, but he dared not move or go near it, even though Gandalf seemed to be asleep.

Actually Gandalf was awake, though lying still and silent. He was deep in thought, trying to recall every memory of his former journey in the Mines, and considering anxiously the next course that he should take; a false turn now might be disastrous. After an hour he rose up and came over to Pippin.

'Get into a corner and have a sleep, my lad,' he said in a kindly tone. 'You want to sleep, I expect. I cannot get a wink, so I may as well do the watching.'

'I know what is the matter with me,' he muttered, as he sat down by the door. 'I need smoke! I have not tasted it since the morning before the snowstorm.'

The last thing that Pippin saw, as sleep took him, was a dark glimpse of the old wizard huddled on the floor, shielding a glowing chip in his gnarled hands between his knees. The flicker for a moment showed his sharp nose, and the puff of smoke.

It was Gandalf who roused them all from sleep. He had sat and watched all alone for about six hours, and had let the others rest. 'And in the watches I have made up my mind,' he said. 'I do not like the feel of the middle way; and I do not like the smell of the left-hand way: there is foul air down there, or I am no guide. I shall take the right-hand passage. It is time we began to climb up again.'

For eight dark hours, not counting two brief halts, they marched on; and they met no danger, and heard nothing, and saw nothing but the faint gleam of the wizard's light, bobbing like a will-o'-the-wisp in front of them. The passage they had chosen wound steadily upwards. As far as they could judge it went in great mounting curves, and as it rose it grew loftier and wider. There were now no openings to other galleries or tunnels on either side, and the floor was level and sound, without pits or cracks. Evidently they had struck what once had been an important road; and they went forward quicker than they had done on their first march.

In this way they advanced some fifteen miles, measured in a direct line east, though they must have actually walked twenty miles or more. As the road climbed upwards, Frodo's spirits rose a little; but he still felt oppressed, and still at times he heard, or thought he heard, away behind the Company and beyond the fall and patter of their feet, a following footstep that was not an echo.

They had marched as far as the hobbits could endure without a rest, and all were thinking of a place where they could sleep, when suddenly the walls to right and left vanished. They seemed to have passed through some arched doorway into a black and empty space. There was a great draught of warmer air behind them, and before them the darkness was cold on their faces. They halted and crowded anxiously together.

Gandalf seemed pleased. 'I chose the right way,' he said. 'At last we are coming to the habitable parts, and I guess that we are not far now from the eastern side. But we are high up, a good deal higher than the Dimrill Gate, unless I am mistaken. From the feeling of the air we must be in a wide hall. I will now risk a little real light.'

He raised his staff, and for a brief instant there was blaze like a flash of lightning. Great shadows sprang up and fled, and for a second they saw a vast roof far above their heads upheld by many mighty pillars hewn of stone. Before them and on either side stretched a huge empty hall; its black walls, polished and smooth as glass, flashed and glittered. Three other entrances they saw, dark black arches: one straight before them eastwards, and one on either side. Then the light went out.

'That is all that I shall venture on for the present,' said Gandalf. 'There used to be great windows on the mountain-side, and shafts leading out to the light in the upper reaches of the Mines. I think we have reached them now, but it is night outside again, and we cannot tell until morning. If I am right, tomorrow we may actually see the morning peeping in. But in the meanwhile we had better go no further. Let us rest, if we can. Things have gone well so far, and the greater part of the dark road is over. But we are not through yet, and it is a long way down to the Gates that open on the world.'

The Company spent that night in the great cavernous hall, huddled close together in a corner to escape the draught: there seemed to be a steady inflow of chill air through the eastern archway. All about them as they lay hung the dark-ness, hollow and immense, and they were oppressed by the loneliness and vastness of the dolven halls and endlessly branching stairs and passages. The wildest imaginings that dark rumour had ever suggested to the hobbits fell altogether short of the actual dread and wonder of Moria.

'There must have been a mighty crowd of dwarves here at one time,' said Sam; 'and every one of them busier than badgers for five hundred years to make all this, and most in hard rock too! What did they do it all for? They didn't live in these darksome holes surely?'

'These are not holes,' said Gimli. 'This is the great realm and city of the Dwarrowdelf. And of old it was not darksome, but full of light and splendour, as is still remembered in our songs.'

He rose and standing in the dark he began to chant in a deep voice, while the echoes ran away into the roof.

The world was young, the mountains green,
No stain yet on the Moon was seen,
No words were laid on stream or stone
When Durin woke and walked alone.
He named the nameless hills and dells;
He drank from yet untasted wells;
He stooped and looked in Mirrormere,
And saw a crown of stars appear,
As gems upon a silver thread,
Above the shadow of his head.

The world was fair, the mountains tall,
In Elder Days before the fall
Of mighty kings in Nargothrond
And Gondolin, who now beyond
The Western Seas have passed away:
The world was fair in Durin's Day.

A king he was on carven throne
In many-pillared halls of stone
With golden roof and silver floor,
And runes of power upon the door.
The light of sun and star and moon
In shining lamps of crystal hewn
Undimmed by cloud or shade of night
There shone for ever fair and bright.

There hammer on the anvil smote,
There chisel clove, and graver wrote;
There forged was blade, and bound was hilt;
The delver mined, the mason built.
There beryl, pearl, and opal pale,
And metal wrought like fishes' mail,
Buckler and corslet, axe and sword,
And shining spears were laid in hoard.

Unwearied then were Durin's folk;
Beneath the mountains music woke:
The harpers harped, the minstrels sang,
And at the gates the trumpets rang.

The world is grey, the mountains old,
The forge's fire is ashen-cold;
No harp is wrung, no hammer falls:
The darkness dwells in Durin's halls;
The shadow lies upon his tomb
In Moria, in Khazad-dûm.
But still the sunken stars appear
In dark and windless Mirrormere;
There lies his crown in water deep,
Till Durin wakes again from sleep.

'I like that!' said Sam. 'I should like to learn it. *In Moria, in Khazad-dûm!* But it makes the darkness seem heavier, thinking of all those lamps. Are there piles of jewels and gold lying about here still?'

Gimli was silent. Having sung his song he would say no more.

'Piles of jewels?' said Gandalf. 'No. The Orcs have often plundered Moria; there is nothing left in the upper halls. And since the dwarves fled, no one dares to seek the shafts and treasuries down in the deep places: they are drowned in water – or in a shadow of fear.'

'Then what do the dwarves want to come back for?' asked Sam.

'For *mithril*,' answered Gandalf. 'The wealth of Moria was not in gold and jewels, the toys of the Dwarves; nor in iron, their servant. Such things they found here, it is true, especially iron; but they did not need to delve for them: all things that they desired they could obtain in traffic. For here alone in the world was found Moria-silver, or true-silver as some have called it: *mithril* is the Elvish name. The Dwarves have a name which they do not tell. Its worth was ten times that of gold, and now it is beyond price; for little is left above ground, and even the Orcs dare not delve here for it. The lodes lead away north towards Caradhras, and down to darkness. The Dwarves tell no tale; but even as *mithril* was the foundation of their wealth, so also it was their destruction: they delved too greedily and too deep, and disturbed that from which they fled, Durin's Bane. Of what they brought to light the Orcs have gathered nearly all, and given it in tribute to Sauron, who covets it.

'*Mithril!* All folk desired it. It could be beaten like copper, and polished like glass; and the Dwarves could make of it a metal, light and yet harder than tempered steel. Its beauty was like to that of common silver, but the beauty of *mithril* did not tarnish or grow dim. The Elves dearly loved it, and among many uses they made of it *ithildin*, starmoon, which you saw upon the doors. Bilbo had a corslet of mithril-rings that Thorin gave him. I wonder what has become of it? Gathering dust still in Michel Delving Mathom-house, I suppose.'

'What?' cried Gimli, startled out of his silence. 'A corslet of Moria-silver? That was a kingly gift!'

'Yes,' said Gandalf. 'I never told him, but its worth was greater than the value of the whole Shire and everything in it.'

Frodo said nothing, but he put his hand under his tunic and touched the rings of his mail-shirt. He felt staggered to think that he had been walking about with the price of the Shire under his jacket. Had Bilbo known? He felt no doubt that Bilbo knew quite well. It was indeed a kingly gift. But now his thoughts had been carried away from the dark Mines, to Rivendell, to Bilbo, and to Bag End in the days while Bilbo was still there. He wished with all his heart that he was back there, and in those days, mowing the lawn, or pottering among the flowers, and that he had never heard of Moria, or *mithril* – or the Ring.

★   ★   ★

A deep silence fell. One by one the others fell asleep. Frodo was on guard. As if it were a breath that came in through unseen doors out of deep places, dread came over him. His hands were cold and his brow damp. He listened. All his mind was given to listening and nothing else for two slow hours; but he heard no sound, not even the imagined echo of a footfall.

His watch was nearly over, when, far off where he guessed that the western archway stood, he fancied that he could see two pale points of light, almost like luminous eyes. He started. His head had nodded. 'I must have nearly fallen asleep on guard,' he thought. 'I was on the edge of a dream.' He stood up and rubbed his eyes, and remained standing, peering into the dark, until he was relieved by Legolas.

When he lay down he quickly went to sleep, but it seemed to him that the dream went on: he heard whispers, and saw the two pale points of light approaching, slowly. He woke and found that the others were speaking softly near him, and that a dim light was falling on his face. High up above the eastern archway through a shaft near the roof came a long pale gleam; and across the hall through the northern arch light also glimmered faint and distantly.

Frodo sat up. 'Good morning!' said Gandalf. 'For morning it is again at last. I was right, you see. We are high up on the east side of Moria. Before today is over we ought to find the Great Gates and see the waters of Mirrormere lying in the Dimrill Dale before us.'

'I shall be glad,' said Gimli. 'I have looked on Moria, and it is very great, but it has become dark and dreadful; and we have found no sign of my kindred. I doubt now that Balin ever came here.'

After they had breakfasted Gandalf decided to go on again at once. 'We are tired, but we shall rest better when we are outside,' he said. 'I think that none of us will wish to spend another night in Moria.'

'No indeed!' said Boromir. 'Which way shall we take? Yonder eastward arch?'

'Maybe,' said Gandalf. 'But I do not know yet exactly where we are. Unless I am quite astray, I guess that we are above and to the north of the Great Gates; and it may not be easy to find the right road down to them. The eastern arch will probably prove to be the way that we must take; but before we make up our minds we ought to look about us. Let us go towards that light in the north door. If we could find a window it would help, but I fear that the light comes only down deep shafts.'

Following his lead the Company passed under the northern arch. They found themselves in a wide corridor. As they went along it the glimmer grew stronger, and they saw that it came through a doorway on their right. It was high and flat-topped, and the stone door was still upon its hinges, standing half open. Beyond it was a large square chamber. It was dimly lit, but to their eyes, after so long a time in the dark, it seemed dazzlingly bright, and they blinked as they entered.

Their feet disturbed a deep dust upon the floor, and stumbled among things lying in the doorway whose shapes they could not at first make out. The chamber was lit by a wide shaft high in the further eastern wall; it slanted up-wards and, far above, a small square patch of blue sky could be seen. The light of the shaft fell directly on a table in the middle of the room: a single oblong block, about two feet high, upon which was laid a great slab of white stone.

'It looks like a tomb,' muttered Frodo, and bent forwards with a curious sense of foreboding, to look more closely at it. Gandalf came quickly to his side. On the slab runes were deeply graven:

'These are Daeron's Runes, such as were used of old in Moria,' said Gandalf. 'Here is written in the tongues of Men and Dwarves:

> BALIN SON OF FUNDIN
> LORD OF MORIA.'

'He is dead then,' said Frodo. 'I feared it was so.' Gimli cast his hood over his face.

CHAPTER V

THE BRIDGE OF KHAZAD-DÛM

The Company of the Ring stood silent beside the tomb of Balin. Frodo thought of Bilbo and his long friendship with the dwarf, and of Balin's visit to the Shire long ago. In that dusty chamber in the mountains it seemed a thousand years ago and on the other side of the world.

At length they stirred and looked up, and began to search for anything that would give them tidings of Balin's fate, or show what had become of his folk. There was another smaller door on the other side of the chamber, under the shaft. By both the doors they could now see that many bones were lying, and among them were broken swords and axe-heads, and cloven shields and helms. Some of the swords were crooked: orc-scimitars with blackened blades.

There were many recesses cut in the rock of the walls, and in them were large iron-bound chests of wood. All had been broken and plundered; but beside the shattered lid of one there lay the remains of a book. It had been slashed and stabbed and partly burned, and it was so stained with black and other dark marks like old blood that little of it could be read. Gandalf lifted it carefully, but the leaves crackled and broke as he laid it on the slab. He pored over it for some time without speaking. Frodo and Gimli standing at his side could see, as he gingerly turned the leaves, that they were written by many different hands, in runes, both of Moria and of Dale, and here and there in Elvish script.

At last Gandalf looked up. 'It seems to be a record of the fortunes of Balin's folk,' he said. 'I guess that it began with their coming to Dimrill Dale nigh on thirty years ago: the pages seem to have numbers referring to the years after their

arrival. The top page is marked *one – three*, so at least two
are missing from the beginning. Listen to this!

'*We drove out orcs from the great gate and guard* – I think;
the next word is blurred and burned: probably *room – we
slew many in the bright* – I think – *sun in the dale. Flói was
killed by an arrow. He slew the great*. Then there is a blur
followed by *Flói under grass near Mirror mere*. The next line
or two I cannot read. Then comes *We have taken the
twentyfirst hall of North end to dwell in. There is* I cannot read
what. A *shaft* is mentioned. Then *Balin has set up his seat in
the Chamber of Mazarbul*.'

'The Chamber of Records,' said Gimli. 'I guess that is
where we now stand.'

'Well, I can read no more for a long way,' said Gandalf,
'except the word *gold*, and *Durin's Axe* and something *helm*.
Then *Balin is now lord of Moria*. That seems to end a chapter.
After some stars another hand begins, and I can see *we found
truesilver*, and later the word *wellforged*, and then something,
I have it! *mithril*; and the last two lines *Óin to seek for the
upper armouries of Third Deep*, something *go westwards*, a blur,
to Hollin gate.'

Gandalf paused and set a few leaves aside. 'There are
several pages of the same sort, rather hastily written and
much damaged,' he said; 'but I can make little of them in
this light. Now there must be a number of leaves missing,
because they begin to be numbered *five*, the fifth year of the
colony, I suppose. Let me see! No, they are too cut and
stained; I cannot read them. We might do better in the sunlight. Wait! Here is something: a large bold hand using an
Elvish script.'

'That would be Ori's hand,' said Gimli, looking over the
wizard's arm. 'He could write well and speedily, and often
used the Elvish characters.'

'I fear he had ill tidings to record in a fair hand,' said
Gandalf. 'The first clear word is *sorrow*, but the rest of the
line is lost, unless it ends in *estre*. Yes, it must be *yestre*

followed by *day being the tenth of novembre Balin lord of Moria fell in Dimrill Dale. He went alone to look in Mirror mere. an orc shot him from behind a stone. we slew the orc, but many more . . . up from east up the Silverlode.* The remainder of the page is so blurred that I can hardly make anything out, but I think I can read *we have barred the gates,* and then *can hold them long if,* and then perhaps *horrible* and *suffer.* Poor Balin! He seems to have kept the title that he took for less than five years. I wonder what happened afterwards; but there is no time to puzzle out the last few pages. Here is the last page of all.' He paused and sighed.

'It is grim reading,' he said. 'I fear their end was cruel. Listen! *We cannot get out. We cannot get out. They have taken the Bridge and second hall. Frár and Lóni and Náli fell there.* Then there are four lines smeared so that I can only read *went 5 days ago.* The last lines run *the pool is up to the wall at Westgate. The Watcher in the Water took Óin. We cannot get out. The end comes,* and then *drums, drums in the deep.* I wonder what that means. The last thing written is in a trailing scrawl of elf-letters: *they are coming.* There is nothing more.' Gandalf paused and stood in silent thought.

A sudden dread and a horror of the chamber fell on the Company. '*We cannot get out,*' muttered Gimli. 'It was well for us that the pool had sunk a little, and that the Watcher was sleeping down at the southern end.'

Gandalf raised his head and looked round. 'They seem to have made a last stand by both doors,' he said; 'but there were not many left by that time. So ended the attempt to retake Moria! It was valiant but foolish. The time is not come yet. Now, I fear, we must say farewell to Balin son of Fundin. Here he must lie in the halls of his fathers. We will take this book, the Book of Mazarbul, and look at it more closely later. You had better keep it, Gimli, and take it back to Dáin, if you get a chance. It will interest him, though it will grieve him deeply. Come, let us go! The morning is passing.'

'Which way shall we go?' asked Boromir.

'Back to the hall,' answered Gandalf. 'But our visit to this room has not been in vain. I now know where we are. This must be, as Gimli says, the Chamber of Mazarbul; and the hall must be the twenty-first of the North-end. Therefore we should leave by the eastern arch of the hall, and bear right and south, and go downwards. The Twenty-first Hall should be on the Seventh Level, that is six above the level of the Gates. Come now! Back to the hall!'

Gandalf had hardly spoken these words, when there came a great noise: a rolling *Boom* that seemed to come from depths far below, and to tremble in the stone at their feet. They sprang towards the door in alarm. *Doom, doom* it rolled again, as if huge hands were turning the very caverns of Moria into a vast drum. Then there came an echoing blast: a great horn was blown in the hall, and answering horns and harsh cries were heard further off. There was a hurrying sound of many feet.

'They are coming!' cried Legolas.

'We cannot get out,' said Gimli.

'Trapped!' cried Gandalf. 'Why did I delay? Here we are, caught, just as they were before. But I was not here then. We will see what———'

Doom, doom came the drum-beat and the walls shook.

'Slam the doors and wedge them!' shouted Aragorn. 'And keep your packs on as long as you can: we may get a chance to cut our way out yet.'

'No!' said Gandalf. 'We must not get shut in. Keep the east door ajar! We will go that way, if we get a chance.'

Another harsh horn-call and shrill cries rang out. Feet were coming down the corridor. There was a ring and clatter as the Company drew their swords. Glamdring shone with a pale light, and Sting glinted at the edges. Boromir set his shoulder against the western door.

'Wait a moment! Do not close it yet!' said Gandalf. He sprang forward to Boromir's side and drew himself up to his full height.

'Who comes hither to disturb the rest of Balin Lord of Moria?' he cried in a loud voice.

There was a rush of hoarse laughter, like the fall of sliding stones into a pit; amid the clamour a deep voice was raised in command. *Doom, boom, doom* went the drums in the deep.

With a quick movement Gandalf stepped before the narrow opening of the door and thrust forward his staff. There was a dazzling flash that lit the chamber and the passage outside. For an instant the wizard looked out. Arrows whined and whistled down the corridor as he sprang back.

'There are Orcs, very many of them,' he said. 'And some are large and evil: black Uruks of Mordor. For the moment they are hanging back, but there is something else there. A great cave-troll, I think, or more than one. There is no hope of escape that way.'

'And no hope at all, if they come at the other door as well,' said Boromir.

'There is no sound outside here yet,' said Aragorn, who was standing by the eastern door listening. 'The passage on this side plunges straight down a stair: it plainly does not lead back towards the hall. But it is no good flying blindly this way with the pursuit just behind. We cannot block the door. Its key is gone and the lock is broken, and it opens inwards. We must do something to delay the enemy first. We will make them fear the Chamber of Mazarbul!' he said grimly, feeling the edge of his sword, Andúril.

Heavy feet were heard in the corridor. Boromir flung himself against the door and heaved it to; then he wedged it with broken sword-blades and splinters of wood. The Company retreated to the other side of the chamber. But they had no chance to fly yet. There was a blow on the door that made it quiver; and then it began to grind slowly open, driving back the wedges. A huge arm and shoulder, with a dark skin of greenish scales, was thrust through the widening gap. Then a great, flat, toeless foot was forced through below. There was a dead silence outside.

Boromir leaped forward and hewed at the arm with all his might; but his sword rang, glanced aside, and fell from his shaken hand. The blade was notched.

Suddenly, and to his own surprise, Frodo felt a hot wrath blaze up in his heart. 'The Shire!' he cried, and springing beside Boromir, he stooped, and stabbed with Sting at the hideous foot. There was a bellow, and the foot jerked back, nearly wrenching Sting from Frodo's arm. Black drops dripped from the blade and smoked on the floor. Boromir hurled himself against the door and slammed it again.

'One for the Shire!' cried Aragorn. 'The hobbit's bite is deep! You have a good blade, Frodo son of Drogo!'

There was a crash on the door, followed by crash after crash. Rams and hammers were beating against it. It cracked and staggered back, and the opening grew suddenly wide. Arrows came whistling in, but struck the northern wall, and fell harmlessly to the floor. There was a horn-blast and a rush of feet, and orcs one after another leaped into the chamber.

How many there were the Company could not count. The affray was sharp, but the orcs were dismayed by the fierceness of the defence. Legolas shot two through the throat. Gimli hewed the legs from under another that had sprung up on Balin's tomb. Boromir and Aragorn slew many. When thirteen had fallen the rest fled shrieking, leaving the defenders unharmed, except for Sam who had a scratch along the scalp. A quick duck had saved him; and he had felled his orc: a sturdy thrust with his Barrow-blade. A fire was smouldering in his brown eyes that would have made Ted Sandyman step backwards, if he had seen it.

'Now is the time!' cried Gandalf. 'Let us go, before the troll returns!'

But even as they retreated, and before Pippin and Merry had reached the stair outside, a huge orc-chieftain, almost man-high, clad in black mail from head to foot, leaped into the chamber; behind him his followers clustered in the door-way. His broad flat face was swart, his eyes were like coals, and his tongue was red; he wielded a great spear. With a thrust of his huge hide shield he turned Boromir's sword and bore him backwards, throwing him to the ground. Diving under Aragorn's blow with the speed of a striking snake he charged into the Company and thrust with his spear straight at Frodo. The blow caught him on the right side, and Frodo was hurled against the wall and pinned. Sam, with a cry, hacked at the spear-shaft, and it broke. But even as the orc flung down the truncheon and swept out his scimitar, Andúril came down upon his helm. There was a flash like flame and the helm burst asunder. The orc fell with cloven head. His followers fled howling, as Boromir and Aragorn sprang at them.

Doom, doom went the drums in the deep. The great voice rolled out again.

'Now!' shouted Gandalf. 'Now is the last chance. Run for it!'

Aragorn picked up Frodo where he lay by the wall and made for the stair, pushing Merry and Pippin in front of him. The others followed; but Gimli had to be dragged away by Legolas: in spite of the peril he lingered by Balin's tomb with his head bowed. Boromir hauled the eastern door to, grinding upon its hinges: it had great iron rings on either side, but could not be fastened.

'I am all right,' gasped Frodo. 'I can walk. Put me down!'

Aragorn nearly dropped him in his amazement. 'I thought you were dead!' he cried.

'Not yet!' said Gandalf. 'But there is no time for wonder. Off you go, all of you, down the stairs! Wait a few minutes for me at the bottom, but if I do not come soon, go on! Go quickly and choose paths leading right and downwards.'

'We cannot leave you to hold the door alone!' said Aragorn.

'Do as I say!' said Gandalf fiercely. 'Swords are no more use here. Go!'

★ ★ ★

The passage was lit by no shaft and was utterly dark. They groped their way down a long flight of steps, and then looked back; but they could see nothing, except high above them the faint glimmer of the wizard's staff. He seemed to be still standing on guard by the closed door. Frodo breathed heavily and leaned against Sam, who put his arms about him. They stood peering up the stairs into the darkness. Frodo thought he could hear the voice of Gandalf above, muttering words that ran down the sloping roof with a sighing echo. He could not catch what was said. The walls seemed to be trembling. Every now and again the drum-beats throbbed and rolled: *doom, doom*.

Suddenly at the top of the stair there was a stab of white light. Then there was a dull rumble and a heavy thud. The drum-beats broke out wildly: *doom-boom, doom-boom*, and then stopped. Gandalf came flying down the steps and fell to the ground in the midst of the Company.

'Well, well! That's over!' said the wizard struggling to his feet. 'I have done all that I could. But I have met my match, and have nearly been destroyed. But don't stand here! Go on! You will have to do without light for a while: I am rather shaken. Go on! Go on! Where are you, Gimli? Come ahead with me! Keep close behind, all of you!'

They stumbled after him wondering what had happened. *Doom, doom* went the drum-beats again: they now sounded muffled and far away, but they were following. There was no other sound of pursuit, neither tramp of feet, nor any voice. Gandalf took no turns, right or left, for the passage seemed to be going in the direction that he desired. Every now and again it descended a flight of steps, fifty or more, to a lower level. At the moment that was their chief danger; for in the dark they could not see a descent, until they came on it and put their feet out into emptiness. Gandalf felt the ground with his staff like a blind man.

At the end of an hour they had gone a mile, or maybe a little more, and had descended many flights of stairs. There was still no sound of pursuit. Almost they began to hope that they would escape. At the bottom of the seventh flight Gandalf halted.

'It is getting hot!' he gasped. 'We ought to be down at least to the level of the Gates now. Soon I think we should look for a left-hand turn to take us east. I hope it is not far. I am very weary. I must rest here a moment, even if all the orcs ever spawned are after us.'

Gimli took his arm and helped him down to a seat on the step. 'What happened away up there at the door?' he asked. 'Did you meet the beater of the drums?'

'I do not know,' answered Gandalf. 'But I found myself suddenly faced by something that I have not met before. I could think of nothing to do but to try and put a shutting-spell on the door. I know many; but to do things of that kind rightly requires time, and even then the door can be broken by strength.

'As I stood there I could hear orc-voices on the other side: at any moment I thought they would burst it open. I could not hear what was said; they seemed to be talking in their own hideous language. All I caught was *ghâsh*: that is "fire". Then something came into the chamber − I felt it through the door, and the orcs themselves were afraid and fell silent. It laid hold of the iron ring, and then it perceived me and my spell.

'What it was I cannot guess, but I have never felt such a challenge. The counter-spell was terrible. It nearly broke me. For an instant the door left my control and began to open! I had to speak a word of Command. That proved too great a strain. The door burst in pieces. Something dark as a cloud was blocking out all the light inside, and I was thrown backwards down the stairs. All the wall gave way, and the roof of the chamber as well, I think.

'I am afraid Balin is buried deep, and maybe something else is buried there too. I cannot say. But at least the passage behind us was completely blocked. Ah! I have never felt so spent, but it is passing. And now what about you, Frodo?

There was not time to say so, but I have never been more delighted in my life than when you spoke. I feared that it was a brave but dead hobbit that Aragorn was carrying.'

'What about me?' said Frodo. 'I am alive, and whole I think. I am bruised and in pain, but it is not too bad.'

'Well,' said Aragorn, 'I can only say that hobbits are made of a stuff so tough that I have never met the like of it. Had I known, I would have spoken softer in the Inn at Bree! That spear-thrust would have skewered a wild boar!'

'Well, it did not skewer me, I am glad to say,' said Frodo; 'though I feel as if I had been caught between a hammer and an anvil.' He said no more. He found breathing painful.

'You take after Bilbo,' said Gandalf. 'There is more about you than meets the eye, as I said of him long ago.' Frodo wondered if the remark meant more than it said.

They now went on again. Before long Gimli spoke. He had keen eyes in the dark. 'I think,' he said, 'that there is a light ahead. But it is not daylight. It is red. What can it be?'

'*Ghâsh!*' muttered Gandalf. 'I wonder if that is what they meant: that the lower levels are on fire? Still, we can only go on.'

Soon the light became unmistakable, and could be seen by all. It was flickering and glowing on the walls away down the passage before them. They could now see their way: in front the road sloped down swiftly, and some way ahead there stood a low archway; through it the growing light came. The air became very hot.

When they came to the arch Gandalf went through, signing to them to wait. As he stood just beyond the opening they saw his face lit by a red glow. Quickly he stepped back.

'There is some new devilry here,' he said, 'devised for our welcome, no doubt. But I know now where we are: we have reached the First Deep, the level immediately below the Gates. This is the Second Hall of Old Moria; and the Gates are near: away beyond the eastern end, on the left, not more than a quarter of a mile. Across the Bridge, up a broad stair, along a wide road, through the First Hall, and out! But come and look!'

They peered out. Before them was another cavernous hall. It was loftier and far longer than the one in which they had slept. They were near its eastern end; westward it ran away into darkness. Down the centre stalked a double line of towering pillars. They were carved like boles of mighty trees whose boughs upheld the roof with a branching tracery of stone. Their stems were smooth and black, but a red glow was darkly mirrored in their sides. Right across the floor, close to the feet of two huge pillars a great fissure had opened. Out of it a fierce red light came, and now and again flames licked at the brink and curled about the bases of the columns. Wisps of dark smoke wavered in the hot air.

'If we had come by the main road down from the upper halls, we should have been trapped here,' said Gandalf. 'Let us hope that the fire now lies between us and pursuit. Come! There is no time to lose.'

Even as he spoke they heard again the pursuing drum-beat: *Doom, doom, doom*. Away beyond the shadows at the western end of the hall there came cries and horn-calls. *Doom, doom*: the pillars seemed to tremble and the flames to quiver.

'Now for the last race!' said Gandalf. 'If the sun is shining outside, we may still escape. After me!'

He turned left and sped across the smooth floor of the hall. The distance was greater than it had looked. As they ran they heard the beat and echo of many hurrying feet behind. A shrill yell went up: they had been seen. There was a ring and clash of steel. An arrow whistled over Frodo's head.

Boromir laughed. 'They did not expect this,' he said. 'The fire has cut them off. We are on the wrong side!'

'Look ahead!' called Gandalf. 'The Bridge is near. It is dangerous and narrow.'

Suddenly Frodo saw before him a black chasm. At the end of the hall the floor vanished and fell to an unknown depth. The outer door could only be reached by a slender bridge of stone, without kerb or rail, that spanned the chasm with one curving spring of fifty feet. It was an ancient defence of the Dwarves against any enemy that might capture the First Hall and the outer passages. They could only pass across it in single file. At the brink Gandalf halted and the others came up in a pack behind.

'Lead the way, Gimli!' he said. 'Pippin and Merry next. Straight on, and up the stair beyond the door!'

Arrows fell among them. One struck Frodo and sprang back. Another pierced Gandalf's hat and stuck there like a black feather. Frodo looked behind. Beyond the fire he saw swarming black figures: there seemed to be hundreds of orcs. They brandished spears and scimitars which shone red as blood in the firelight. *Doom, doom* rolled the drum-beats, growing louder and louder, *doom, doom*.

Legolas turned and set an arrow to the string, though it was a long shot for his small bow. He drew, but his hand fell, and the arrow slipped to the ground. He gave a cry of dismay and fear. Two great trolls appeared; they bore great slabs of stone, and flung them down to serve as gangways over the fire. But it was not the trolls that had filled the Elf with terror. The ranks of the orcs had opened, and they crowded away, as if they themselves were afraid. Something was coming up behind them. What it was could not be seen: it was like a great shadow, in the middle of which was a dark form, of man-shape maybe, yet greater; and a power and terror seemed to be in it and to go before it.

It came to the edge of the fire and the light faded as if a cloud had bent over it. Then with a rush it leaped across the fissure. The flames roared up to greet it, and wreathed about it; and a black smoke swirled in the air. Its streaming mane kindled, and blazed behind it. In its right hand was a blade like a stabbing tongue of fire; in its left it held a whip of many thongs.

'Ai! ai!' wailed Legolas. 'A Balrog! A Balrog is come!'

Gimli stared with wide eyes. 'Durin's Bane!' he cried, and letting his axe fall he covered his face.

'A Balrog,' muttered Gandalf. 'Now I understand.' He faltered and leaned heavily on his staff. 'What an evil fortune! And I am already weary.'

The dark figure streaming with fire raced towards them. The orcs yelled and poured over the stone gangways. Then Boromir raised his horn and blew. Loud the challenge rang and bellowed, like the shout of many throats under the cavernous roof. For a moment the orcs quailed and the fiery shadow halted. Then the echoes died as suddenly as a flame blown out by a dark wind, and the enemy advanced again.

'Over the bridge!' cried Gandalf, recalling his strength. 'Fly! This is a foe beyond any of you. I must hold the narrow way. Fly!' Aragorn and Boromir did not heed the command, but still held their ground, side by side, behind Gandalf at the far end of the bridge. The others halted just within the doorway at the hall's end, and turned, unable to leave their leader to face the enemy alone.

The Balrog reached the bridge. Gandalf stood in the middle of the span, leaning on the staff in his left hand, but in his other hand Glamdring gleamed, cold and white. His enemy halted again, facing him, and the shadow about it reached out like two vast wings. It raised the whip, and the thongs whined and cracked. Fire came from its nostrils. But Gandalf stood firm.

'You cannot pass,' he said. The orcs stood still, and a dead silence fell. 'I am a servant of the Secret Fire, wielder of the flame of Anor. You cannot pass. The dark fire will not avail you, flame of Udûn. Go back to the Shadow! You cannot pass.'

The Balrog made no answer. The fire in it seemed to die, but the darkness grew. It stepped forward slowly on to the bridge, and suddenly it drew itself up to a great height, and its wings were spread from wall to wall; but still Gandalf could be seen, glimmering in the gloom; he seemed small, and altogether alone: grey and bent, like a wizened tree before the onset of a storm.

From out of the shadow a red sword leaped flaming.

Glamdring glittered white in answer.

There was a ringing clash and a stab of white fire. The Balrog fell back and its sword flew up in molten fragments. The wizard swayed on the bridge, stepped back a pace, and then again stood still.

'You cannot pass!' he said.

With a bound the Balrog leaped full upon the bridge. Its whip whirled and hissed.

'He cannot stand alone!' cried Aragorn suddenly and ran back along the bridge. '*Elendil!*' he shouted. 'I am with you, Gandalf!'

'Gondor!' cried Boromir and leaped after him.

At that moment Gandalf lifted his staff, and crying aloud he smote the bridge before him. The staff broke asunder and fell from his hand. A blinding sheet of white flame sprang up. The bridge cracked. Right at the Balrog's feet it broke, and the stone upon which it stood crashed into the gulf, while the rest remained, poised, quivering like a tongue of rock thrust out into emptiness.

With a terrible cry the Balrog fell forward, and its shadow plunged down and vanished. But even as it fell it swung its whip, and the thongs lashed and curled about the wizard's knees, dragging him to the brink. He staggered and fell, grasped vainly at the stone, and slid into the abyss. 'Fly, you fools!' he cried, and was gone.

The fires went out, and blank darkness fell. The Company stood rooted with horror staring into the pit. Even as Aragorn and Boromir came flying back, the rest of the bridge cracked and fell. With a cry Aragorn roused them.

'Come! I will lead you now!' he called. 'We must obey his last command. Follow me!'

They stumbled wildly up the great stairs beyond the door. Aragorn leading, Boromir at the rear. At the top was a wide echoing passage. Along this they fled. Frodo heard Sam at his side weeping, and then he found that he himself was weeping as he ran. *Doom, doom, doom* the drum-beats rolled behind, mournful now and slow; *doom!*

They ran on. The light grew before them; great shafts pierced the roof. They ran swifter. They passed into a hall, bright with daylight from its high windows in the east. They fled across it. Through its huge broken doors they passed, and suddenly before them the Great Gates opened, an arch of blazing light.

There was a guard of orcs crouching in the shadows behind the great door-posts towering on either side, but the gates were shattered and cast down. Aragorn smote to the ground the captain that stood in his path, and the rest fled in terror of his wrath. The Company swept past them and took no heed of them. Out of the Gates they ran and sprang down the huge and age-worn steps, the threshold of Moria.

Thus, at last, they came beyond hope under the sky and felt the wind on their faces.

They did not halt until they were out of bowshot from the walls. Dimrill Dale lay about them. The shadow of the Misty Mountains lay upon it, but eastwards there was a golden light on the land. It was but one hour after noon. The sun was shining; the clouds were white and high.

They looked back. Dark yawned the archway of the Gates under the mountain-shadow. Faint and far beneath the earth rolled the slow drum-beats: *doom.* A thin black smoke trailed out. Nothing else was to be seen; the dale all around was empty. *Doom.* Grief at last wholly overcame them, and they wept long: some standing and silent, some cast upon the ground. *Doom, doom.* The drum-beats faded.

CHAPTER VI

LOTHLÓRIEN

'Alas! I fear we cannot stay here longer,' said Aragorn. He looked towards the mountains and held up his sword. 'Farewell, Gandalf!' he cried. 'Did I not say to you: *if you pass the doors of Moria, beware*? Alas that I spoke true! What hope have we without you?'

He turned to the Company. 'We must do without hope,' he said. 'At least we may yet be avenged. Let us gird ourselves and weep no more! Come! We have a long road, and much to do.'

They rose and looked about them. Northward the dale ran up into a glen of shadows between two great arms of the mountains, above which three white peaks were shining: Celebdil, Fanuidhol, Caradhras, the Mountains of Moria. At the head of the glen a torrent flowed like a white lace over an endless ladder of short falls, and a mist of foam hung in the air about the mountains' feet.

'Yonder is the Dimrill Stair,' said Aragorn, pointing to the falls. 'Down the deep-cloven way that climbs beside the torrent we should have come, if fortune had been kinder.'

'Or Caradhras less cruel,' said Gimli. 'There he stands smiling in the sun!' He shook his fist at the furthest of the snow-capped peaks and turned away.

To the east the outflung arm of the mountains marched to a sudden end, and far lands could be descried beyond them, wide and vague. To the south the Misty Mountains receded endlessly as far as sight could reach. Less than a mile away, and a little below them, for they still stood high up on the west side of the dale, there lay a mere. It was long and oval, shaped like a great spear-head thrust deep into the northern glen; but its southern end was beyond the shadows under the sunlit sky. Yet its waters were dark: a deep blue like clear evening sky seen from a lamp-lit room. Its face was still and unruffled. About it lay a smooth sward, shelving down on all sides to its bare unbroken rim.

'There lies the Mirrormere, deep Kheled-zâram!' said Gimli sadly. 'I remember that he said: "May you have joy of the sight! But we cannot linger there." Now long shall I journey ere I have joy again. It is I that must hasten away, and he that must remain.'

The Company now went down the road from the Gates. It was rough and broken, fading to a winding track between heather and whin that thrust amid the cracking stones. But still it could be seen that once long ago a great paved way had wound upwards from the lowlands of the Dwarf-kingdom. In places there were ruined works of stone beside the path, and mounds of green topped with slender birches, or fir-trees sighing in the wind. An eastward bend led them hard by the sward of Mirrormere, and there not far from the roadside stood a single column broken at the top.

'That is Durin's Stone!' cried Gimli. 'I cannot pass without turning aside for a moment to look at the wonder of the dale!'

'Be swift then!' said Aragorn, looking back towards the Gates. 'The Sun sinks early. The Orcs will not, maybe, come out till after dusk, but we must be far away before nightfall. The Moon is almost spent, and it will be dark tonight.'

'Come with me, Frodo!' cried the dwarf, springing from the road. 'I would not have you go without seeing Kheled-zâram.' He ran down the long green slope. Frodo followed slowly, drawn by the still blue water in spite of hurt and weariness; Sam came up behind.

Beside the standing stone Gimli halted and looked up. It was cracked and weather-worn, and the faint runes upon its side could not be read. 'This pillar marks the spot where Durin first looked in the Mirrormere,' said the dwarf. 'Let us look ourselves once, ere we go!'

They stooped over the dark water. At first they could see

nothing. Then slowly they saw the forms of the encircling mountains mirrored in a profound blue, and the peaks were like plumes of white flame above them; beyond there was a space of sky. There like jewels sunk in the deep shone glinting stars, though sunlight was in the sky above. Of their own stooping forms no shadow could be seen.

'O Kheled-zâram fair and wonderful!' said Gimli. 'There lies the Crown of Durin till he wakes. Farewell!' He bowed, and turned away, and hastened back up the green-sward to the road again.

'What did you see?' said Pippin to Sam, but Sam was too deep in thought to answer.

The road now turned south and went quickly downwards, running out from between the arms of the dale. Some way below the mere they came on a deep well of water, clear as crystal, from which a freshet fell over a stone lip and ran glistening and gurgling down a steep rocky channel.

'Here is the spring from which the Silverlode rises,' said Gimli. 'Do not drink of it! It is icy cold.'

'Soon it becomes a swift river, and it gathers water from many other mountain-streams,' said Aragorn. 'Our road leads beside it for many miles. For I shall take you by the road that Gandalf chose, and first I hope to come to the woods where the Silverlode flows into the Great River – out yonder.' They looked as he pointed, and before them they could see the stream leaping down to the trough of the valley, and then running on and away into the lower lands, until it was lost in a golden haze.

'There lie the woods of Lothlórien!' said Legolas. 'That is the fairest of all the dwellings of my people. There are no trees like the trees of that land. For in the autumn their leaves fall not, but turn to gold. Not till the spring comes and the new green opens do they fall, and then the boughs are laden with yellow flowers; and the floor of the wood is golden, and golden is the roof, and its pillars are of silver, for the bark of the trees is smooth and grey. So still our songs in Mirkwood

say. My heart would be glad if I were beneath the eaves of
that wood, and it were springtime!'

'My heart will be glad, even in the winter,' said Aragorn.
'But it lies many miles away. Let us hasten!'

For some time Frodo and Sam managed to keep up with
the others; but Aragorn was leading them at a great pace,
and after a while they lagged behind. They had eaten nothing
since the early morning. Sam's cut was burning like fire, and
his head felt light. In spite of the shining sun the wind seemed
chill after the warm darkness of Moria. He shivered. Frodo
felt every step more painful and he gasped for breath.

At last Legolas turned, and seeing them now far behind,
he spoke to Aragorn. The others halted, and Aragorn ran
back, calling to Boromir to come with him.

'I am sorry, Frodo!' he cried, full of concern. 'So much
has happened this day and we have such need of haste, that
I have forgotten that you were hurt; and Sam too. You should
have spoken. We have done nothing to ease you, as we ought,
though all the orcs of Moria were after us. Come now! A
little further on there is a place where we can rest for a little.
There I will do what I can for you. Come, Boromir! We will
carry them.'

Soon afterwards they came upon another stream that ran
down from the west, and joined its bubbling water with the
hurrying Silverlode. Together they plunged over a fall of
green-hued stone, and foamed down into a dell. About it
stood fir-trees, short and bent, and its sides were steep
and clothed with harts-tongue and shrubs of whortle-berry.
At the bottom there was a level space through which the
stream flowed noisily over shining pebbles. Here they rested.
It was now nearly three hours after noon, and they had
come only a few miles from the Gates. Already the sun was
westering.

While Gimli and the two younger hobbits kindled a fire of
brush- and fir-wood, and drew water, Aragorn tended Sam
and Frodo. Sam's wound was not deep, but it looked ugly,

and Aragorn's face was grave as he examined it. After a moment he looked up with relief.

'Good luck, Sam!' he said. 'Many have received worse than this in payment for the slaying of their first orc. The cut is not poisoned, as the wounds of orc-blades too often are. It should heal well when I have tended it. Bathe it when Gimli has heated water.'

He opened his pouch and drew out some withered leaves. 'They are dry, and some of their virtue has gone,' he said, 'but here I have still some of the leaves of *athelas* that I gathered near Weathertop. Crush one in the water, and wash the wound clean, and I will bind it. Now it is your turn, Frodo!'

'I am all right,' said Frodo, reluctant to have his garments touched. 'All I needed was some food and a little rest.'

'No!' said Aragorn. 'We must have a look and see what the hammer and the anvil have done to you. I still marvel that you are alive at all.' Gently he stripped off Frodo's old jacket and worn tunic, and gave a gasp of wonder. Then he laughed. The silver corslet shimmered before his eyes like the light upon a rippling sea. Carefully he took it off and held it up, and the gems on it glittered like stars, and the sound of the shaken rings was like the tinkle of rain in a pool.

'Look, my friends!' he called. 'Here's a pretty hobbit-skin to wrap an elven-princeling in! If it were known that hobbits had such hides, all the hunters of Middle-earth would be riding to the Shire.'

'And all the arrows of all the hunters in the world would be in vain,' said Gimli, gazing at the mail in wonder. 'It is a mithril-coat. Mithril! I have never seen or heard tell of one so fair. Is this the coat that Gandalf spoke of? Then he undervalued it. But it was well given!'

'I have often wondered what you and Bilbo were doing, so close in his little room,' said Merry. 'Bless the old hobbit! I love him more than ever. I hope we get a chance of telling him about it!'

There was a dark and blackened bruise on Frodo's right

side and breast. Under the mail there was a shirt of soft leather, but at one point the rings had been driven through it into the flesh. Frodo's left side also was scored and bruised where he had been hurled against the wall. While the others set the food ready, Aragorn bathed the hurts with water in which *athelas* was steeped. The pungent fragrance filled the dell, and all those who stooped over the steaming water felt refreshed and strengthened. Soon Frodo felt the pain leave him, and his breath grew easy: though he was stiff and sore to the touch for many days. Aragorn bound some soft pads of cloth at his side.

'The mail is marvellously light,' he said. 'Put it on again, if you can bear it. My heart is glad to know that you have such a coat. Do not lay it aside, even in sleep, unless fortune brings you where you are safe for a while; and that will seldom chance while your quest lasts.'

When they had eaten, the Company got ready to go on. They put out the fire and hid all traces of it. Then climbing out of the dell they took to the road again. They had not gone far before the sun sank behind the westward heights and great shadows crept down the mountain-sides. Dusk veiled their feet, and mist rose in the hollows. Away in the east the evening light lay pale upon the dim lands of distant plain and wood. Sam and Frodo now feeling eased and greatly refreshed were able to go at a fair pace, and with only one brief halt Aragorn led the Company on for nearly three more hours.

It was dark. Deep night had fallen. There were many clear stars, but the fast-waning moon would not be seen till late. Gimli and Frodo were at the rear, walking softly and not speaking, listening for any sound upon the road behind. At length Gimli broke the silence.

'Not a sound but the wind,' he said. 'There are no goblins near, or my ears are made of wood. It is to be hoped that the Orcs will be content with driving us from Moria. And maybe that was all their purpose, and they had nothing else

to do with us – with the Ring. Though Orcs will often pursue
foes for many leagues into the plain, if they have a fallen
captain to avenge.'

Frodo did not answer. He looked at Sting, and the blade
was dull. Yet he had heard something, or thought he had.
As soon as the shadows had fallen about them and the road
behind was dim, he had heard again the quick patter of feet.
Even now he heard it. He turned swiftly. There were two
tiny gleams of light behind, or for a moment he thought he
saw them, but at once they slipped aside and vanished.

'What is it?' said the dwarf.

'I don't know,' answered Frodo. 'I thought I heard feet,
and I thought I saw a light – like eyes. I have thought so
often, since we first entered Moria.'

Gimli halted and stooped to the ground. 'I hear nothing
but the night-speech of plant and stone,' he said. 'Come! Let
us hurry! The others are out of sight.'

The night-wind blew chill up the valley to meet them.
Before them a wide grey shadow loomed, and they heard an
endless rustle of leaves like poplars in the breeze.

'Lothlórien!' cried Legolas. 'Lothlórien! We have come to
the eaves of the Golden Wood. Alas that it is winter!'

Under the night the trees stood tall before them, arched
over the road and stream that ran suddenly beneath their
spreading boughs. In the dim light of the stars their stems
were grey, and their quivering leaves a hint of fallow
gold.

'Lothlórien!' said Aragorn. 'Glad I am to hear again the
wind in the trees! We are still little more than five leagues
from the Gates, but we can go no further. Here let us hope
that the virtue of the Elves will keep us tonight from the peril
that comes behind.'

'If Elves indeed still dwell here in the darkening world,'
said Gimli.

'It is long since any of my own folk journeyed hither back
to the land whence we wandered in ages long ago,' said

Legolas, 'but we hear that Lórien is not yet deserted, for there is a secret power here that holds evil from the land. Nevertheless its folk are seldom seen, and maybe they dwell now deep in the woods and far from the northern border.'

'Indeed deep in the wood they dwell,' said Aragorn, and sighed as if some memory stirred in him. 'We must fend for ourselves tonight. We will go forward a short way, until the trees are all about us, and then we will turn aside from the path and seek a place to rest in.'

He stepped forward; but Boromir stood irresolute and did not follow. 'Is there no other way?' he said.

'What other fairer way would you desire?' said Aragorn.

'A plain road, though it led through a hedge of swords,' said Boromir. 'By strange paths has this Company been led, and so far to evil fortune. Against my will we passed under the shades of Moria, to our loss. And now we must enter the Golden Wood, you say. But of that perilous land we have heard in Gondor, and it is said that few come out who once go in; and of that few none have escaped unscathed.'

'Say not *unscathed*, but if you say *unchanged*, then maybe you will speak the truth,' said Aragorn. 'But lore wanes in Gondor, Boromir, if in the city of those who once were wise they now speak evil of Lothlórien. Believe what you will, there is no other way for us – unless you would go back to Moria-gate, or scale the pathless mountains, or swim the Great River all alone.'

'Then lead on!' said Boromir. 'But it is perilous.'

'Perilous indeed,' said Aragorn, 'fair and perilous; but only evil need fear it, or those who bring some evil with them. Follow me!'

They had gone little more than a mile into the forest when they came upon another stream flowing down swiftly from the tree-clad slopes that climbed back westward towards the mountains. They heard it splashing over a fall away among the shadows on their right. Its dark hurrying waters ran across

the path before them, and joined the Silverlode in a swirl of
dim pools among the roots of trees.

'Here is Nimrodel!' said Legolas. 'Of this stream the Silvan
Elves made many songs long ago, and still we sing them in
the North, remembering the rainbow on its falls, and the
golden flowers that floated in its foam. All is dark now and
the Bridge of Nimrodel is broken down. I will bathe my feet,
for it is said that the water is healing to the weary.' He went
forward and climbed down the deep-cloven bank and stepped
into the stream.

'Follow me!' he cried. 'The water is not deep. Let us wade
across! On the further bank we can rest, and the sound of
the falling water may bring us sleep and forgetfulness of
grief.'

One by one they climbed down and followed Legolas. For
a moment Frodo stood near the brink and let the water flow
over his tired feet. It was cold but its touch was clean, and
as he went on and it mounted to his knees, he felt that the
stain of travel and all weariness was washed from his limbs.

When all the Company had crossed, they sat and rested
and ate a little food; and Legolas told them tales of Lothlórien
that the Elves of Mirkwood still kept in their hearts, of sunlight and starlight upon the meadows by the Great River
before the world was grey.

At length a silence fell, and they heard the music of the
waterfall running sweetly in the shadows. Almost Frodo fancied that he could hear a voice singing, mingled with the
sound of the water.

'Do you hear the voice of Nimrodel?' asked Legolas. 'I
will sing you a song of the maiden Nimrodel, who bore the
same name as the stream beside which she lived long ago. It
is a fair song in our woodland tongue; but this is how it runs
in the Westron Speech, as some in Rivendell now sing it.' In
a soft voice hardly to be heard amid the rustle of the leaves
above them he began:

An Elven-maid there was of old,
    A shining star by day:
Her mantle white was hemmed with gold,
    Her shoes of silver-grey.

A star was bound upon her brows,
    A light was on her hair
As sun upon the golden boughs
    In Lórien the fair.

Her hair was long, her limbs were white,
    And fair she was and free;
And in the wind she went as light
    As leaf of linden-tree.

Beside the falls of Nimrodel,
    By water clear and cool,
Her voice as falling silver fell
    Into the shining pool.

Where now she wanders none can tell,
    In sunlight or in shade;
For lost of yore was Nimrodel
    And in the mountains strayed.

The elven-ship in haven grey
    Beneath the mountain-lee
Awaited her for many a day
    Beside the roaring sea.

A wind by night in Northern lands
    Arose, and loud it cried,
And drove the ship from elven-strands
    Across the streaming tide.

When dawn came dim the land was lost,
The mountains sinking grey
Beyond the heaving waves that tossed
Their plumes of blinding spray.

Amroth beheld the fading shore
Now low beyond the swell,
And cursed the faithless ship that bore
Him far from Nimrodel.

Of old he was an Elven-king,
A lord of tree and glen,
When golden were the boughs in spring
In fair Lothlórien.

From helm to sea they saw him leap,
As arrow from the string,
And dive into the water deep,
As mew upon the wing.

The wind was in his flowing hair,
The foam about him shone;
Afar they saw him strong and fair
Go riding like a swan.

But from the West has come no word,
And on the Hither Shore
No tidings Elven-folk have heard
Of Amroth evermore.

The voice of Legolas faltered, and the song ceased. 'I cannot sing any more,' he said. 'That is but a part, for I have forgotten much. It is long and sad, for it tells how sorrow came upon Lothlórien, Lórien of the Blossom, when the Dwarves awakened evil in the mountains.'

'But the Dwarves did not make the evil,' said Gimli.

'I said not so; yet evil came,' answered Legolas sadly. 'Then

many of the Elves of Nimrodel's kindred left their dwellings
and departed, and she was lost far in the South, in the passes
of the White Mountains; and she came not to the ship where
Amroth her lover waited for her. But in the spring when the
wind is in the new leaves the echo of her voice may still be
heard by the falls that bear her name. And when the wind is
in the South the voice of Amroth comes up from the sea;
for Nimrodel flows into Silverlode, that Elves call Celebrant,
and Celebrant into Anduin the Great, and Anduin flows into
the Bay of Belfalas whence the Elves of Lórien set sail. But
neither Nimrodel nor Amroth ever came back.

'It is told that she had a house built in the branches of a
tree that grew near the falls; for that was the custom of the
Elves of Lórien, to dwell in the trees, and maybe it is so still.
Therefore they were called the Galadhrim, the Tree-people.
Deep in their forest the trees are very great. The people of
the woods did not delve in the ground like Dwarves, nor
build strong places of stone before the Shadow came.'

'And even in these latter days dwelling in the trees might
be thought safer than sitting on the ground,' said Gimli. He
looked across the stream to the road that led back to Dimrill
Dale, and then up into the roof of dark boughs above.

'Your words bring good counsel, Gimli,' said Aragorn.
'We cannot build a house, but tonight we will do as the
Galadhrim and seek refuge in the tree-tops, if we can. We
have sat here beside the road already longer than was wise.'

The Company now turned aside from the path, and went
into the shadow of the deeper woods, westward along the
mountain-stream away from Silverlode. Not far from the falls
of Nimrodel they found a cluster of trees, some of which
overhung the stream. Their great grey trunks were of mighty
girth, but their height could not be guessed.

'I will climb up,' said Legolas. 'I am at home among trees,
by root or bough, though these trees are of a kind strange to
me, save as a name in song. *Mellyrn* they are called, and are
those that bear the yellow blossom, but I have never climbed

in one. I will see now what is their shape and way of growth.'

'Whatever it may be,' said Pippin, 'they will be marvellous trees indeed if they can offer any rest at night, except to birds. I cannot sleep on a perch!'

'Then dig a hole in the ground,' said Legolas, 'if that is more after the fashion of your kind. But you must dig swift and deep, if you wish to hide from Orcs.' He sprang lightly up from the ground and caught a branch that grew from the trunk high above his head. But even as he swung there for a moment, a voice spoke suddenly from the tree-shadows above him.

'*Daro!*' it said in commanding tone, and Legolas dropped back to earth in surprise and fear. He shrank against the bole of the tree.

'Stand still!' he whispered to the others. 'Do not move or speak!'

There was a sound of soft laughter over their heads, and then another clear voice spoke in an elven-tongue. Frodo could understand little of what was said, for the speech that the Silvan folk east of the mountains used among themselves was unlike that of the West. Legolas looked up and answered in the same language.★

'Who are they, and what do they say?' asked Merry.

'They're Elves,' said Sam. 'Can't you hear their voices?'

'Yes, they are Elves,' said Legolas; 'and they say that you breathe so loud that they could shoot you in the dark.' Sam hastily put his hand over his mouth. 'But they say also that you need have no fear. They have been aware of us for a long while. They heard my voice across the Nimrodel, and knew that I was one of their Northern kindred, and therefore they did not hinder our crossing; and afterwards they heard my song. Now they bid me climb up with Frodo; for they seem to have had some tidings of him and of our journey. The others they ask to wait a little, and to keep watch at the foot of the tree, until they have decided what is to be done.'

★   ★   ★

★ See note in Appendix F: *Of the Elves*.

Out of the shadows a ladder was let down: it was made of rope, silver-grey and glimmering in the dark, and though it looked slender it proved strong enough to bear many men. Legolas ran lightly up, and Frodo followed slowly; behind came Sam trying not to breathe loudly. The branches of the mallorn-tree grew out nearly straight from the trunk, and then swept upward; but near the top the main stem divided into a crown of many boughs, and among these they found that there had been built a wooden platform, or *flet* as such things were called in those days: the Elves called it a *talan*. It was reached by a round hole in the centre through which the ladder passed.

When Frodo came at last up on to the flet he found Legolas seated with three other Elves. They were clad in shadowy-grey, and could not be seen among the tree-stems, unless they moved suddenly. They stood up, and one of them uncovered a small lamp that gave out a slender silver beam. He held it up, looking at Frodo's face, and Sam's. Then he shut off the light again, and spoke words of welcome in his elven-tongue. Frodo spoke haltingly in return.

'Welcome!' the Elf then said again in the Common Language, speaking slowly. 'We seldom use any tongue but our own; for we dwell now in the heart of the forest, and do not willingly have dealings with any other folk. Even our own kindred in the North are sundered from us. But there are some of us still who go abroad for the gathering of news and the watching of our enemies, and they speak the languages of other lands. I am one. Haldir is my name. My brothers, Rúmil and Orophin, speak little of your tongue.

'But we have heard rumours of your coming, for the messengers of Elrond passed by Lórien on their way home up the Dimrill Stair. We had not heard of – hobbits, of halflings, for many a long year, and did not know that any yet dwelt in Middle-earth. You do not look evil! And since you come with an Elf of our kindred, we are willing to befriend you, as Elrond asked; though it is not our custom to lead strangers through our land. But you must stay here tonight. How many are you?'

'Eight,' said Legolas. 'Myself, four hobbits; and two men, one of whom, Aragorn, is an Elf-friend of the folk of Westernesse.'

'The name of Aragorn son of Arathorn is known in Lórien,' said Haldir, 'and he has the favour of the Lady. All then is well. But you have yet spoken only of seven.'

'The eighth is a dwarf,' said Legolas.

'A dwarf!' said Haldir. 'That is not well. We have not had dealings with the Dwarves since the Dark Days. They are not permitted in our land. I cannot allow him to pass.'

'But he is from the Lonely Mountain, one of Dáin's trusty people, and friendly to Elrond,' said Frodo. 'Elrond himself chose him to be one of our companions, and he has been brave and faithful.'

The Elves spoke together in soft voices, and questioned Legolas in their own tongue. 'Very good,' said Haldir at last. 'We will do this, though it is against our liking. If Aragorn and Legolas will guard him, and answer for him, he shall pass; but he must go blindfold through Lothlórien.

'But now we must debate no longer. Your folk must not remain on the ground. We have been keeping watch on the rivers, ever since we saw a great troop of Orcs going north toward Moria, along the skirts of the mountains, many days ago. Wolves are howling on the wood's borders. If you have indeed come from Moria, the peril cannot be far behind. Tomorrow early you must go on.

'The four hobbits shall climb up here and stay with us – we do not fear them! There is another *talan* in the next tree. There the others must take refuge. You, Legolas, must answer to us for them. Call us, if anything is amiss! And have an eye on that dwarf!'

Legolas at once went down the ladder to take Haldir's message; and soon afterwards Merry and Pippin clambered up on to the high flet. They were out of breath and seemed rather scared.

'There!' said Merry panting. 'We have lugged up your blankets as well as our own. Strider has hidden all the rest of our baggage in a deep drift of leaves.'

'You had no need of your burdens,' said Haldir. 'It is cold in the tree-tops in winter, though the wind tonight is in the South; but we have food and drink to give you that will drive away the night-chill, and we have skins and cloaks to spare.'

The hobbits accepted this second (and far better) supper very gladly. Then they wrapped themselves warmly, not only in the fur-cloaks of the Elves, but in their own blankets as well, and tried to go to sleep. But weary as they were only Sam found that easy to do. Hobbits do not like heights, and do not sleep upstairs, even when they have any stairs. The flet was not at all to their liking as a bedroom. It had no walls, not even a rail; only on one side was there a light plaited screen, which could be moved and fixed in different places according to the wind.

Pippin went on talking for a while. 'I hope, if I do go to sleep in this bed-loft, that I shan't roll off,' he said.

'Once I do get to sleep,' said Sam, 'I shall go on sleeping, whether I roll off or no. And the less said, the sooner I'll drop off, if you take my meaning.'

Frodo lay for some time awake, and looked up at the stars glinting through the pale roof of quivering leaves. Sam was snoring at his side long before he himself closed his eyes. He could dimly see the grey forms of two elves sitting motionless with their arms about their knees, speaking in whispers. The other had gone down to take up his watch on one of the lower branches. At last lulled by the wind in the boughs above, and the sweet murmur of the falls of Nimrodel below, Frodo fell asleep with the song of Legolas running in his mind.

Late in the night he awoke. The other hobbits were asleep.

The Elves were gone. The sickle Moon was gleaming dimly among the leaves. The wind was still. A little way off he heard a harsh laugh and the tread of many feet on the ground below. There was a ring of metal. The sounds died slowly away, and seemed to go southward, on into the wood.

A head appeared suddenly through the hole in the flet. Frodo sat up in alarm and saw that it was a grey-hooded Elf. He looked towards the hobbits.

'What is it?' said Frodo.

'*Yrch!*' said the Elf in a hissing whisper, and cast on to the flet the rope-ladder rolled up.

'Orcs!' said Frodo. 'What are they doing?' But the Elf had gone.

There were no more sounds. Even the leaves were silent, and the very falls seemed to be hushed. Frodo sat and shivered in his wraps. He was thankful that they had not been caught on the ground; but he felt that the trees offered little protection, except concealment. Orcs were as keen as hounds on a scent, it was said, but they could also climb. He drew out Sting: it flashed and glittered like a blue flame; and then slowly faded again and grew dull. In spite of the fading of his sword the feeling of immediate danger did not leave Frodo, rather it grew stronger. He got up and crawled to the opening and peered down. He was almost certain that he could hear stealthy movements at the tree's foot far below.

Not Elves; for the woodland folk were altogether noiseless in their movements. Then he heard faintly a sound like sniffing; and something seemed to be scrabbling on the bark of the tree-trunk. He stared down into the dark, holding his breath.

Something was now climbing slowly, and its breath came like a soft hissing through closed teeth. Then coming up, close to the stem, Frodo saw two pale eyes. They stopped and gazed upward unwinking. Suddenly they turned away, and a shadowy figure slipped round the trunk of the tree and vanished.

Immediately afterwards Haldir came climbing swiftly up through the branches. 'There was something in this tree that I have never seen before,' he said. 'It was not an orc. It fled as soon as I touched the tree-stem. It seemed to be wary, and to have some skill in trees, or I might have thought that it was one of you hobbits.

'I did not shoot, for I dared not arouse any cries: we cannot risk battle. A strong company of Orcs has passed. They crossed the Nimrodel – curse their foul feet in its clean water! – and went on down the old road beside the river. They seemed to pick up some scent, and they searched the ground for a while near the place where you halted. The three of us could not challenge a hundred, so we went ahead and spoke with feigned voices, leading them on into the wood.

'Orophin has now gone in haste back to our dwellings to warn our people. None of the Orcs will ever return out of Lórien. And there will be many Elves hidden on the northern border before another night falls. But you must take the road south as soon as it is fully light.'

Day came pale from the East. As the light grew it filtered through the yellow leaves of the mallorn, and it seemed to the hobbits that the early sun of a cool summer's morning was shining. Pale-blue sky peeped among the moving branches. Looking through an opening on the south side of the flet Frodo saw all the valley of the Silverlode lying like a sea of fallow gold tossing gently in the breeze.

The morning was still young and cold when the Company set out again, guided now by Haldir and his brother Rúmil. 'Farewell, sweet Nimrodel!' cried Legolas. Frodo looked back and caught a gleam of white foam among the grey tree-stems. 'Farewell,' he said. It seemed to him that he would never hear again a running water so beautiful, for ever blending its innumerable notes in an endless changeful music.

They went back to the path that still went on along the west side of the Silverlode, and for some way they followed it southward. There were the prints of orc-feet in the earth.

But soon Haldir turned aside into the trees and halted on the bank of the river under their shadows.

'There is one of my people yonder across the stream,' he said, 'though you may not see him.' He gave a call like the low whistle of a bird, and out of a thicket of young trees an Elf stepped, clad in grey, but with his hood thrown back; his hair glinted like gold in the morning sun. Haldir skilfully cast over the stream a coil of grey rope, and he caught it and bound the end about a tree near the bank.

'Celebrant is already a strong stream here, as you see,' said Haldir, 'and it runs both swift and deep, and is very cold. We do not set foot in it so far north, unless we must. But in these days of watchfulness we do not make bridges. This is how we cross! Follow me!' He made his end of the rope fast about another tree, and then ran lightly along it, over the river and back again, as if he were on a road.

'I can walk this path,' said Legolas; 'but the others have not this skill. Must they swim?'

'No!' said Haldir. 'We have two more ropes. We will fasten them above the other, one shoulder-high, and another half-high, and holding these the strangers should be able to cross with care.'

When this slender bridge had been made, the Company passed over, some cautiously and slowly, others more easily. Of the hobbits Pippin proved the best for he was sure-footed, and he walked over quickly, holding only with one hand; but he kept his eyes on the bank ahead and did not look down. Sam shuffled along, clutching hard, and looking down into the pale eddying water as if it was a chasm in the mountains.

He breathed with relief when he was safely across. 'Live and learn! as my gaffer used to say. Though he was thinking of gardening, not of roosting like a bird, nor of trying to walk like a spider. Not even my uncle Andy ever did a trick like that!'

When at length all the Company was gathered on the east bank of the Silverlode, the Elves untied the ropes and coiled two of them. Rúmil, who had remained on the other side, drew back the last one, slung it on his shoulder, and with a wave of his hand went away, back to Nimrodel to keep watch.

'Now, friends,' said Haldir, 'you have entered the Naith of Lórien, or the Gore, as you would say, for it is the land that lies like a spearhead between the arms of Silverlode and Anduin the Great. We allow no strangers to spy out the secrets of the Naith. Few indeed are permitted even to set foot there.

'As was agreed, I shall here blindfold the eyes of Gimli the Dwarf. The others may walk free for a while, until we come nearer to our dwellings, down in Egladil, in the Angle between the waters.'

This was not at all to the liking of Gimli. 'The agreement was made without my consent,' he said. 'I will not walk blindfold, like a beggar or a prisoner. And I am no spy. My folk have never had dealings with any of the servants of the Enemy. Neither have we done harm to the Elves. I am no more likely to betray you than Legolas, or any other of my companions.'

'I do not doubt you,' said Haldir. 'Yet this is our law. I am not the master of the law, and cannot set it aside. I have done much in letting you set foot over Celebrant.'

Gimli was obstinate. He planted his feet firmly apart, and laid his hand upon the haft of his axe. 'I will go forward free,' he said, 'or I will go back and seek my own land, where I am known to be true of word, though I perish alone in the wilderness.'

'You cannot go back,' said Haldir sternly. 'Now you have come thus far, you must be brought before the Lord and the Lady. They shall judge you, to hold you or to give you leave, as they will. You cannot cross the rivers again, and behind you there are now secret sentinels that you cannot pass. You would be slain before you saw them.'

Gimli drew his axe from his belt. Haldir and his companion bent their bows. 'A plague on Dwarves and their stiff necks!' said Legolas.

'Come!' said Aragorn. 'If I am still to lead this Company,

you must do as I bid. It is hard upon the Dwarf to be thus
singled out. We will all be blindfold, even Legolas. That will
be best, though it will make the journey slow and dull.'

Gimli laughed suddenly. 'A merry troop of fools we shall
look! Will Haldir lead us all on a string, like many blind
beggars with one dog? But I will be content, if only Legolas
here shares my blindness.'

'I am an Elf and a kinsman here,' said Legolas, becoming
angry in his turn.

'Now let us cry: "a plague on the stiff necks of Elves!"'
said Aragorn. 'But the Company shall all fare alike. Come,
bind our eyes, Haldir!'

'I shall claim full amends for every fall and stubbed toe, if
you do not lead us well,' said Gimli as they bound a cloth
about his eyes.

'You will have no claim,' said Haldir. 'I shall lead you well,
and the paths are smooth and straight.'

'Alas for the folly of these days!' said Legolas. 'Here all
are enemies of the one Enemy, and yet I must walk
blind, while the sun is merry in the woodland under leaves
of gold!'

'Folly it may seem,' said Haldir. 'Indeed in nothing is the
power of the Dark Lord more clearly shown than in the
estrangement that divides all those who still oppose him. Yet
so little faith and trust do we find now in the world beyond
Lothlórien, unless maybe in Rivendell, that we dare not by
our own trust endanger our land. We live now upon an island
amid many perils, and our hands are more often upon the
bowstring than upon the harp.

'The rivers long defended us, but they are a sure guard
no more; for the Shadow has crept northward all about us.
Some speak of departing, yet for that it already seems too
late. The mountains to the west are growing evil; to the east
the lands are waste, and full of Sauron's creatures; and it is
rumoured that we cannot now safely pass southward through
Rohan, and the mouths of the Great River are watched by
the Enemy. Even if we could come to the shores of the Sea,

we should find no longer any shelter there. It is said that there are still havens of the High Elves, but they are far north and west, beyond the land of the Halflings. But where that may be, though the Lord and Lady may know, I do not.'

'You ought at least to guess, since you have seen us,' said Merry. 'There are Elf-havens west of my land, the Shire, where Hobbits live.'

'Happy folk are Hobbits to dwell near the shores of the sea!' said Haldir. 'It is long indeed since any of my folk have looked on it, yet still we remember it in song. Tell me of these havens as we walk.'

'I cannot,' said Merry. 'I have never seen them. I have never been out of my own land before. And if I had known what the world outside was like, I don't think I should have had the heart to leave it.'

'Not even to see fair Lothlórien?' said Haldir. 'The world is indeed full of peril, and in it there are many dark places; but still there is much that is fair, and though in all lands love is now mingled with grief, it grows perhaps the greater.

'Some there are among us who sing that the Shadow will draw back, and peace shall come again. Yet I do not believe that the world about us will ever again be as it was of old, or the light of the Sun as it was aforetime. For the Elves, I fear, it will prove at best a truce, in which they may pass to the Sea unhindered and leave the Middle-earth for ever. Alas for Lothlórien that I love! It would be a poor life in a land where no mallorn grew. But if there are mallorn-trees beyond the Great Sea, none have reported it.'

As they spoke thus, the Company filed slowly along the paths in the wood, led by Haldir, while the other Elf walked behind. They felt the ground beneath their feet smooth and soft, and after a while they walked more freely, without fear of hurt or fall. Being deprived of sight, Frodo found his hearing and other senses sharpened. He could smell the trees and the trodden grass. He could hear many different notes in the rustle of the leaves overhead, the river murmuring away on his right, and the thin clear voices of birds in the sky. He felt the sun upon his face and hands when they passed through an open glade.

As soon as he set foot upon the far bank of Silverlode a strange feeling had come upon him, and it deepened as he walked on into the Naith: it seemed to him that he had stepped over a bridge of time into a corner of the Elder Days, and was now walking in a world that was no more. In Rivendell there was memory of ancient things; in Lórien the ancient things still lived on in the waking world. Evil had been seen and heard there, sorrow had been known; the Elves feared and distrusted the world outside: wolves were howling on the wood's borders: but on the land of Lórien no shadow lay.

All that day the Company marched on, until they felt the cool evening come and heard the early night-wind whispering among many leaves. Then they rested and slept without fear upon the ground; for their guides would not permit them to unbind their eyes, and they could not climb. In the morning they went on again, walking without haste. At noon they halted, and Frodo was aware that they had passed out under the shining Sun. Suddenly he heard the sound of many voices all around him.

A marching host of Elves had come up silently: they were hastening toward the northern borders to guard against any attack from Moria; and they brought news, some of which Haldir reported. The marauding orcs had been waylaid and almost all destroyed; the remnant had fled westward towards the mountains, and were being pursued. A strange creature also had been seen, running with bent back and with hands near the ground, like a beast and yet not of beast-shape. It had eluded capture, and they had not shot it, not knowing whether it was good or ill, and it had vanished down the Silverlode southward.

'Also,' said Haldir, 'they bring me a message from the Lord and Lady of the Galadhrim. You are all to walk free, even the dwarf Gimli. It seems that the Lady knows who and what

is each member of your Company. New messages have come
from Rivendell perhaps.'

He removed the bandage first from Gimli's eyes. 'Your
pardon!' he said, bowing low. 'Look on us now with friendly
eyes! Look and be glad, for you are the first dwarf to behold
the trees of the Naith of Lórien since Durin's Day!'

When his eyes were in turn uncovered, Frodo looked up
and caught his breath. They were standing in an open space.
To the left stood a great mound, covered with a sward of
grass as green as Springtime in the Elder Days. Upon it, as
a double crown, grew two circles of trees: the outer had bark
of snowy white, and were leafless but beautiful in their
shapely nakedness; the inner were mallorn-trees of great
height, still arrayed in pale gold. High amid the branches of
a towering tree that stood in the centre of all there gleamed
a white flet. At the feet of the trees, and all about the green
hillsides the grass was studded with small golden flowers
shaped like stars. Among them, nodding on slender stalks,
were other flowers, white and palest green: they glimmered
as a mist amid the rich hue of the grass. Over all the sky was
blue, and the sun of afternoon glowed upon the hill and cast
long green shadows beneath the trees.

'Behold! You are come to Cerin Amroth,' said Haldir. 'For
this is the heart of the ancient realm as it was long ago, and
here is the mound of Amroth, where in happier days his high
house was built. Here ever bloom the winter flowers in the
unfading grass: the yellow *elanor*, and the pale *niphredil*. Here
we will stay awhile, and come to the city of the Galadhrim
at dusk.'

The others cast themselves down upon the fragrant grass,
but Frodo stood awhile still lost in wonder. It seemed to him
that he had stepped through a high window that looked on
a vanished world. A light was upon it for which his language
had no name. All that he saw was shapely, but the shapes
seemed at once clear cut, as if they had been first conceived
and drawn at the uncovering of his eyes, and ancient as if

they had endured for ever. He saw no colour but those he knew, gold and white and blue and green, but they were fresh and poignant, as if he had at that moment first perceived them and made for them names new and wonderful. In winter here no heart could mourn for summer or for spring. No blemish or sickness or deformity could be seen in anything that grew upon the earth. On the land of Lórien there was no stain.

He turned and saw that Sam was now standing beside him, looking round with a puzzled expression, and rubbing his eyes as if he was not sure that he was awake. 'It's sunlight and bright day, right enough,' he said. 'I thought that Elves were all for moon and stars: but this is more elvish than anything I ever heard tell of. I feel as if I was *inside* a song, if you take my meaning.'

Haldir looked at them, and he seemed indeed to take the meaning of both thought and word. He smiled. 'You feel the power of the Lady of the Galadhrim,' he said. 'Would it please you to climb with me up Cerin Amroth?'

They followed him as he stepped lightly up the grass-clad slopes. Though he walked and breathed, and about him living leaves and flowers were stirred by the same cool wind as fanned his face, Frodo felt that he was in a timeless land that did not fade or change or fall into forgetfulness. When he had gone and passed again into the outer world, still Frodo the wanderer from the Shire would walk there, upon the grass among *elanor* and *niphredil* in fair Lothlórien.

They entered the circle of white trees. As they did so the South Wind blew upon Cerin Amroth and sighed among the branches. Frodo stood still, hearing far off great seas upon beaches that had long ago been washed away, and sea-birds crying whose race had perished from the earth.

Haldir had gone on and was now climbing to the high flet. As Frodo prepared to follow him, he laid his hand upon the tree beside the ladder: never before had he been so suddenly and so keenly aware of the feel and texture of a tree's skin and of the life within it. He felt a delight in wood and the touch of it, neither as forester nor as carpenter; it was the delight of the living tree itself.

As he stepped out at last upon the lofty platform, Haldir took his hand and turned him toward the South. 'Look this way first!' he said.

Frodo looked and saw, still at some distance, a hill of many mighty trees, or a city of green towers: which it was he could not tell. Out of it, it seemed to him that the power and light came that held all the land in sway. He longed suddenly to fly like a bird to rest in the green city. Then he looked eastward and saw all the land of Lórien running down to the pale gleam of Anduin, the Great River. He lifted his eyes across the river and all the light went out, and he was back again in the world he knew. Beyond the river the land appeared flat and empty, formless and vague, until far away it rose again like a wall, dark and drear. The sun that lay on Lothlórien had no power to enlighten the shadow of that distant height.

'There lies the fastness of Southern Mirkwood,' said Haldir. 'It is clad in a forest of dark fir, where the trees strive one against another and their branches rot and wither. In the midst upon a stony height stands Dol Guldur, where long the hidden Enemy had his dwelling. We fear that now it is inhabited again, and with power sevenfold. A black cloud lies often over it of late. In this high place you may see the two powers that are opposed one to another; and ever they strive now in thought, but whereas the light perceives the very heart of the darkness, its own secret has not been discovered. Not yet.' He turned and climbed swiftly down, and they followed him.

At the hill's foot Frodo found Aragorn, standing still and silent as a tree; but in his hand was a small golden bloom of *elanor*, and a light was in his eyes. He was wrapped in some fair memory: and as Frodo looked at him he knew that he beheld things as they once had been in this same place. For the grim years were removed from the face of Aragorn, and he seemed clothed in white, a young lord tall and fair; and he spoke words in the Elvish tongue to one whom Frodo could not see. *Arwen vanimelda, namarië!* he said, and then he drew a breath, and returning out of his thought he looked at Frodo and smiled.

'Here is the heart of Elvendom on earth,' he said, 'and here my heart dwells ever, unless there be a light beyond the dark roads that we still must tread, you and I. Come with me!' And taking Frodo's hand in his, he left the hill of Cerin Amroth and came there never again as living man.

CHAPTER VII

THE MIRROR OF GALADRIEL

The sun was sinking behind the mountains, and the shadows were deepening in the woods, when they went on again. Their paths now went into thickets where the dusk had already gathered. Night came beneath the trees as they walked, and the Elves uncovered their silver lamps.

Suddenly they came out into the open again and found themselves under a pale evening sky pricked by a few early stars. There was a wide treeless space before them, running in a great circle and bending away on either hand. Beyond it was a deep fosse lost in soft shadow, but the grass upon its brink was green, as if it glowed still in memory of the sun that had gone. Upon the further side there rose to a great height a green wall encircling a green hill thronged with mallorn-trees taller than any they had yet seen in all the land. Their height could not be guessed, but they stood up in the twilight like living towers. In their many-tiered branches and amid their ever-moving leaves countless lights were gleaming, green and gold and silver. Haldir turned towards the Company.

'Welcome to Caras Galadhon!' he said. 'Here is the city of the Galadhrim where dwell the Lord Celeborn and Galadriel the Lady of Lórien. But we cannot enter here, for the gates do not look northward. We must go round to the southern side, and the way is not short, for the city is great.'

There was a road paved with white stone running on the outer brink of the fosse. Along this they went westward, with the city ever climbing up like a green cloud upon their left; and as the night deepened more lights sprang forth, until all the hill seemed afire with stars. They came at last to a white bridge, and crossing found the great gates of the city: they faced south-west, set between the ends of the encircling wall that here overlapped, and they were tall and strong, and hung with many lamps.

Haldir knocked and spoke, and the gates opened sound-lessly; but of guards Frodo could see no sign. The travellers passed within, and the gates shut behind them. They were in a deep lane between the ends of the wall, and passing quickly through it they entered the City of the Trees. No folk could they see, nor hear any feet upon the paths; but there were many voices, about them, and in the air above. Far away up on the hill they could hear the sound of singing falling from on high like soft rain upon leaves.

They went along many paths and climbed many stairs, until they came to the high places and saw before them amid a wide lawn a fountain shimmering. It was lit by silver lamps that swung from the boughs of trees, and it fell into a basin of silver, from which a white stream spilled. Upon the south side of the lawn there stood the mightiest of all the trees; its great smooth bole gleamed like grey silk, and up it towered, until its first branches, far above, opened their huge limbs under shadowy clouds of leaves. Beside it a broad white ladder stood, and at its foot three Elves were seated. They sprang up as the travellers approached, and Frodo saw that they were tall and clad in grey mail, and from their shoulders hung long white cloaks.

'Here dwell Celeborn and Galadriel,' said Haldir. 'It is their wish that you should ascend and speak with them.'

One of the Elf-wardens then blew a clear note on a small horn, and it was answered three times from far above. 'I will go first,' said Haldir. 'Let Frodo come next and with him Legolas. The others may follow as they wish. It is a long climb for those that are not accustomed to such stairs, but you may rest upon the way.'

As he climbed slowly up Frodo passed many flets: some on one side, some on another, and some set about the bole of the tree, so that the ladder passed through them. At a great height above the ground he came to a wide *talan*, like the deck of a great ship. On it was built a house, so large that almost it would have served for a hall of Men upon the earth. He entered behind Haldir, and found that he was in a chamber of oval shape, in the midst of which grew the trunk of the great mallorn, now tapering towards its crown, and yet making still a pillar of wide girth.

The chamber was filled with a soft light; its walls were green and silver and its roof of gold. Many Elves were seated there. On two chairs beneath the bole of the tree and canopied by a living bough there sat, side by side, Celeborn and Galadriel. They stood up to greet their guests, after the manner of Elves, even those who were accounted mighty kings. Very tall they were, and the Lady no less tall than the Lord; and they were grave and beautiful. They were clad wholly in white; and the hair of the Lady was of deep gold, and the hair of the Lord Celeborn was of silver long and bright; but no sign of age was upon them, unless it were in the depths of their eyes; for these were keen as lances in the starlight, and yet profound, the wells of deep memory.

Haldir led Frodo before them, and the Lord welcomed him in his own tongue. The Lady Galadriel said no word but looked long upon his face.

'Sit now beside my chair, Frodo of the Shire!' said Celeborn. 'When all have come we will speak together.'

Each of the companions he greeted courteously by name as they entered. 'Welcome Aragorn son of Arathorn!' he said. 'It is eight and thirty years of the world outside since you came to this land; and those years lie heavy on you. But the end is near, for good or ill. Here lay aside your burden for a while!'

'Welcome son of Thranduil! Too seldom do my kindred journey hither from the North.'

'Welcome Gimli son of Glóin! It is long indeed since we saw one of Durin's folk in Caras Galadhon. But today we have broken our long law. May it be a sign that though the world is now dark better days are at hand, and that friendship shall be renewed between our peoples.' Gimli bowed low.

When all the guests were seated before his chair the Lord looked at them again. 'Here there are eight,' he said. 'Nine were to set out: so said the messages. But maybe there has been some change of counsel that we have not heard. Elrond is far away, and darkness gathers between us, and all this year the shadows have grown longer.'

'Nay, there was no change of counsel,' said the Lady Galadriel, speaking for the first time. Her voice was clear and musical, but deeper than woman's wont. 'Gandalf the Grey set out with the Company, but he did not pass the borders of this land. Now tell us where he is; for I much desired to speak with him again. But I cannot see him from afar, unless he comes within the fences of Lothlórien: a grey mist is about him, and the ways of his feet and of his mind are hidden from me.'

'Alas!' said Aragorn. 'Gandalf the Grey fell into shadow. He remained in Moria and did not escape.'

At these words all the Elves in the hall cried aloud in grief and amazement. 'These are evil tidings,' said Celeborn, 'the most evil that have been spoken here in long years full of grievous deeds.' He turned to Haldir. 'Why has nothing of this been told to me before?' he asked in the Elven-tongue.

'We have not spoken to Haldir of our deeds or our purpose,' said Legolas. 'At first we were weary and danger was too close behind; and afterwards we almost forgot our grief for a time, as we walked in gladness on the fair paths of Lórien.'

'Yet our grief is great and our loss cannot be mended,' said Frodo. 'Gandalf was our guide, and he led us through Moria; and when our escape seemed beyond hope he saved us, and he fell.'

'Tell us now the full tale!' said Celeborn.

Then Aragorn recounted all that had happened upon the

pass of Caradhras, and in the days that followed; and he spoke of Balin and his book, and the fight in the Chamber of Mazarbul, and the fire, and the narrow bridge, and the coming of the Terror. 'An evil of the Ancient World it seemed, such as I have never seen before,' said Aragorn. 'It was both a shadow and a flame, strong and terrible.'

'It was a Balrog of Morgoth,' said Legolas; 'of all elf-banes the most deadly, save the One who sits in the Dark Tower.'

'Indeed I saw upon the bridge that which haunts our darkest dreams, I saw Durin's Bane,' said Gimli in a low voice, and dread was in his eyes.

'Alas!' said Celeborn. 'We long have feared that under Caradhras a terror slept. But had I known that the Dwarves had stirred up this evil in Moria again, I would have forbidden you to pass the northern borders, you and all that went with you. And if it were possible, one would say that at the last Gandalf fell from wisdom into folly, going needlessly into the net of Moria.'

'He would be rash indeed that said that thing,' said Galadriel gravely. 'Needless were none of the deeds of Gandalf in life. Those that followed him knew not his mind and cannot report his full purpose. But however it may be with the guide, the followers are blameless. Do not repent of your welcome to the Dwarf. If our folk had been exiled long and far from Lothlórien, who of the Galadhrim, even Celeborn the Wise, would pass nigh and would not wish to look upon their ancient home, though it had become an abode of dragons?

'Dark is the water of Kheled-zâram, and cold are the springs of Kibil-nâla, and fair were the many-pillared halls of Khazad-dûm in Elder Days before the fall of mighty kings beneath the stone.' She looked upon Gimli, who sat glowering and sad, and she smiled. And the Dwarf, hearing the names given in his own ancient tongue, looked up and met her eyes; and it seemed to him that he looked suddenly into the heart of an enemy and saw there love and understanding. Wonder came into his face, and then he smiled in answer.

He rose clumsily and bowed in dwarf-fashion, saying: 'Yet more fair is the living land of Lórien, and the Lady Galadriel is above all the jewels that lie beneath the earth!'

There was a silence. At length Celeborn spoke again. 'I did not know that your plight was so evil,' he said. 'Let Gimli forget my harsh words: I spoke in the trouble of my heart. I will do what I can to aid you, each according to his wish and need, but especially that one of the little folk who bears the burden.'

'Your quest is known to us,' said Galadriel, looking at Frodo. 'But we will not here speak of it more openly. Yet not in vain will it prove, maybe, that you came to this land seeking aid, as Gandalf himself plainly purposed. For the Lord of the Galadhrim is accounted the wisest of the Elves of Middle-earth, and a giver of gifts beyond the power of kings. He has dwelt in the West since the days of dawn, and I have dwelt with him years uncounted; for ere the fall of Nargothrond or Gondolin I passed over the mountains, and together through ages of the world we have fought the long defeat.

'I it was who first summoned the White Council. And if my designs had not gone amiss, it would have been governed by Gandalf the Grey, and then mayhap things would have gone otherwise. But even now there is hope left. I will not give you counsel, saying do this, or do that. For not in doing or contriving, nor in choosing between this course and another, can I avail; but only in knowing what was and is, and in part also what shall be. But this I will say to you: your Quest stands upon the edge of a knife. Stray but a little and it will fail, to the ruin of all. Yet hope remains while all the Company is true.'

And with that word she held them with her eyes, and in silence looked searchingly at each of them in turn. None save Legolas and Aragorn could long endure her glance. Sam quickly blushed and hung his head.

At length the Lady Galadriel released them from her eyes,

and she smiled. 'Do not let your hearts be troubled,' she said. 'Tonight you shall sleep in peace.' Then they sighed and felt suddenly weary, as those who have been questioned long and deeply, though no words had been spoken openly.

'Go now!' said Celeborn. 'You are worn with sorrow and much toil. Even if your Quest did not concern us closely, you should have refuge in this City, until you were healed and refreshed. Now you shall rest, and we will not speak of your further road for a while.'

That night the Company slept upon the ground, much to the satisfaction of the hobbits. The Elves spread for them a pavilion among the trees near the fountain, and in it they laid soft couches; then speaking words of peace with fair elvish voices they left them. For a little while the travellers talked of their night before in the tree-tops, and of their day's journey, and of the Lord and Lady; for they had not yet the heart to look further back.

'What did you blush for, Sam?' said Pippin. 'You soon broke down. Anyone would have thought you had a guilty conscience. I hope it was nothing worse than a wicked plot to steal one of my blankets.'

'I never thought no such thing,' answered Sam, in no mood for jest. 'If you want to know, I felt as if I hadn't got nothing on, and I didn't like it. She seemed to be looking inside me and asking me what I would do if she gave me the chance of flying back home to the Shire to a nice little hole with – with a bit of garden of my own.'

'That's funny,' said Merry. 'Almost exactly what I felt myself; only, only well, I don't think I'll say any more,' he ended lamely.

All of them, it seemed, had fared alike: each had felt that he was offered a choice between a shadow full of fear that lay ahead, and something that he greatly desired: clear before his mind it lay, and to get it he had only to turn aside from the road and leave the Quest and the war against Sauron to others.

'And it seemed to me, too,' said Gimli, 'that my choice would remain secret and known only to myself.'

'To me it seemed exceedingly strange,' said Boromir. 'Maybe it was only a test, and she thought to read our thoughts for her own good purpose; but almost I should have said that she was tempting us, and offering what she pretended to have the power to give. It need not be said that I refused to listen. The Men of Minas Tirith are true to their word.' But what he thought that the Lady had offered him Boromir did not tell.

And as for Frodo, he would not speak, though Boromir pressed him with questions. 'She held you long in her gaze, Ring-bearer,' he said.

'Yes,' said Frodo; 'but whatever came into my mind then I will keep there.'

'Well, have a care!' said Boromir. 'I do not feel too sure of this Elvish Lady and her purposes.'

'Speak no evil of the Lady Galadriel!' said Aragorn sternly. 'You know not what you say. There is in her and in this land no evil, unless a man bring it hither himself. Then let him beware! But tonight I shall sleep without fear for the first time since I left Rivendell. And may I sleep deep, and forget for a while my grief! I am weary in body and in heart.' He cast himself down upon his couch and fell at once into a long sleep.

The others soon did the same, and no sound or dream disturbed their slumber. When they woke they found that the light of day was broad upon the lawn before the pavilion, and the fountain rose and fell glittering in the sun.

They remained some days in Lothlórien, so far as they could tell or remember. All the while that they dwelt there the sun shone clear, save for a gentle rain that fell at times, and passed away leaving all things fresh and clean. The air was cool and soft, as if it were early spring, yet they felt about them the deep and thoughtful quiet of winter. It seemed to them that they did little but eat and drink and rest, and walk among the trees; and it was enough.

They had not seen the Lord and Lady again, and they had little speech with the Elven-folk; for few of these knew or would use the Westron tongue. Haldir had bidden them farewell and gone back again to the fences of the North, where great watch was now kept since the tidings of Moria that the Company had brought. Legolas was away much among the Galadhrim, and after the first night he did not sleep with the other companions, though he returned to eat and talk with them. Often he took Gimli with him when he went abroad in the land, and the others wondered at this change.

Now as the companions sat or walked together they spoke of Gandalf, and all that each had known and seen of him came clear before their minds. As they were healed of hurt and weariness of body the grief of their loss grew more keen. Often they heard nearby Elvish voices singing, and knew that they were making songs of lamentation for his fall, for they caught his name among the sweet sad words that they could not understand.

Mithrandir, Mithrandir sang the Elves, *O Pilgrim Grey!* For so they loved to call him. But if Legolas was with the Company, he would not interpret the songs for them, saying that he had not the skill, and that for him the grief was still too near, a matter for tears and not yet for song.

It was Frodo who first put something of his sorrow into halting words. He was seldom moved to make song or rhyme; even in Rivendell he had listened and had not sung himself, though his memory was stored with many things that others had made before him. But now as he sat beside the fountain in Lórien and heard about him the voices of the Elves, his thought took shape in a song that seemed fair to him; yet when he tried to repeat it to Sam only snatches remained, faded as a handful of withered leaves.

When evening in the Shire was grey
his footsteps on the Hill were heard;
before the dawn he went away
on journey long without a word.

From Wilderland to Western shore,
from northern waste to southern hill,
through dragon-lair and hidden door
and darkling woods he walked at will.

With Dwarf and Hobbit, Elves and Men,
with mortal and immortal folk,
with bird on bough and beast in den,
in their own secret tongues he spoke.

A deadly sword, a healing hand,
a back that bent beneath its load;
a trumpet-voice, a burning brand,
a weary pilgrim on the road.

A lord of wisdom throned he sat,
swift in anger, quick to laugh;
an old man in a battered hat
who leaned upon a thorny staff.

He stood upon the bridge alone
and Fire and Shadow both defied;
his staff was broken on the stone,
in Khazad-dûm his wisdom died.

'Why, you'll be beating Mr. Bilbo next!' said Sam.

'No, I am afraid not,' said Frodo. 'But that is the best I can do yet.'

'Well, Mr. Frodo, if you do have another go, I hope you'll say a word about his fireworks,' said Sam. 'Something like this:

> *The finest rockets ever seen:*
> *they burst in stars of blue and green,*
> *or after thunder golden showers*
> *came falling like a rain of flowers.*

Though that doesn't do them justice by a long road.'

'No, I'll leave that to you, Sam. Or perhaps to Bilbo. But – well, I can't talk of it any more. I can't bear to think of bringing the news to him.'

One evening Frodo and Sam were walking together in the cool twilight. Both of them felt restless again. On Frodo suddenly the shadow of parting had fallen: he knew somehow that the time was very near when he must leave Lothlórien.

'What do you think of Elves now, Sam?' he said. 'I asked you the same question once before – it seems a very long while ago; but you have seen more of them since then.'

'I have indeed!' said Sam. 'And I reckon there's Elves and Elves. They're all elvish enough, but they're not all the same. Now these folk aren't wanderers or homeless, and seem a bit nearer to the likes of us: they seem to belong here, more even than Hobbits do in the Shire. Whether they've made the land, or the land's made them, it's hard to say, if you take my meaning. It's wonderfully quiet here. Nothing seems to be going on, and nobody seems to want it to. If there's any magic about, it's right down deep, where I can't lay my hands on it, in a manner of speaking.'

'You can see and feel it everywhere,' said Frodo.

'Well,' said Sam, 'you can't see nobody working it. No fireworks like poor Gandalf used to show. I wonder we don't see nothing of the Lord and Lady in all these days. I fancy now that *she* could do some wonderful things, if she had a mind. I'd dearly love to see some Elf-magic, Mr. Frodo!'

'I wouldn't,' said Frodo. 'I am content. And I don't miss Gandalf's fireworks, but his bushy eyebrows, and his quick temper, and his voice.'

'You're right,' said Sam. 'And don't think I'm finding fault. I've often wanted to see a bit of magic like what it tells of in old tales, but I've never heard of a better land than this. It's like being at home and on a holiday at the same time, if you understand me. I don't want to leave. All the same, I'm beginning to feel that if we've got to go on, then we'd best get it over.

'*It's the job that's never started as takes longest to finish*, as my old gaffer used to say. And I don't reckon that these folk can do much more to help us, magic or no. It's when we leave this land that we shall miss Gandalf worse, I'm thinking.'

'I am afraid that's only too true, Sam,' said Frodo. 'Yet I hope very much that before we leave we shall see the Lady of the Elves again.'

Even as he spoke, they saw, as if she came in answer to their words, the Lady Galadriel approaching. Tall and white and fair she walked beneath the trees. She spoke no word, but beckoned to them.

Turning aside, she led them toward the southern slopes of the hill of Caras Galadhon, and passing through a high green hedge they came into an enclosed garden. No trees grew there, and it lay open to the sky. The evening star had risen and was shining with white fire above the western woods. Down a long flight of steps the Lady went into the deep green hollow, through which ran murmuring the silver stream that issued from the fountain on the hill. At the bottom, upon a low pedestal carved like a branching tree, stood a basin of silver, wide and shallow, and beside it stood a silver ewer.

With water from the stream Galadriel filled the basin to the brim, and breathed on it, and when the water was still again she spoke. 'Here is the Mirror of Galadriel,' she said. 'I have brought you here so that you may look in it, if you will.'

The air was very still, and the dell was dark, and the Elf-lady beside him was tall and pale. 'What shall we look for, and what shall we see?' asked Frodo, filled with awe.

'Many things I can command the Mirror to reveal,' she answered, 'and to some I can show what they desire to see. But the Mirror will also show things unbidden, and those are often stranger and more profitable than things which we wish to behold. What you will see, if you leave the Mirror free to work, I cannot tell. For it shows things that were, and things that are, and things that yet may be. But which it is that he sees, even the wisest cannot always tell. Do you wish to look?'

Frodo did not answer.

'And you?' she said, turning to Sam. 'For this is what your folk would call magic, I believe; though I do not understand clearly what they mean; and they seem to use the same word of the deceits of the Enemy. But this, if you will, is the magic of Galadriel. Did you not say that you wished to see Elf-magic?'

'I did,' said Sam, trembling a little between fear and curiosity. 'I'll have a peep, Lady, if you're willing.

'And I'd not mind a glimpse of what's going on at home,' he said in an aside to Frodo. 'It seems a terrible long time that I've been away. But there, like as not I'll only see the stars, or something that I won't understand.'

'Like as not,' said the Lady with a gentle laugh. 'But come, you shall look and see what you may. Do not touch the water!'

Sam climbed up on the foot of the pedestal and leaned over the basin. The water looked hard and dark. Stars were reflected in it.

'There's only stars, as I thought,' he said. Then he gave a low gasp, for the stars went out. As if a dark veil had been withdrawn, the Mirror grew grey, and then clear. There was sun shining, and the branches of trees were waving and tossing in the wind. But before Sam could make up his mind what it was that he saw, the light faded; and now he thought he saw Frodo with a pale face lying fast asleep under a great dark cliff. Then he seemed to see himself going along a dim passage, and climbing an endless winding stair. It came to him suddenly that he was looking urgently for something, but what it was he did not know. Like a dream the vision shifted and went back, and he saw the trees again. But this time they were not so close, and he could see what was going on: they were not waving in the wind, they were falling, crashing to the ground.

'Hi!' cried Sam in an outraged voice. 'There's that Ted Sandyman a-cutting down trees as he shouldn't. They didn't ought to be felled: it's that avenue beyond the Mill that shades the road to Bywater. I wish I could get at Ted, and I'd fell *him*!'

But now Sam noticed that the Old Mill had vanished, and a large red-brick building was being put up where it had stood. Lots of folk were busily at work. There was a tall red chimney nearby. Black smoke seemed to cloud the surface of the Mirror.

'There's some devilry at work in the Shire,' he said. 'Elrond knew what he was about when he wanted to send Mr. Merry back.' Then suddenly Sam gave a cry and sprang away. 'I can't stay here,' he said wildly. 'I must go home. They've dug up Bagshot Row, and there's the poor old gaffer going down the Hill with his bits of things on a barrow. I must go home!'

'You cannot go home alone,' said the Lady. 'You did not wish to go home without your master before you looked in the Mirror, and yet you knew that evil things might well be happening in the Shire. Remember that the Mirror shows many things, and not all have yet come to pass. Some never come to be, unless those that behold the visions turn aside from their path to prevent them. The Mirror is dangerous as a guide of deeds.'

Sam sat on the ground and put his head in his hands. 'I wish I had never come here, and I don't want to see no more magic,' he said and fell silent. After a moment he spoke again thickly, as if struggling with tears. 'No, I'll go home by the long road with Mr. Frodo, or not at all,' he said. 'But I hope

I do get back some day. If what I've seen turns out true, somebody's going to catch it hot!'

'Do you now wish to look, Frodo?' said the Lady Galadriel. 'You did not wish to see Elf-magic and were content.'

'Do you advise me to look?' asked Frodo.

'No,' she said. 'I do not counsel you one way or the other. I am not a counsellor. You may learn something, and whether what you see be fair or evil, that may be profitable, and yet it may not. Seeing is both good and perilous. Yet I think, Frodo, that you have courage and wisdom enough for the venture, or I would not have brought you here. Do as you will!'

'I will look,' said Frodo, and he climbed on the pedestal and bent over the dark water. At once the Mirror cleared and he saw a twilit land. Mountains loomed dark in the distance against a pale sky. A long grey road wound back out of sight. Far away a figure came slowly down the road, faint and small at first, but growing larger and clearer as it approached. Suddenly Frodo realized that it reminded him of Gandalf. He almost called aloud the wizard's name, and then he saw that the figure was clothed not in grey but in white, in a white that shone faintly in the dusk; and in its hand there was a white staff. The head was so bowed that he could see no face, and presently the figure turned aside round a bend in the road and went out of the Mirror's view. Doubt came into Frodo's mind: was this a vision of Gandalf on one of his many lonely journeys long ago, or was it Saruman?

The vision now changed. Brief and small but very vivid he caught a glimpse of Bilbo walking restlessly about his room. The table was littered with disordered papers; rain was beating on the windows.

Then there was a pause, and after it many swift scenes followed that Frodo in some way knew to be parts of a great history in which he had become involved. The mist cleared and he saw a sight which he had never seen before but knew

at once: the Sea. Darkness fell. The sea rose and raged in a
great storm. Then he saw against the Sun, sinking blood-red
into a wrack of clouds, the black outline of a tall ship with
torn sails riding up out of the West. Then a wide river flowing
through a populous city. Then a white fortress with seven
towers. And then again a ship with black sails, but now it
was morning again, and the water rippled with light, and a
banner bearing the emblem of a white tree shone in the sun.
A smoke as of fire and battle arose, and again the sun went
down in a burning red that faded into a grey mist; and into
the mist a small ship passed away, twinkling with lights. It
vanished, and Frodo sighed and prepared to draw away.

But suddenly the Mirror went altogether dark, as dark as
if a hole had opened in the world of sight, and Frodo looked
into emptiness. In the black abyss there appeared a single
Eye that slowly grew, until it filled nearly all the Mirror. So
terrible was it that Frodo stood rooted, unable to cry out or
to withdraw his gaze. The Eye was rimmed with fire, but
was itself glazed, yellow as a cat's, watchful and intent, and
the black slit of its pupil opened on a pit, a window into
nothing.

Then the Eye began to rove, searching this way and that;
and Frodo knew with certainty and horror that among the
many things that it sought he himself was one. But he also
knew that it could not see him – not yet, not unless he willed
it. The Ring that hung upon its chain about his neck grew
heavy, heavier than a great stone, and his head was dragged
downwards. The Mirror seemed to be growing hot and curls
of steam were rising from the water. He was slipping forward.

'Do not touch the water!' said the Lady Galadriel softly.
The vision faded, and Frodo found that he was looking at
the cool stars twinkling in the silver basin. He stepped back
shaking all over and looked at the Lady.

'I know what it was that you last saw,' she said; 'for that
is also in my mind. Do not be afraid! But do not think that
only by singing amid the trees, nor even by the slender arrows
of elven-bows, is this land of Lothlórien maintained and

defended against its Enemy. I say to you, Frodo, that even as I speak to you, I perceive the Dark Lord and know his mind, or all of his mind that concerns the Elves. And he gropes ever to see me and my thought. But still the door is closed!'

She lifted up her white arms, and spread out her hands towards the East in a gesture of rejection and denial. Eärendil, the Evening Star, most beloved of the Elves, shone clear above. So bright was it that the figure of the Elven-lady cast a dim shadow on the ground. Its rays glanced upon a ring about her finger; it glittered like polished gold overlaid with silver light, and a white stone in it twinkled as if the Even-star had come down to rest upon her hand. Frodo gazed at the ring with awe; for suddenly it seemed to him that he understood.

'Yes,' she said, divining his thought, 'it is not permitted to speak of it, and Elrond could not do so. But it cannot be hidden from the Ring-bearer, and one who has seen the Eye. Verily it is in the land of Lórien upon the finger of Galadriel that one of the Three remains. This is Nenya, the Ring of Adamant, and I am its keeper.

'He suspects, but he does not know – not yet. Do you not see now wherefore your coming is to us as the footstep of Doom? For if you fail, then we are laid bare to the Enemy. Yet if you succeed, then our power is diminished, and Loth-lórien will fade, and the tides of Time will sweep it away. We must depart into the West, or dwindle to a rustic folk of dell and cave, slowly to forget and to be forgotten.'

Frodo bent his head. 'And what do you wish?' he said at last.

'That what should be shall be,' she answered. 'The love of the Elves for their land and their works is deeper than the deeps of the Sea, and their regret is undying and cannot ever wholly be assuaged. Yet they will cast all away rather than submit to Sauron: for they know him now. For the fate of Lothlórien you are not answerable, but only for the doing of your own task. Yet I could wish, were it of any avail, that the One Ring had never been wrought, or had remained for ever lost.'

'You are wise and fearless and fair, Lady Galadriel,' said Frodo. 'I will give you the One Ring, if you ask for it. It is too great a matter for me.'

Galadriel laughed with a sudden clear laugh. 'Wise the Lady Galadriel may be,' she said, 'yet here she has met her match in courtesy. Gently are you revenged for my testing of your heart at our first meeting. You begin to see with a keen eye. I do not deny that my heart has greatly desired to ask what you offer. For many long years I had pondered what I might do, should the Great Ring come into my hands, and behold! it was brought within my grasp. The evil that was devised long ago works on in many ways, whether Sauron himself stands or falls. Would not that have been a noble deed to set to the credit of his Ring, if I had taken it by force or fear from my guest?

'And now at last it comes. You will give me the Ring freely! In place of the Dark Lord you will set up a Queen. And I shall not be dark, but beautiful and terrible as the Morning and the Night! Fair as the Sea and the Sun and the Snow upon the Mountain! Dreadful as the Storm and the Lightning! Stronger than the foundations of the earth. All shall love me and despair!'

She lifted up her hand and from the ring that she wore there issued a great light that illumined her alone and left all else dark. She stood before Frodo seeming now tall beyond measurement, and beautiful beyond enduring, terrible and worshipful. Then she let her hand fall, and the light faded, and suddenly she laughed again, and lo! she was shrunken: a slender elf-woman, clad in simple white, whose gentle voice was soft and sad.

'I pass the test,' she said. 'I will diminish, and go into the West, and remain Galadriel.'

They stood for a long while in silence. At length the Lady spoke again. 'Let us return!' she said. 'In the morning you must depart, for now we have chosen, and the tides of fate are flowing.'

'I would ask one thing before we go,' said Frodo, 'a thing which I often meant to ask Gandalf in Rivendell. I am permitted to wear the One Ring: why cannot I see all the others and know the thoughts of those that wear them?'

'You have not tried,' she said. 'Only thrice have you set the Ring upon your finger since you knew what you possessed. Do not try! It would destroy you. Did not Gandalf tell you that the rings give power according to the measure of each possessor? Before you could use that power you would need to become far stronger, and to train your will to the domination of others. Yet even so, as Ring-bearer and as one that has borne it on finger and seen that which is hidden, your sight is grown keener. You have perceived my thought more clearly than many that are accounted wise. You saw the Eye of him that holds the Seven and the Nine. And did you not see and recognize the ring upon my finger? Did you see my ring?' she asked turning again to Sam.

'No, Lady,' he answered. 'To tell you the truth, I wondered what you were talking about. I saw a star through your fingers. But if you'll pardon my speaking out, I think my master was right. I wish you'd take his Ring. You'd put things to rights. You'd stop them digging up the gaffer and turning him adrift. You'd make some folk pay for their dirty work.'

'I would,' she said. 'That is how it would begin. But it would not stop with that, alas! We will not speak more of it. Let us go!'

CHAPTER VIII

FAREWELL TO LÓRIEN

That night the Company was again summoned to the chamber of Celeborn, and there the Lord and Lady greeted them with fair words. At length Celeborn spoke of their departure.

'Now is the time,' he said, 'when those who wish to continue the Quest must harden their hearts to leave this land. Those who no longer wish to go forward may remain here, for a while. But whether they stay or go, none can be sure of peace. For we are come now to the edge of doom. Here those who wish may await the oncoming of the hour till either the ways of the world lie open again, or we summon them to the last need of Lórien. Then they may return to their own lands, or else go to the long home of those that fall in battle.'

There was a silence. 'They all resolved to go forward,' said Galadriel looking in their eyes.

'As for me,' said Boromir, 'my way home lies onward and not back.'

'That is true,' said Celeborn, 'but is all this Company going with you to Minas Tirith?'

'We have not decided our course,' said Aragorn. 'Beyond Lothlórien I do not know what Gandalf intended to do. Indeed I do not think that even he had any clear purpose.'

'Maybe not,' said Celeborn, 'yet when you leave this land, you can no longer forget the Great River. As some of you know well, it cannot be crossed by travellers with baggage between Lórien and Gondor, save by boat. And are not the bridges of Osgiliath broken down and all the landings held now by the Enemy?

'On which side will you journey? The way to Minas Tirith

lies upon this side, upon the west; but the straight road of the Quest lies east of the River, upon the darker shore. Which shore will you now take?'

'If my advice is heeded, it will be the western shore, and the way to Minas Tirith,' answered Boromir. 'But I am not the leader of the Company.' The others said nothing, and Aragorn looked doubtful and troubled.

'I see that you do not yet know what to do,' said Celeborn. 'It is not my part to choose for you; but I will help you as I may. There are some among you who can handle boats: Legolas, whose folk know the swift Forest River; and Boromir of Gondor; and Aragorn the traveller.'

'And one Hobbit!' cried Merry. 'Not all of us look on boats as wild horses. My people live by the banks of the Brandywine.'

'That is well,' said Celeborn. 'Then I will furnish your Company with boats. They must be small and light, for if you go far by water, there are places where you will be forced to carry them. You will come to the rapids of Sarn Gebir, and maybe at last to the great falls of Rauros where the River thunders down from Nen Hithoel; and there are other perils. Boats may make your journey less toilsome for a while. Yet they will not give you counsel: in the end you must leave them and the River, and turn west – or east.'

Aragorn thanked Celeborn many times. The gift of boats comforted him much, not least because there would now be no need to decide his course for some days. The others, too, looked more hopeful. Whatever perils lay ahead, it seemed better to float down the broad tide of Anduin to meet them than to plod forward with bent backs. Only Sam was doubtful: he at any rate still thought boats as bad as wild horses, or worse, and not all the dangers that he had survived made him think better of them.

'All shall be prepared for you and await you at the haven before noon tomorrow,' said Celeborn. 'I will send my people to you in the morning to help you make ready for the journey. Now we will wish you all a fair night and untroubled sleep.'

'Good night, my friends!' said Galadriel. 'Sleep in peace! Do not trouble your hearts overmuch with thought of the road tonight. Maybe the paths that you each shall tread are already laid before your feet, though you do not see them. Good night!'

The Company now took their leave and returned to their pavilion. Legolas went with them, for this was to be their last night in Lothlórien, and in spite of the words of Galadriel they wished to take counsel together.

For a long time they debated what they should do, and how it would be best to attempt the fulfilling of their purpose with the Ring; but they came to no decision. It was plain that most of them desired to go first to Minas Tirith, and to escape at least for a while from the terror of the Enemy. They would have been willing to follow a leader over the River and into the shadow of Mordor; but Frodo spoke no word, and Aragorn was still divided in his mind.

His own plan, while Gandalf remained with them, had been to go with Boromir, and with his sword help to deliver Gondor. For he believed that the message of the dreams was a summons, and that the hour had come at last when the heir of Elendil should come forth and strive with Sauron for the mastery. But in Moria the burden of Gandalf had been laid on him; and he knew that he could not now forsake the Ring, if Frodo refused in the end to go with Boromir. And yet what help could he or any of the Company give to Frodo, save to walk blindly with him into the darkness?

'I shall go to Minas Tirith, alone if need be, for it is my duty,' said Boromir; and after that he was silent for a while, sitting with his eyes fixed on Frodo, as if he was trying to read the Halfling's thoughts. At length he spoke again, softly, as if he was debating with himself. 'If you wish only to destroy the Ring,' he said, 'then there is little use in war and weapons; and the Men of Minas Tirith cannot help. But if you wish to destroy the armed might of the Dark Lord, then it is folly to go without force into his domain; and folly to throw away.' He paused suddenly, as if he had become aware that he was speaking his thoughts aloud. 'It would be folly to throw lives away, I mean,' he ended. 'It is a choice between defending a strong place and walking openly into the arms of death. At least, that is how I see it.'

Frodo caught something new and strange in Boromir's glance, and he looked hard at him. Plainly Boromir's thought was different from his final words. It would be folly to throw away: what? The Ring of Power? He had said something like this at the Council, but then he had accepted the correction of Elrond. Frodo looked at Aragorn, but he seemed deep in his own thought and made no sign that he had heeded Boromir's words. And so their debate ended. Merry and Pippin were already asleep, and Sam was nodding. The night was growing old.

In the morning, as they were beginning to pack their slender goods, Elves that could speak their tongue came to them and brought them many gifts of food and clothing for the journey. The food was mostly in the form of very thin cakes, made of a meal that was baked a light brown on the outside, and inside was the colour of cream. Gimli took up one of the cakes and looked at it with a doubtful eye.

'*Cram*,' he said under his breath, as he broke off a crisp corner and nibbled at it. His expression quickly changed, and he ate all the rest of the cake with relish.

'No more, no more!' cried the Elves laughing. 'You have eaten enough already for a long day's march.'

'I thought it was only a kind of *cram*, such as the Dale-men make for journeys in the wild,' said the Dwarf.

'So it is,' they answered. 'But we call it *lembas* or waybread, and it is more strengthening than any food made by Men, and it is more pleasant than *cram*, by all accounts.'

'Indeed it is,' said Gimli. 'Why, it is better than the honey-cakes of the Beornings, and that is great praise, for the Beornings are the best bakers that I know of; but they are none too willing to deal out their cakes to travellers in these days. You are kindly hosts!'

'All the same, we bid you spare the food,' they said. 'Eat little at a time, and only at need. For these things are given to serve you when all else fails. The cakes will keep sweet for many many days, if they are unbroken and left in their leaf-wrappings, as we have brought them. One will keep a traveller on his feet for a day of long labour, even if he be one of the tall Men of Minas Tirith.'

The Elves next unwrapped and gave to each of the Company the clothes they had brought. For each they had provided a hood and cloak, made according to his size, of the light but warm silken stuff that the Galadhrim wove. It was hard to say of what colour they were: grey with the hue of twilight under the trees they seemed to be; and yet if they were moved, or set in another light, they were green as shadowed leaves, or brown as fallow fields by night, dusksilver as water under the stars. Each cloak was fastened about the neck with a brooch like a green leaf veined with silver.

'Are these magic cloaks?' asked Pippin, looking at them with wonder.

'I do not know what you mean by that,' answered the leader of the Elves. 'They are fair garments, and the web is good, for it was made in this land. They are elvish robes certainly, if that is what you mean. Leaf and branch, water and stone: they have the hue and beauty of all these things under the twilight of Lórien that we love; for we put the thought of all that we love into all that we make. Yet they are garments, not armour, and they will not turn shaft or blade. But they should serve you well: they are light to wear, and warm enough or cool enough at need. And you will find them a great aid in keeping out of the sight of unfriendly eyes, whether you walk among the stones or the trees. You are indeed high in the favour of the Lady! For she herself and her maidens wove this stuff; and never before have we clad strangers in the garb of our own people.'

*   *   *

After their morning meal the Company said farewell to the lawn by the fountain. Their hearts were heavy; for it was a fair place, and it had become like home to them, though they could not count the days and nights that they had passed there. As they stood for a moment looking at the white water in the sunlight, Haldir came walking towards them over the green grass of the glade. Frodo greeted him with delight.

'I have returned from the Northern Fences,' said the Elf, 'and I am sent now to be your guide again. The Dimrill Dale is full of vapour and clouds of smoke, and the mountains are troubled. There are noises in the deeps of the earth. If any of you had thought of returning northwards to your homes, you would not have been able to pass that way. But come! Your path now goes south.'

As they walked through Caras Galadhon the green ways were empty; but in the trees above them many voices were murmuring and singing. They themselves went silently. At last Haldir led them down the southward slopes of the hill, and they came again to the great gate hung with lamps, and to the white bridge; and so they passed out and left the city of the Elves. Then they turned away from the paved road and took a path that went off into a deep thicket of mallorn-trees, and passed on, winding through rolling woodlands of silver shadow, leading them ever down, southwards and eastwards, towards the shores of the River.

They had gone some ten miles and noon was at hand when they came on a high green wall. Passing through an opening they came suddenly out of the trees. Before them lay a long lawn of shining grass, studded with golden *elanor* that glinted in the sun. The lawn ran out into a narrow tongue between bright margins: on the right and west the Silverlode flowed glittering; on the left and east the Great River rolled its broad waters, deep and dark. On the further shores the woodlands still marched on southwards as far as the eye could see, but all the banks were bleak and bare. No mallorn lifted its gold-hung boughs beyond the Land of Lórien.

On the bank of the Silverlode, at some distance up from

the meeting of the streams, there was a hythe of white stones and white wood. By it were moored many boats and barges. Some were brightly painted, and shone with silver and gold and green, but most were either white or grey. Three small grey boats had been made ready for the travellers, and in these the Elves stowed their goods. And they added also coils of rope, three to each boat. Slender they looked, but strong, silken to the touch, grey of hue like the elven-cloaks.

'What are these?' asked Sam, handling one that lay upon the greensward.

'Ropes indeed!' answered an Elf from the boats. 'Never travel far without a rope! And one that is long and strong and light. Such are these. They may be a help in many needs.'

'You don't need to tell me that!' said Sam. 'I came without any, and I've been worried ever since. But I was wondering what these were made of, knowing a bit about rope-making: it's in the family as you might say.'

'They are made of *hithlain*,' said the Elf, 'but there is no time now to instruct you in the art of their making. Had we known that this craft delighted you, we could have taught you much. But now alas! unless you should at some time return hither, you must be content with our gift. May it serve you well!'

'Come!' said Haldir. 'All is now ready for you. Enter the boats! But take care at first!'

'Heed the words!' said the other Elves. 'These boats are light-built, and they are crafty and unlike the boats of other folk. They will not sink, lade them as you will; but they are wayward if mishandled. It would be wise if you accustomed yourselves to stepping in and out, here where there is a landing-place, before you set off downstream.'

The Company was arranged in this way: Aragorn, Frodo, and Sam were in one boat; Boromir, Merry, and Pippin in another; and in the third were Legolas and Gimli, who had now become fast friends. In this last boat most of the goods and packs were stowed. The boats were moved and steered with short-handled paddles that had broad leaf-shaped blades. When all was ready Aragorn led them on a trial up the Silverlode. The current was swift and they went forward slowly. Sam sat in the bows, clutching the sides, and looking back wistfully to the shore. The sunlight glittering on the water dazzled his eyes. As they passed beyond the green field of the Tongue, the trees drew down to the river's brink. Here and there golden leaves tossed and floated on the rippling stream. The air was very bright and still, and there was a silence, except for the high distant song of larks.

They turned a sharp bend in the river, and there, sailing proudly down the stream toward them, they saw a swan of great size. The water rippled on either side of the white breast beneath its curving neck. Its beak shone like burnished gold, and its eyes glinted like jet set in yellow stones; its huge white wings were half lifted. A music came down the river as it drew nearer; and suddenly they perceived that it was a ship, wrought and carved with elven-skill in the likeness of a bird. Two elves clad in white steered it with black paddles. In the midst of the vessel sat Celeborn, and behind him stood Galadriel, tall and white; a circlet of golden flowers was in her hair, and in her hand she held a harp, and she sang. Sad and sweet was the sound of her voice in the cool clear air:

> I sang of leaves, of leaves of gold, and leaves of gold there
>   grew:
> Of wind I sang, a wind there came and in the branches blew.
> Beyond the Sun, beyond the Moon, the foam was on the Sea,
> And by the strand of Ilmarin there grew a golden Tree.
> Beneath the stars of Ever-eve in Eldamar it shone,
> In Eldamar beside the walls of Elven Tirion.
> There long the golden leaves have grown upon the branching
>   years,
> While here beyond the Sundering Seas now fall the
>   Elven-tears.
> O Lórien! The Winter comes, the bare and leafless Day;

The leaves are falling in the stream, the River flows away.
O Lórien! Too long I have dwelt upon this Hither Shore
And in a fading crown have twined the golden elanor.
But if of ships I now should sing, what ship would come to
    me,
What ship would bear me ever back across so wide a Sea?

Aragorn stayed his boat as the Swan-ship drew alongside. The Lady ended her song and greeted them. 'We have come to bid our last farewell,' she said, 'and to speed you with blessings from our land.'

'Though you have been our guests,' said Celeborn, 'you have not yet eaten with us, and we bid you, therefore, to a parting feast, here between the flowing waters that will bear you far from Lórien.'

The Swan passed on slowly to the hythe, and they turned their boats and followed it. There in the last end of Egladil upon the green grass the parting feast was held; but Frodo ate and drank little, heeding only the beauty of the Lady and her voice. She seemed no longer perilous or terrible, nor filled with hidden power. Already she seemed to him, as by men of later days Elves still at times are seen: present and yet remote, a living vision of that which has already been left far behind by the flowing streams of Time.

After they had eaten and drunk, sitting upon the grass, Celeborn spoke to them again of their journey, and lifting his hand he pointed south to the woods beyond the Tongue.

'As you go down the water,' he said, 'you will find that the trees will fail, and you will come to a barren country. There the River flows in stony vales amid high moors, until at last after many leagues it comes to the tall island of the Tindrock, that we call Tol Brandir. There it casts its arms about the steep shores of the isle, and falls then with a great noise and smoke over the cataracts of Rauros down into the Nindalf, the Wetwang as it is called in your tongue. That is a wide region of sluggish fen where the stream becomes

tortuous and much divided. There the Entwash flows in by
many mouths from the Forest of Fangorn in the west. About
that stream, on this side of the Great River, lies Rohan. On
the further side are the bleak hills of the Emyn Muil. The
wind blows from the East there, for they look out over the
Dead Marshes and the Noman-lands to Cirith Gorgor and
the black gates of Mordor.

'Boromir, and any that go with him seeking Minas Tirith,
will do well to leave the Great River above Rauros and cross
the Entwash before it finds the marshes. Yet they should not
go too far up that stream, nor risk becoming entangled in
the Forest of Fangorn. That is a strange land, and is now
little known. But Boromir and Aragorn doubtless do not need
this warning.'

'Indeed we have heard of Fangorn in Minas Tirith,' said
Boromir. 'But what I have heard seems to me for the most
part old wives' tales, such as we tell to our children. All that
lies north of Rohan is now to us so far away that fancy can
wander freely there. Of old Fangorn lay upon the borders of
our realm; but it is now many lives of men since any of us
visited it, to prove or disprove the legends that have come
down from distant years.

'I have myself been at whiles in Rohan, but I have never
crossed it northwards. When I was sent out as a messenger,
I passed through the Gap by the skirts of the White Mountains, and crossed the Isen and the Greyflood into Norther-
land. A long and wearisome journey. Four hundred leagues
I reckoned it, and it took me many months; for I lost my
horse at Tharbad, at the fording of the Greyflood. After that
journey, and the road I have trodden with this Company, I
do not much doubt that I shall find a way through Rohan,
and Fangorn too, if need be.'

'Then I need say no more,' said Celeborn. 'But do not
despise the lore that has come down from distant years; for
oft it may chance that old wives keep in memory word of
things that once were needful for the wise to know.'

*　　*　　*

Now Galadriel rose from the grass, and taking a cup from one of her maidens she filled it with white mead and gave it to Celeborn.

'Now it is time to drink the cup of farewell,' she said. 'Drink, Lord of the Galadhrim! And let not your heart be sad, though night must follow noon, and already our evening draweth nigh.'

Then she brought the cup to each of the Company, and bade them drink and farewell. But when they had drunk she commanded them to sit again on the grass, and chairs were set for her and for Celeborn. Her maidens stood silent about her, and a while she looked upon her guests. At last she spoke again.

'We have drunk the cup of parting,' she said, 'and the shadows fall between us. But before you go, I have brought in my ship gifts which the Lord and Lady of the Galadhrim now offer you in memory of Lothlórien.' Then she called to each in turn.

'Here is the gift of Celeborn and Galadriel to the leader of your Company,' she said to Aragorn, and she gave him a sheath that had been made to fit his sword. It was overlaid with a tracery of flowers and leaves wrought of silver and gold, and on it were set in elven-runes formed of many gems the name Andúril and the lineage of the sword.

'The blade that is drawn from this sheath shall not be stained or broken even in defeat,' she said. 'But is there aught else that you desire of me at our parting? For darkness will flow between us, and it may be that we shall not meet again, unless it be far hence upon a road that has no returning.'

And Aragorn answered: 'Lady, you know all my desire, and long held in keeping the only treasure that I seek. Yet it is not yours to give me, even if you would; and only through darkness shall I come to it.'

'Yet maybe this will lighten your heart,' said Galadriel; 'for it was left in my care to be given to you, should you pass through this land.' Then she lifted from her lap a great stone of a clear green, set in a silver brooch that was wrought in the likeness of an eagle with outspread wings; and as she held it up the gem flashed like the sun shining through the leaves of spring. 'This stone I gave to Celebrían my daughter, and she to hers; and now it comes to you as a token of hope. In this hour take the name that was foretold for you, Elessar, the Elfstone of the house of Elendil!'

Then Aragorn took the stone and pinned the brooch upon his breast, and those who saw him wondered; for they had not marked before how tall and kingly he stood, and it seemed to them that many years of toil had fallen from his shoulders. 'For the gifts that you have given me I thank you,' he said, 'O Lady of Lórien of whom were sprung Celebrían and Arwen Evenstar. What praise could I say more?'

The Lady bowed her head, and she turned then to Boromir, and to him she gave a belt of gold; and to Merry and Pippin she gave small silver belts, each with a clasp wrought like a golden flower. To Legolas she gave a bow such as the Galadhrim used, longer and stouter than the bows of Mirkwood, and strung with a string of elf-hair. With it went a quiver of arrows.

'For you little gardener and lover of trees,' she said to Sam, 'I have only a small gift.' She put into his hand a little box of plain grey wood, unadorned save for a single silver rune upon the lid. 'Here is set G for Galadriel,' she said; 'but also it may stand for garden in your tongue. In this box there is earth from my orchard, and such blessing as Galadriel has still to bestow is upon it. It will not keep you on your road, nor defend you against any peril; but if you keep it and see your home again at last, then perhaps it may reward you. Though you should find all barren and laid waste, there will be few gardens in Middle-earth that will bloom like your garden, if you sprinkle this earth there. Then you may remember Galadriel, and catch a glimpse far off of Lórien, that you have seen only in our winter. For our spring and our summer are gone by, and they will never be seen on earth again save in memory.'

Sam went red to the ears and muttered something inaudible, as he clutched the box and bowed as well as he could.

'And what gift would a Dwarf ask of the Elves?' said Galadriel, turning to Gimli.

'None, Lady,' answered Gimli. 'It is enough for me to have seen the Lady of the Galadhrim, and to have heard her gentle words.'

'Hear all ye Elves!' she cried to those about her. 'Let none say again that Dwarves are grasping and ungracious! Yet surely, Gimli son of Glóin, you desire something that I could give? Name it, I bid you! You shall not be the only guest without a gift.'

'There is nothing, Lady Galadriel,' said Gimli, bowing low and stammering. 'Nothing, unless it might be – unless it is permitted to ask, nay, to name a single strand of your hair, which surpasses the gold of the earth as the stars surpass the gems of the mine. I do not ask for such a gift. But you commanded me to name my desire.'

The Elves stirred and murmured with astonishment, and Celeborn gazed at the Dwarf in wonder, but the Lady smiled. 'It is said that the skill of the Dwarves is in their hands rather than in their tongues,' she said; 'yet that is not true of Gimli. For none have ever made to me a request so bold and yet so courteous. And how shall I refuse, since I commanded him to speak? But tell me, what would you do with such a gift?'

'Treasure it, Lady,' he answered, 'in memory of your words to me at our first meeting. And if ever I return to the smithies of my home, it shall be set in imperishable crystal to be an heirloom of my house, and a pledge of good will between the Mountain and the Wood until the end of days.'

Then the Lady unbraided one of her long tresses, and cut off three golden hairs, and laid them in Gimli's hand. 'These words shall go with the gift,' she said. 'I do not foretell, for all foretelling is now vain: on the one hand lies darkness, and on the other only hope. But if hope should not fail, then I say to you, Gimli son of Glóin, that your hands shall flow with gold, and yet over you gold shall have no dominion.

'And you, Ring-bearer,' she said, turning to Frodo. 'I come to you last who are not last in my thoughts. For you I have prepared this.' She held up a small crystal phial: it glittered as she moved it, and rays of white light sprang from her hand. 'In this phial,' she said, 'is caught the light of Eärendil's star, set amid the waters of my fountain. It will shine still brighter when night is about you. May it be a light to you in dark places, when all other lights go out. Remember Galadriel and her Mirror!'

Frodo took the phial, and for a moment as it shone between them, he saw her again standing like a queen, great and beautiful, but no longer terrible. He bowed, but found no words to say.

Now the Lady arose, and Celeborn led them back to the hythe. A yellow noon lay on the green land of the Tongue, and the water glittered with silver. All at last was made ready. The Company took their places in the boats as before. Crying farewell, the Elves of Lórien with long grey poles thrust them out into the flowing stream, and the rippling waters bore them slowly away. The travellers sat still without moving or speaking. On the green bank near to the very point of the Tongue the Lady Galadriel stood alone and silent. As they passed her they turned and their eyes watched her slowly floating away from them. For so it seemed to them: Lórien was slipping backward, like a bright ship masted with enchanted trees, sailing on to forgotten shores, while they sat helpless upon the margin of the grey and leafless world.

Even as they gazed, the Silverlode passed out into the currents of the Great River, and their boats turned and began to speed southward. Soon the white form of the Lady was small and distant. She shone like a window of glass upon a far hill in the westering sun, or as a remote lake seen from a mountain: a crystal fallen in the lap of the land. Then it seemed to Frodo that she lifted her arms in a final farewell, and far but piercing-clear on the following wind came the sound of her voice singing. But now she sang in the ancient

tongue of the Elves beyond the Sea, and he did not understand the words: fair was the music, but it did not comfort
him.

Yet as is the way of Elvish words, they remained graven
in his memory, and long afterwards he interpreted them, as
well as he could: the language was that of Elven-song and
spoke of things little known on Middle-earth.

> *Ai! laurië lantar lassi súrinen,*
> *yéni únótimë ve rámar aldaron!*
> *Yéni ve lintë yuldar avánier*
> *mi oromardi lisse-miruvóreva*
> *Andúnë pella, Vardo tellumar*
> *nu luini yassen tintilar i eleni*
> *ómaryo airetári-lírinen.*

> *Sí man i yulma nin enquantuva?*

> *An sí Tintallë Varda Oiolossëo*
> *ve fanyar máryat Elentári ortanë,*
> *ar ilyë tier undulávë lumbulë;*
> *ar sindanóriello caita mornië*
> *i falmalinnar imbë met, ar hísië*
> *untúpa Calaciryo míri oialë.*
> *Sí vanwa ná, Rómello vanwa, Valimar!*

> *Namárië! Nai hiruvalyë Valimar.*
> *Nai elyë hiruva. Namárië!*

'Ah! like gold fall the leaves in the wind, long years number-
less as the wings of trees! The years have passed like swift
draughts of the sweet mead in lofty halls beyond the West,
beneath the blue vaults of Varda wherein the stars tremble
in the song of her voice, holy and queenly. Who now shall
refill the cup for me? For now the Kindler, Varda, the Queen
of the Stars, from Mount Everwhite has uplifted her hands
like clouds, and all paths are drowned deep in shadow; and

out of a grey country darkness lies on the foaming waves between us, and mist covers the jewels of Calacirya for ever. Now lost, lost to those from the East is Valimar! Farewell! Maybe thou shalt find Valimar. Maybe even thou shalt find it. Farewell!' Varda is the name of that Lady whom the Elves in these lands of exile name Elbereth.

Suddenly the River swept round a bend, and the banks rose upon either side, and the light of Lórien was hidden. To that fair land Frodo never came again.

The travellers now turned their faces to the journey; the sun was before them, and their eyes were dazzled, for all were filled with tears. Gimli wept openly.

'I have looked the last upon that which was fairest,' he said to Legolas his companion. 'Henceforward I will call nothing fair, unless it be her gift.' He put his hand to his breast.

'Tell me, Legolas, why did I come on this Quest? Little did I know where the chief peril lay! Truly Elrond spoke, saying that we could not foresee what we might meet upon our road. Torment in the dark was the danger that I feared, and it did not hold me back. But I would not have come, had I known the danger of light and joy. Now I have taken my worst wound in this parting, even if I were to go this night straight to the Dark Lord. Alas for Gimli son of Glóin!'

'Nay!' said Legolas. 'Alas for us all! And for all that walk the world in these after-days. For such is the way of it: to find and lose, as it seems to those whose boat is on the running stream. But I count you blessed, Gimli son of Glóin: for your loss you suffer of your own free will, and you might have chosen otherwise. But you have not forsaken your companions, and the least reward that you shall have is that the memory of Lothlórien shall remain ever clear and unstained in your heart, and shall neither fade nor grow stale.'

'Maybe,' said Gimli; 'and I thank you for your words. True words doubtless; yet all such comfort is cold. Memory is not what the heart desires. That is only a mirror, be it clear as Kheled-zâram. Or so says the heart of Gimli the Dwarf. Elves

may see things otherwise. Indeed I have heard that for them
memory is more like to the waking world than to a dream.
Not so for Dwarves.

'But let us talk no more of it. Look to the boat! She is too
low in the water with all this baggage, and the Great River
is swift. I do not wish to drown my grief in cold water.' He
took up a paddle, and steered towards the western bank,
following Aragorn's boat ahead, which had already moved
out of the middle stream.

So the Company went on their long way, down the wide
hurrying waters, borne ever southwards. Bare woods stalked
along either bank, and they could not see any glimpse of the
lands behind. The breeze died away and the River flowed
without a sound. No voice of bird broke the silence. The sun
grew misty as the day grew old, until it gleamed in a pale
sky like a high white pearl. Then it faded into the West, and
dusk came early, followed by a grey and starless night. Far
into the dark quiet hours they floated on, guiding their boats
under the overhanging shadows of the western woods. Great
trees passed by like ghosts, thrusting their twisted thirsty roots
through the mist down into the water. It was dreary and cold.
Frodo sat and listened to the faint lap and gurgle of the River
fretting among the tree-roots and driftwood near the shore,
until his head nodded and he fell into an uneasy sleep.

CHAPTER IX

THE GREAT RIVER

Frodo was roused by Sam. He found that he was lying, well wrapped, under tall grey-skinned trees in a quiet corner of the woodlands on the west bank of the Great River, Anduin. He had slept the night away, and the grey of morning was dim among the bare branches. Gimli was busy with a small fire near at hand.

They started again before the day was broad. Not that most of the Company were eager to hurry southwards: they were content that the decision, which they must make at latest when they came to Rauros and the Tindrock Isle, still lay some days ahead; and they let the River bear them on at its own pace, having no desire to hasten towards the perils that lay beyond, whichever course they took in the end. Aragorn let them drift with the stream as they wished, husbanding their strength against weariness to come. But he insisted that at least they should start early each day and journey on far into the evening; for he felt in his heart that time was pressing, and he feared that the Dark Lord had not been idle while they lingered in Lórien.

Nonetheless they saw no sign of an enemy that day, nor the next. The dull grey hours passed without event. As the third day of their voyage wore on the lands changed slowly: the trees thinned and then failed altogether. On the eastern bank to their left they saw long formless slopes stretching up and away toward the sky; brown and withered they looked, as if fire had passed over them, leaving no living blade of green: an unfriendly waste without even a broken tree or a bold stone to relieve the emptiness. They had come to the Brown Lands that lay, vast and desolate, between Southern Mirkwood and the hills of the Emyn Muil. What pestilence

or war or evil deed of the Enemy had so blasted all that
region even Aragorn could not tell.

Upon the west to their right the land was treeless also, but
it was flat, and in many places green with wide plains of
grass. On this side of the River they passed forests of great
reeds, so tall that they shut out all view to the west, as the
little boats went rustling by along their fluttering borders.
Their dark withered plumes bent and tossed in the light cold
airs, hissing softly and sadly. Here and there through openings Frodo could catch sudden glimpses of rolling meads,
and far beyond them hills in the sunset, and away on the
edge of sight a dark line, where marched the southernmost
ranks of the Misty Mountains.

There was no sign of living moving things, save birds. Of
these there were many: small fowl whistling and piping in
the reeds, but they were seldom seen. Once or twice the
travellers heard the rush and whine of swan-wings, and looking up they saw a great phalanx streaming along the sky.

'Swans!' said Sam. 'And mighty big ones too!'

'Yes,' said Aragorn, 'and they are black swans.'

'How wide and empty and mournful all this country looks!'
said Frodo. 'I always imagined that as one journeyed south
it got warmer and merrier, until winter was left behind for
ever.'

'But we have not journeyed far south yet,' answered Aragorn. 'It is still winter, and we are far from the sea. Here the
world is cold until the sudden spring, and we may yet have
snow again. Far away down in the Bay of Belfalas, to which
Anduin runs, it is warm and merry, maybe, or would be but
for the Enemy. But here we are not above sixty leagues, I
guess, south of the Southfarthing away in your Shire, hundreds of long miles yonder. You are looking now south-west
across the north plains of the Riddermark, Rohan the land
of the Horse-lords. Ere long we shall come to the mouth of
the Limlight that runs down from Fangorn to join the Great
River. That is the north boundary of Rohan; and of old all
that lay between Limlight and the White Mountains belonged

to the Rohirrim. It is a rich and pleasant land, and its grass has no rival; but in these evil days folk do not dwell by the River or ride often to its shores. Anduin is wide, yet the orcs can shoot their arrows far across the stream; and of late, it is said, they have dared to cross the water and raid the herds and studs of Rohan.'

Sam looked from bank to bank uneasily. The trees had seemed hostile before, as if they harboured secret eyes and lurking dangers; now he wished that the trees were still there. He felt that the Company was too naked, afloat in little open boats in the midst of shelterless lands, and on a river that was the frontier of war.

In the next day or two, as they went on, borne steadily southwards, this feeling of insecurity grew on all the Company. For a whole day they took to their paddles and hastened forward. The banks slid by. Soon the River broadened and grew more shallow; long stony beaches lay upon the east, and there were gravel-shoals in the water, so that careful steering was needed. The Brown Lands rose into bleak wolds, over which flowed a chill air from the East. On the other side the meads had become rolling downs of withered grass amidst a land of fen and tussock. Frodo shivered, thinking of the lawns and fountains, the clear sun and gentle rains of Lothlórien. There was little speech and no laughter in any of the boats. Each member of the Company was busy with his own thoughts.

The heart of Legolas was running under the stars of a summer night in some northern glade amid the beech-woods; Gimli was fingering gold in his mind, and wondering if it were fit to be wrought into the housing of the Lady's gift. Merry and Pippin in the middle boat were ill at ease, for Boromir sat muttering to himself, sometimes biting his nails, as if some restlessness or doubt consumed him, sometimes seizing a paddle and driving the boat close behind Aragorn's. Then Pippin, who sat in the bow looking back, caught a queer gleam in his eye, as he peered forward gazing at Frodo. Sam had long ago made up his mind that, though boats were maybe not as dangerous as he had been brought up to believe, they were far more uncomfortable than even he had imagined. He was cramped and miserable, having nothing to do but stare at the winter-lands crawling by and the grey water on either side of him. Even when the paddles were in use they did not trust Sam with one.

As dusk drew down on the fourth day, he was looking back over the bowed heads of Frodo and Aragorn and the following boats; he was drowsy and longed for camp and the feel of earth under his toes. Suddenly something caught his sight: at first he stared at it listlessly, then he sat up and rubbed his eyes; but when he looked again he could not see it any more.

That night they camped on a small eyot close to the western bank. Sam lay rolled in blankets beside Frodo. 'I had a funny dream an hour or two before we stopped, Mr. Frodo,' he said. 'Or maybe it wasn't a dream. Funny it was anyway.'

'Well, what was it?' said Frodo, knowing that Sam would not settle down until he had told his tale, whatever it was. 'I haven't seen or thought of anything to make me smile since we left Lothlórien.'

'It wasn't funny that way, Mr. Frodo. It was queer. All wrong, if it wasn't a dream. And you had best hear it. It was like this: I saw a log with eyes!'

'The log's all right,' said Frodo. 'There are many in the River. But leave out the eyes!'

'That I won't,' said Sam. ''Twas the eyes as made me sit up, so to speak. I saw what I took to be a log floating along in the half-light behind Gimli's boat; but I didn't give much heed to it. Then it seemed as if the log was slowly catching us up. And that was peculiar, as you might say, seeing as we were all floating on the stream together. Just then I saw the eyes: two pale sort of points, shiny-like, on a hump at the near end of the log. What's more, it wasn't a log, for it had paddle-feet, like a swan's almost, only they seemed bigger, and kept dipping in and out of the water.

'That's when I sat right up and rubbed my eyes, meaning to give a shout, if it was still there when I had rubbed the drowse out of my head. For the whatever-it-was was coming along fast now and getting close behind Gimli. But whether those two lamps spotted me moving and staring, or whether I came to my senses, I don't know. When I looked again, it wasn't there. Yet I think I caught a glimpse, with the tail of my eye, as the saying is, of something dark shooting under the shadow of the bank. I couldn't see no more eyes, though.

'I said to myself: "dreaming again, Sam Gamgee," I said; and I said no more just then. But I've been thinking since, and now I'm not so sure. What do you make of it, Mr. Frodo?'

'I should make nothing of it but a log and the dusk and sleep in your eyes, Sam,' said Frodo, 'if this was the first time that those eyes had been seen. But it isn't. I saw them away back north before we reached Lórien. And I saw a strange creature with eyes climbing to the flet that night. Haldir saw it too. And do you remember the report of the Elves that went after the orc-band?'

'Ah,' said Sam, 'I do; and I remember more too. I don't like my thoughts; but thinking of one thing and another, and Mr. Bilbo's stories and all, I fancy I could put a name on the creature, at a guess. A nasty name. Gollum, maybe?'

'Yes, that is what I have feared for some time,' said Frodo. 'Ever since the night on the flet. I suppose he was lurking in Moria, and picked up our trail then; but I hoped that our stay in Lórien would throw him off the scent again. The miserable creature must have been hiding in the woods by the Silverlode, watching us start off!'

'That's about it,' said Sam. 'And we'd better be a bit more watchful ourselves, or we'll feel some nasty fingers round our necks one of these nights, if we ever wake up to feel anything. And that's what I was leading up to. No need to trouble Strider or the others tonight. I'll keep watch. I can sleep tomorrow, being no more than luggage in a boat, as you might say.'

'I might,' said Frodo, 'and I might say "luggage with eyes".
You shall watch; but only if you promise to wake me half-way
towards morning, if nothing happens before then.'

In the dead hours Frodo came out of a deep dark sleep to
find Sam shaking him. 'It's a shame to wake you,' whispered
Sam, 'but that's what you said. There's nothing to tell, or
not much. I thought I heard some soft plashing and a sniffing
noise, a while back; but you hear a lot of such queer sounds
by a river at night.'

He lay down, and Frodo sat up, huddled in his blankets,
and fought off his sleep. Minutes or hours passed slowly,
and nothing happened. Frodo was just yielding to the tempta-
tion to lie down again when a dark shape, hardly visible,
floated close to one of the moored boats. A long whitish hand
could be dimly seen as it shot out and grabbed the gunwale;
two pale lamplike eyes shone coldly as they peered inside,
and then they lifted and gazed up at Frodo on the eyot. They
were not more than a yard or two away, and Frodo heard
the soft hiss of intaken breath. He stood up, drawing Sting
from its sheath, and faced the eyes. Immediately their light
was shut off. There was another hiss and a splash, and the
dark log-shape shot away downstream into the night. Aragorn
stirred in his sleep, turned over, and sat up.

'What is it?' he whispered, springing up and coming to
Frodo. 'I felt something in my sleep. Why have you drawn
your sword?'

'Gollum,' answered Frodo. 'Or at least, so I guess.'

'Ah!' said Aragorn. 'So you know about our little footpad,
do you? He padded after us all through Moria and right
down to Nimrodel. Since we took to boats, he has been lying
on a log and paddling with hands and feet. I have tried to
catch him once or twice at night; but he is slier than a fox,
and as slippery as a fish. I hoped the river-voyage would beat
him, but he is too clever a waterman.

'We shall have to try going faster tomorrow. You lie down
now, and I will keep watch for what is left of the night. I

wish I could lay my hands on the wretch. We might make him useful. But if I cannot, we shall have to try and lose him. He is very dangerous. Quite apart from murder by night on his own account, he may put any enemy that is about on our track.'

The night passed without Gollum showing so much as a shadow again. After that the Company kept a sharp look-out, but they saw no more of Gollum while the voyage lasted. If he was still following, he was very wary and cunning. At Aragorn's bidding they paddled now for long spells, and the banks went swiftly by. But they saw little of the country, for they journeyed mostly by night and twilight, resting by day, and lying as hidden as the land allowed. In this way the time passed without event until the seventh day.

The weather was still grey and overcast, with wind from the East, but as evening drew into night the sky away westward cleared, and pools of faint light, yellow and pale green, opened under the grey shores of cloud. There the white rind of the new Moon could be seen glimmering in the remote lakes. Sam looked at it and puckered his brows.

The next day the country on either side began to change rapidly. The banks began to rise and grow stony. Soon they were passing through a hilly rocky land, and on both shores there were steep slopes buried in deep brakes of thorn and sloe, tangled with brambles and creepers. Behind them stood low crumbling cliffs, and chimneys of grey weathered stone dark with ivy; and beyond these again there rose high ridges crowned with wind-writhen firs. They were drawing near to the grey hill-country of the Emyn Muil, the southern march of Wilderland.

There were many birds about the cliffs and the rock-chimneys, and all day high in the air flocks of birds had been circling, black against the pale sky. As they lay in their camp that day Aragorn watched the flights doubtfully, wondering if Gollum had been doing some mischief and the news of their voyage was now moving in the wilderness. Later as the sun was setting, and the Company was stirring and getting ready to start again, he descried a dark spot against the fading light: a great bird high and far off, now wheeling, now flying on slowly southwards.

'What is that, Legolas?' he asked, pointing to the northern sky. 'Is it, as I think, an eagle?'

'Yes,' said Legolas. 'It is an eagle, a hunting eagle. I wonder what that forebodes. It is far from the mountains.'

'We will not start until it is fully dark,' said Aragorn.

The eighth night of their journey came. It was silent and windless; the grey east wind had passed away. The thin crescent of the Moon had fallen early into the pale sunset, but the sky was clear above, and though far away in the South there were great ranges of cloud that still shone faintly, in the West stars glinted bright.

'Come!' said Aragorn. 'We will venture one more journey by night. We are coming to reaches of the River that I do not know well; for I have never journeyed by water in these parts before, not between here and the rapids of Sarn Gebir. But if I am right in my reckoning, those are still many miles ahead. Still there are dangerous places even before we come there: rocks and stony eyots in the stream. We must keep a sharp watch and not try to paddle swiftly.'

To Sam in the leading boat was given the task of watchman. He lay forward peering into the gloom. The night grew dark, but the stars above were strangely bright, and there was a glimmer on the face of the River. It was close on midnight, and they had been drifting for some while, hardly using the paddles, when suddenly Sam cried out. Only a few yards ahead dark shapes loomed up in the stream and he heard the swirl of racing water. There was a swift current which swung left, towards the eastern shore where the channel was clear. As they were swept aside the travellers could see, now very close, the pale foam of the River lashing against sharp rocks that were thrust out far into the stream like a ridge of teeth. The boats were all huddled together.

'Hoy there, Aragorn!' shouted Boromir, as his boat bumped into the leader. 'This is madness! We cannot dare the Rapids by night! But no boat can live in Sarn Gebir, be it night or day.'

'Back, back!' cried Aragorn. 'Turn! Turn if you can!' He drove his paddle into the water, trying to hold the boat and bring it round.

'I am out of my reckoning,' he said to Frodo. 'I did not know that we had come so far: Anduin flows faster than I thought. Sarn Gebir must be close at hand already.'

With great efforts they checked the boats and slowly brought them about; but at first they could make only small headway against the current, and all the time they were carried nearer and nearer to the eastern bank. Now dark and ominous it loomed up in the night.

'All together, paddle!' shouted Boromir. 'Paddle! Or we shall be driven on the shoals.' Even as he spoke Frodo felt the keel beneath him grate upon stone.

At that moment there was a twang of bowstrings: several arrows whistled over them, and some fell among them. One smote Frodo between the shoulders and he lurched forward with a cry, letting go his paddle: but the arrow fell back, foiled by his hidden coat of mail. Another passed through Aragorn's hood; and a third stood fast in the gunwale of the second boat, close by Merry's hand. Sam thought he could glimpse black figures running to and fro upon the long shingle-banks that lay under the eastern shore. They seemed very near.

'*Yrch!*' said Legolas, falling into his own tongue.

'Orcs!' cried Gimli.

'Gollum's doing, I'll be bound,' said Sam to Frodo. 'And a nice place to choose, too. The River seems set on taking us right into their arms!'

They all leaned forward straining at the paddles: even Sam took a hand. Every moment they expected to feel the bite of black-feathered arrows. Many whined overhead or struck the water nearby; but there were no more hits. It was dark, but not too dark for the night-eyes of Orcs, and in the star-glimmer they must have offered their cunning foes some mark, unless it was that the grey cloaks of Lórien and the grey timber of the elf-wrought boats defeated the malice of the archers of Mordor.

Stroke by stroke they laboured on. In the darkness it was hard to be sure that they were indeed moving at all; but slowly the swirl of the water grew less, and the shadow of the eastern bank faded back into the night. At last, as far as they could judge, they had reached the middle of the stream again and had driven their boats back some distance above the jutting rocks. Then half turning they thrust them with all their strength towards the western shore. Under the shadow of bushes leaning out over the water they halted and drew breath.

Legolas laid down his paddle and took up the bow that he had brought from Lórien. Then he sprang ashore and climbed a few paces up the bank. Stringing the bow and fitting an arrow he turned, peering back over the River into the darkness. Across the water there were shrill cries, but nothing could be seen.

Frodo looked up at the Elf standing tall above him, as he gazed into the night, seeking a mark to shoot at. His head was dark, crowned with sharp white stars that glittered in the black pools of the sky behind. But now rising and sailing up from the South the great clouds advanced, sending out dark outriders into the starry fields. A sudden dread fell on the Company.

'*Elbereth Gilthoniel!*' sighed Legolas as he looked up. Even as he did so, a dark shape, like a cloud and yet not a cloud, for it moved far more swiftly, came out of the blackness in the South, and sped towards the Company, blotting out all light as it approached. Soon it appeared as a great winged creature, blacker than the pits in the night. Fierce voices rose up to greet it from across the water. Frodo felt a sudden chill running through him and clutching at his heart; there was a deadly cold, like the memory of an old wound, in his shoulder. He crouched down, as if to hide.

Suddenly the great bow of Lórien sang. Shrill went the arrow from the elven-string. Frodo looked up. Almost above him the winged shape swerved. There was a harsh croaking scream, as it fell out of the air, vanishing down into the gloom of the eastern shore. The sky was clean again. There was a tumult of many voices far away, cursing and wailing in the darkness, and then silence. Neither shaft nor cry came again from the east that night.

After a while Aragorn led the boats back upstream. They felt their way along the water's edge for some distance, until they found a small shallow bay. A few low trees grew there close to the water, and behind them rose a steep rocky bank. Here the Company decided to stay and await the dawn: it was useless to attempt to move further by night. They made no camp and lit no fire, but lay huddled in the boats, moored close together.

'Praised be the bow of Galadriel, and the hand and eye of Legolas!' said Gimli, as he munched a wafer of *lembas*. 'That was a mighty shot in the dark, my friend!'

'But who can say what it hit?' said Legolas.

'I cannot,' said Gimli. 'But I am glad that the shadow came no nearer. I liked it not at all. Too much it reminded me of the shadow in Moria – the shadow of the Balrog,' he ended in a whisper.

'It was not a Balrog,' said Frodo, still shivering with the chill that had come upon him. 'It was something colder. I think it was———' Then he paused and fell silent.

'What do you think?' asked Boromir eagerly, leaning from his boat, as if he was trying to catch a glimpse of Frodo's face.

'I think – No, I will not say,' answered Frodo. 'Whatever it was, its fall has dismayed our enemies.'

'So it seems,' said Aragorn. 'Yet where they are, and how many, and what they will do next, we do not know. This

night we must all be sleepless! Dark hides us now. But what
the day will show who can tell? Have your weapons close to
hand!'

Sam sat tapping the hilt of his sword as if he were counting
on his fingers, and looking up at the sky. 'It's very strange,'
he murmured. 'The Moon's the same in the Shire and in
Wilderland, or it ought to be. But either it's out of its running,
or I'm all wrong in my reckoning. You'll remember, Mr.
Frodo, the Moon was waning as we lay on the flet up in that
tree: a week from the full, I reckon. And we'd been a week
on the way last night, when up pops a New Moon as thin
as a nail-paring, as if we had never stayed no time in the
Elvish country.

'Well, I can remember three nights there for certain, and
I seem to remember several more, but I would take my oath
it was never a whole month. Anyone would think that time
did not count in there!'

'And perhaps that was the way of it,' said Frodo. 'In that
land, maybe, we were in a time that has elsewhere long gone
by. It was not, I think, until Silverlode bore us back to Anduin
that we returned to the time that flows through mortal lands to
the Great Sea. And I don't remember any moon, either new or
old, in Caras Galadhon: only stars by night and sun by day.'

Legolas stirred in his boat. 'Nay, time does not tarry ever,'
he said; 'but change and growth is not in all things and places
alike. For the Elves the world moves, and it moves both very
swift and very slow. Swift, because they themselves change
little, and all else fleets by: it is a grief to them. Slow, because
they do not count the running years, not for themselves. The
passing seasons are but ripples ever repeated in the long long
stream. Yet beneath the Sun all things must wear to an end
at last.'

'But the wearing is slow in Lórien,' said Frodo. 'The power
of the Lady is on it. Rich are the hours, though short they
seem, in Caras Galadhon, where Galadriel wields the
Elven-ring.'

'That should not have been said outside Lórien, not even to me,' said Aragorn. 'Speak no more of it! But so it is, Sam: in that land you lost your count. There time flowed swiftly by us, as for the Elves. The old moon passed, and a new moon waxed and waned in the world outside, while we tarried there. And yestereve a new moon came again. Winter is nearly gone. Time flows on to a spring of little hope.'

The night passed silently. No voice or call was heard again across the water. The travellers huddled in their boats felt the changing of the weather. The air grew warm and very still under the great moist clouds that had floated up from the South and the distant seas. The rushing of the River over the rocks of the rapids seemed to grow louder and closer. The twigs of the trees above them began to drip.

When the day came the mood of the world about them had become soft and sad. Slowly the dawn grew to a pale light, diffused and shadowless. There was mist on the River, and white fog swathed the shore; the far bank could not be seen.

'I can't abide fog,' said Sam; 'but this seems to be a lucky one. Now perhaps we can get away without those cursed goblins seeing us.'

'Perhaps so,' said Aragorn. 'But it will be hard to find the path unless the fog lifts a little later on. And we must find the path, if we are to pass Sarn Gebir and come to the Emyn Muil.'

'I do not see why we should pass the Rapids or follow the River any further,' said Boromir. 'If the Emyn Muil lie before us, then we can abandon these cockle-boats, and strike westward and southward, until we come to the Entwash and cross into my own land.'

'We can, if we are making for Minas Tirith,' said Aragorn, 'but that is not yet agreed. And such a course may be more perilous than it sounds. The vale of Entwash is flat and fenny, and fog is a deadly peril there for those on foot and laden.

I would not abandon our boats until we must. The River is at least a path that cannot be missed.'

'But the Enemy holds the eastern bank,' objected Boromir. 'And even if you pass the Gates of Argonath and come unmolested to the Tindrock, what will you do then? Leap down the Falls and land in the marshes?'

'No!' answered Aragorn. 'Say rather that we will bear our boats by the ancient way to Rauros-foot, and there take to the water again. Do you not know, Boromir, or do you choose to forget the North Stair, and the high seat upon Amon Hen, that were made in the days of the great kings? I at least have a mind to stand in that high place again, before I decide my further course. There, maybe, we shall see some sign that will guide us.'

Boromir held out long against this choice; but when it became plain that Frodo would follow Aragorn, wherever he went, he gave in. 'It is not the way of the Men of Minas Tirith to desert their friends at need,' he said, 'and you will need my strength, if ever you are to reach the Tindrock. To the tall isle I will go, but no further. There I shall turn to my home, alone if my help has not earned the reward of any companionship.'

The day was now growing, and the fog had lifted a little. It was decided that Aragorn and Legolas should at once go forward along the shore, while the others remained by the boats. Aragorn hoped to find some way by which they could carry both their boats and their baggage to the smoother water beyond the Rapids.

'Boats of the Elves would not sink, maybe,' he said, 'but that does not say that we should come through Sarn Gebir alive. None have ever done so yet. No road was made by the Men of Gondor in this region, for even in their great days their realm did not reach up Anduin beyond the Emyn Muil; but there is a portage-way somewhere on the western shore, if I can find it. It cannot yet have perished; for light boats used to journey out of Wilderland down to Osgiliath, and still did so until a few years ago, when the Orcs of Mordor began to multiply.'

'Seldom in my life has any boat come out of the North, and the Orcs prowl on the east-shore,' said Boromir. 'If you go forward, peril will grow with every mile, even if you find a path.'

'Peril lies ahead on every southward road,' answered Aragorn. 'Wait for us one day. If we do not return in that time, you will know that evil has indeed befallen us. Then you must take a new leader and follow him as best you can.'

It was with a heavy heart that Frodo saw Aragorn and Legolas climb the steep bank and vanish into the mists; but his fears proved groundless. Only two or three hours had passed, and it was barely mid-day, when the shadowy shapes of the explorers appeared again.

'All is well,' said Aragorn, as he clambered down the bank. 'There is a track, and it leads to a good landing that is still serviceable. The distance is not great: the head of the Rapids is but half a mile below us, and they are little more than a mile long. Not far beyond them the stream becomes clear and smooth again, though it runs swiftly. Our hardest task will be to get our boats and baggage to the old portage-way. We have found it, but it lies well back from the water-side here, and runs under the lee of a rock-wall, a furlong or more from the shore. We did not find where the northward landing lies. If it still remains, we must have passed it yesterday night. We might labour far upstream and yet miss it in the fog. I fear we must leave the River now, and make for the portage-way as best we can from here.'

'That would not be easy, even if we were all Men,' said Boromir.

'Yet such as we are we will try it,' said Aragorn.

'Aye, we will,' said Gimli. 'The legs of Men will lag on a rough road, while a Dwarf goes on, be the burden twice his own weight, Master Boromir!'

The task proved hard indeed, yet in the end it was done. The goods were taken out of the boats and brought to the top of the bank, where there was a level space. Then the boats were drawn out of the water and carried up. They were far less heavy than any had expected. Of what tree growing in the elvish country they were made not even Legolas knew; but the wood was tough and yet strangely light. Merry and Pippin alone could carry their boat with ease along the flat. Nonetheless it needed the strength of the two Men to lift and haul them over the ground that the Company now had to cross. It sloped up away from the River, a tumbled waste of grey limestone-boulders, with many hidden holes shrouded with weeds and bushes; there were thickets of brambles, and sheer dells; and here and there boggy pools fed by waters trickling from the terraces further inland.

One by one Boromir and Aragorn carried the boats, while the others toiled and scrambled after them with the baggage. At last all was removed and laid on the portage-way. Then with little further hindrance, save from sprawling briars and many fallen stones, they moved forward all together. Fog still hung in veils upon the crumbling rock-wall, and to their left mist shrouded the River: they could hear it rushing and foaming over the sharp shelves and stony teeth of Sarn Gebir, but they could not see it. Twice they made the journey, before all was brought safe to the southern landing.

There the portage-way, turning back to the water-side, ran gently down to the shallow edge of a little pool. It seemed to have been scooped in the river-side, not by hand, but by the water swirling down from Sarn Gebir against a low pier of rock that jutted out some way into the stream. Beyond it the shore rose sheer into a grey cliff, and there was no further passage for those on foot.

Already the short afternoon was past, and a dim cloudy dusk was closing in. They sat beside the water listening to the confused rush and roar of the Rapids hidden in the mist; they were tired and sleepy, and their hearts were as gloomy as the dying day.

'Well, here we are, and here we must pass another night,' said Boromir. 'We need sleep, and even if Aragorn had a mind to pass the Gates of Argonath by night, we are all too tired – except, no doubt, our sturdy dwarf.'

Gimli made no reply: he was nodding as he sat.

'Let us rest as much as we can now,' said Aragorn. 'Tomorrow we must journey by day again. Unless the weather changes once more and cheats us, we shall have a good chance of slipping through, unseen by any eyes on the eastern shore. But tonight two must watch together in turns: three hours off and one on guard.'

Nothing happened that night worse than a brief drizzle of rain an hour before dawn. As soon as it was fully light they started. Already the fog was thinning. They kept as close as they could to the western side, and they could see the dim shapes of the low cliffs rising ever higher, shadowy walls with their feet in the hurrying river. In the mid-morning the clouds drew down lower, and it began to rain heavily. They drew the skin-covers over their boats to prevent them from being flooded, and drifted on; little could be seen before them or about them through the grey falling curtains.

The rain, however, did not last long. Slowly the sky above grew lighter, and then suddenly the clouds broke, and their draggled fringes trailed away northward up the River. The fogs and mists were gone. Before the travellers lay a wide ravine, with great rocky sides to which clung, upon shelves and in narrow crevices, a few thrawn trees. The channel grew narrower and the River swifter. Now they were speeding along with little hope of stopping or turning, whatever they might meet ahead. Over them was a lane of pale-blue sky, around them the dark overshadowed River, and before them black, shutting out the sun, the hills of Emyn Muil, in which no opening could be seen.

Frodo peering forward saw in the distance two great rocks approaching: like great pinnacles or pillars of stone they seemed. Tall and sheer and ominous they stood upon either side of the stream. A narrow gap appeared between them, and the River swept the boats towards it.

'Behold the Argonath, the Pillars of the Kings!' cried Aragorn. 'We shall pass them soon. Keep the boats in line, and as far apart as you can! Hold the middle of the stream!'

As Frodo was borne towards them the great pillars rose like towers to meet him. Giants they seemed to him, vast grey figures silent but threatening. Then he saw that they were indeed shaped and fashioned: the craft and power of old had wrought upon them, and still they preserved through the suns and rains of forgotten years the mighty likenesses in which they had been hewn. Upon great pedestals founded in the deep waters stood two great kings of stone: still with blurred eyes and crannied brows they frowned upon the North. The left hand of each was raised palm outwards in gesture of warning; in each right hand there was an axe; upon each head there was a crumbling helm and crown. Great power and majesty they still wore, the silent wardens of a long-vanished kingdom. Awe and fear fell upon Frodo, and he cowered down, shutting his eyes and not daring to look up as the boat drew near. Even Boromir bowed his head as the boats whirled by, frail and fleeting as little leaves, under the enduring shadow of the sentinels of Númenor. So they passed into the dark chasm of the Gates.

Sheer rose the dreadful cliffs to unguessed heights on either side. Far off was the dim sky. The black waters roared and echoed, and a wind screamed over them. Frodo crouching over his knees heard Sam in front muttering and groaning: 'What a place! What a horrible place! Just let me get out of this boat, and I'll never wet my toes in a puddle again, let alone a river!'

'Fear not!' said a strange voice behind him. Frodo turned and saw Strider, and yet not Strider; for the weatherworn Ranger was no longer there. In the stern sat Aragorn son of Arathorn, proud and erect, guiding the boat with skilful strokes; his hood was cast back, and his dark hair was blowing in the wind, a light was in his eyes: a king returning from exile to his own land.

'Fear not!' he said. 'Long have I desired to look upon the

likenesses of Isildur and Anárion, my sires of old. Under their shadow Elessar, the Elfstone son of Arathorn of the House of Valandil Isildur's son, heir of Elendil, has nought to dread!'

Then the light of his eyes faded, and he spoke to himself: 'Would that Gandalf were here! How my heart yearns for Minas Anor and the walls of my own city! But whither now shall I go?'

The chasm was long and dark, and filled with the noise of wind and rushing water and echoing stone. It bent somewhat towards the west so that at first all was dark ahead; but soon Frodo saw a tall gap of light before him, ever growing. Swiftly it drew near, and suddenly the boats shot through, out into a wide clear light.

The sun, already long fallen from the noon, was shining in a windy sky. The pent waters spread out into a long oval lake, pale Nen Hithoel, fenced by steep grey hills whose sides were clad with trees, but their heads were bare, cold-gleaming in the sunlight. At the far southern end rose three peaks. The midmost stood somewhat forward from the others and sundered from them, an island in the waters, about which the flowing River flung pale shimmering arms. Distant but deep there came up on the wind a roaring sound like the roll of thunder heard far away.

'Behold Tol Brandir!' said Aragorn, pointing south to the tall peak. 'Upon the left stands Amon Lhaw, and upon the right is Amon Hen, the Hills of Hearing and of Sight. In the days of the great kings there were high seats upon them, and watch was kept there. But it is said that no foot of man or beast has ever been set upon Tol Brandir. Ere the shade of night falls we shall come to them. I hear the endless voice of Rauros calling.'

The Company rested now for a while, drifting south on the current that flowed through the middle of the lake. They ate some food, and then they took to their paddles and hastened on their way. The sides of the westward hills fell into shadow, and the Sun grew round and red. Here and there a misty star peered out. The three peaks loomed before them, darkling in the twilight. Rauros was roaring with a great voice. Already night was laid on the flowing waters when the travellers came at last under the shadow of the hills.

The tenth day of their journey was over. Wilderland was behind them. They could go no further without choice between the east-way and the west. The last stage of the Quest was before them.

CHAPTER X

THE BREAKING OF THE FELLOWSHIP

Aragorn led them to the right arm of the River. Here upon its western side under the shadow of Tol Brandir a green lawn ran down to the water from the feet of Amon Hen. Behind it rose the first gentle slopes of the hill clad with trees, and trees marched away westward along the curving shores of the lake. A little spring fell tumbling down and fed the grass.

'Here we will rest tonight,' said Aragorn. 'This is the lawn of Parth Galen: a fair place in the summer days of old. Let us hope that no evil has yet come here.'

They drew up their boats on the green banks, and beside them they made their camp. They set a watch, but had no sight nor sound of their enemies. If Gollum had contrived to follow them, he remained unseen and unheard. Nonetheless as the night wore on Aragorn grew uneasy, tossing often in his sleep and waking. In the small hours he got up and came to Frodo, whose turn it was to watch.

'Why are you waking?' asked Frodo. 'It is not your watch.'

'I do not know,' answered Aragorn; 'but a shadow and a threat has been growing in my sleep. It would be well to draw your sword.'

'Why?' said Frodo. 'Are enemies at hand?'

'Let us see what Sting may show,' answered Aragorn.

Frodo then drew the elf-blade from its sheath. To his dismay the edges gleamed dimly in the night. 'Orcs!' he said. 'Not very near, and yet too near, it seems.'

'I feared as much,' said Aragorn. 'But maybe they are not on this side of the River. The light of Sting is faint, and it may point to no more than spies of Mordor roaming on the slopes of Amon Lhaw. I have never heard before of Orcs upon Amon Hen. Yet who knows what may happen in these evil days, now that Minas Tirith no longer holds secure the passages of Anduin. We must go warily tomorrow.'

The day came like fire and smoke. Low in the East there were black bars of cloud like the fumes of a great burning. The rising sun lit them from beneath with flames of murky red; but soon it climbed above them into a clear sky. The summit of Tol Brandir was tipped with gold. Frodo looked out eastward and gazed at the tall island. Its sides sprang sheer out of the running water. High up above the tall cliffs were steep slopes upon which trees climbed, mounting one head above another; and above them again were grey faces of inaccessible rock, crowned by a great spire of stone. Many birds were circling about it, but no sign of other living things could be seen.

When they had eaten, Aragorn called the Company together. 'The day has come at last,' he said: 'the day of choice which we have long delayed. What shall now become of our Company that has travelled so far in fellowship? Shall we turn west with Boromir and go to the wars of Gondor; or turn east to the Fear and Shadow; or shall we break our fellowship and go this way and that as each may choose? Whatever we do must be done soon. We cannot long halt here. The enemy is on the eastern shore, we know; but I fear that the Orcs may already be on this side of the water.'

There was a long silence in which no one spoke or moved.

'Well, Frodo,' said Aragorn at last. 'I fear that the burden is laid upon you. You are the Bearer appointed by the Council. Your own way you alone can choose. In this matter I cannot advise you. I am not Gandalf, and though I have tried to bear his part, I do not know what design or hope he had for this hour, if indeed he had any. Most likely it seems that if he were here now the choice would still wait on you. Such is your fate.'

Frodo did not answer at once. Then he spoke slowly. 'I know that haste is needed, yet I cannot choose. The burden is heavy. Give me an hour longer, and I will speak. Let me be alone!'

Aragorn looked at him with kindly pity. 'Very well, Frodo son of Drogo,' he said. 'You shall have an hour, and you shall be alone. We will stay here for a while. But do not stray far or out of call.'

Frodo sat for a moment with his head bowed. Sam, who had been watching his master with great concern, shook his head and muttered: 'Plain as a pikestaff it is, but it's no good Sam Gamgee putting in his spoke just now.'

Presently Frodo got up and walked away; and Sam saw that while the others restrained themselves and did not stare at him, the eyes of Boromir followed Frodo intently, until he passed out of sight in the trees at the foot of Amon Hen.

Wandering aimlessly at first in the wood, Frodo found that his feet were leading him up towards the slopes of the hill. He came to a path, the dwindling ruins of a road of long ago. In steep places stairs of stone had been hewn, but now they were cracked and worn, and split by the roots of trees. For some while he climbed, not caring which way he went, until he came to a grassy place. Rowan-trees grew about it, and in the midst was a wide flat stone. The little upland lawn was open upon the East and was filled now with the early sunlight. Frodo halted and looked out over the River, far below him, to Tol Brandir and the birds wheeling in the great gulf of air between him and the untrodden isle. The voice of Rauros was a mighty roaring mingled with a deep throbbing boom.

He sat down upon the stone and cupped his chin in his hands, staring eastwards but seeing little with his eyes. All that had happened since Bilbo left the Shire was passing through his mind, and he recalled and pondered everything that he could remember of Gandalf's words. Time went on, and still he was no nearer to a choice.

Suddenly he awoke from his thoughts: a strange feeling came to him that something was behind him, that unfriendly eyes were upon him. He sprang up and turned; but all that he saw to his surprise was Boromir, and his face was smiling and kind.

'I was afraid for you, Frodo,' he said, coming forward. 'If Aragorn is right and Orcs are near, then none of us should wander alone, and you least of all: so much depends on you. And my heart too is heavy. May I stay now and talk for a while, since I have found you? It would comfort me. Where there are so many, all speech becomes a debate without end. But two together may perhaps find wisdom.'

'You are kind,' answered Frodo. 'But I do not think that any speech will help me. For I know what I should do, but I am afraid of doing it, Boromir: afraid.'

Boromir stood silent. Rauros roared endlessly on. The wind murmured in the branches of the trees. Frodo shivered.

Suddenly Boromir came and sat beside him. 'Are you sure that you do not suffer needlessly?' he said. 'I wish to help you. You need counsel in your hard choice. Will you not take mine?'

'I think I know already what counsel you would give, Boromir,' said Frodo. 'And it would seem like wisdom but for the warning of my heart.'

'Warning? Warning against what?' said Boromir sharply.

'Against delay. Against the way that seems easier. Against refusal of the burden that is laid on me. Against – well, if it must be said, against trust in the strength and truth of Men.'

'Yet that strength has long protected you far away in your little country, though you knew it not.'

'I do not doubt the valour of your people. But the world is changing. The walls of Minas Tirith may be strong, but they are not strong enough. If they fail, what then?'

'We shall fall in battle valiantly. Yet there is still hope that they will not fail.'

'No hope while the Ring lasts,' said Frodo.

'Ah! The Ring!' said Boromir, his eyes lighting. 'The Ring! Is it not a strange fate that we should suffer so much fear and doubt for so small a thing? So small a thing! And I have

THE BREAKING OF THE FELLOWSHIP

seen it only for an instant in the House of Elrond. Could I not have a sight of it again?'

Frodo looked up. His heart went suddenly cold. He caught the strange gleam in Boromir's eyes, yet his face was still kind and friendly. 'It is best that it should lie hidden,' he answered.

'As you wish. I care not,' said Boromir. 'Yet may I not even speak of it? For you seem ever to think only of its power in the hands of the Enemy: of its evil uses not of its good. The world is changing, you say. Minas Tirith will fall, if the Ring lasts. But why? Certainly, if the Ring were with the Enemy. But why, if it were with us?'

'Were you not at the Council?' answered Frodo. 'Because we cannot use it, and what is done with it turns to evil.'

Boromir got up and walked about impatiently. 'So you go on,' he cried. 'Gandalf, Elrond – all these folk have taught you to say so. For themselves they may be right. These elves and half-elves and wizards, they would come to grief perhaps. Yet often I doubt if they are wise and not merely timid. But each to his own kind. True-hearted Men, they will not be corrupted. We of Minas Tirith have been staunch through long years of trial. We do not desire the power of wizard-lords, only strength to defend ourselves, strength in a just cause. And behold! in our need chance brings to light the Ring of Power. It is a gift, I say; a gift to the foes of Mordor. It is mad not to use it, to use the power of the Enemy against him. The fearless, the ruthless, these alone will achieve victory. What could not a warrior do in this hour, a great leader? What could not Aragorn do? Or if he refuses, why not Boromir? The Ring would give me power of Command. How I would drive the hosts of Mordor, and all men would flock to my banner!'

Boromir strode up and down, speaking ever more loudly. Almost he seemed to have forgotten Frodo, while his talk dwelt on walls and weapons, and the mustering of men; and he drew plans for great alliances and glorious victories to be; and he cast down Mordor, and became himself a mighty

king, benevolent and wise. Suddenly he stopped and waved
his arms.

'And they tell us to throw it away!' he cried. 'I do not say
destroy it. That might be well, if reason could show any hope
of doing so. It does not. The only plan that is proposed to
us is that a halfling should walk blindly into Mordor and
offer the Enemy every chance of recapturing it for himself.
Folly!

'Surely you see it, my friend?' he said, turning now suddenly to Frodo again. 'You say that you are afraid. If it is
so, the boldest should pardon you. But is it not really your
good sense that revolts?'

'No, I am afraid,' said Frodo. 'Simply afraid. But I am
glad to have heard you speak so fully. My mind is clearer
now.'

'Then you will come to Minas Tirith?' cried Boromir. His
eyes were shining and his face eager.

'You misunderstand me,' said Frodo.

'But you will come, at least for a while?' Boromir persisted.
'My city is not far now; and it is little further from there to
Mordor than from here. We have been long in the wilderness,
and you need news of what the Enemy is doing before you
make a move. Come with me, Frodo,' he said. 'You need
rest before your venture, if go you must.' He laid his hand
on the hobbit's shoulder in friendly fashion; but Frodo felt
the hand trembling with suppressed excitement. He stepped
quickly away, and eyed with alarm the tall Man, nearly twice
his height and many times his match in strength.

'Why are you so unfriendly?' said Boromir. 'I am a true
man, neither thief nor tracker. I need your Ring: that you
know now; but I give you my word that I do not desire to
keep it. Will you not at least let me make trial of my plan?
Lend me the Ring!'

'No! no!' cried Frodo. 'The Council laid it upon me to
bear it.'

'It is by our own folly that the Enemy will defeat us,' cried
Boromir. 'How it angers me! Fool! Obstinate fool! Running

wilfully to death and ruining our cause. If any mortals have claim to the Ring, it is the men of Númenor, and not Halflings. It is not yours save by unhappy chance. It might have been mine. It should be mine. Give it to me!'

Frodo did not answer, but moved away till the great flat stone stood between them. 'Come, come, my friend!' said Boromir in a softer voice. 'Why not get rid of it? Why not be free of your doubt and fear? You can lay the blame on me, if you will. You can say that I was too strong and took it by force. For I am too strong for you, halfling,' he cried; and suddenly he sprang over the stone and leaped at Frodo. His fair and pleasant face was hideously changed; a raging fire was in his eyes.

Frodo dodged aside and again put the stone between them. There was only one thing he could do: trembling he pulled out the Ring upon its chain and quickly slipped it on his finger, even as Boromir sprang at him again. The Man gasped, stared for a moment amazed, and then ran wildly about, seeking here and there among the rocks and trees.

'Miserable trickster!' he shouted. 'Let me get my hands on you! Now I see your mind. You will take the Ring to Sauron and sell us all. You have only waited your chance to leave us in the lurch. Curse you and all halflings to death and darkness!' Then, catching his foot on a stone, he fell sprawling and lay upon his face. For a while he was as still as if his own curse had struck him down; then suddenly he wept.

He rose and passed his hand over his eyes, dashing away the tears. 'What have I said?' he cried. 'What have I done? Frodo, Frodo!' he called. 'Come back! A madness took me, but it has passed. Come back!'

There was no answer. Frodo did not even hear his cries. He was already far away, leaping blindly up the path to the hill-top. Terror and grief shook him, seeing in his thought the mad fierce face of Boromir, and his burning eyes.

Soon he came out alone on the summit of Amon Hen, and halted, gasping for breath. He saw as through a mist a wide

flat circle, paved with mighty flags, and surrounded with a
crumbling battlement; and in the middle, set upon four
carven pillars, was a high seat, reached by a stair of many
steps. Up he went and sat upon the ancient chair, feeling like
a lost child that had clambered upon the throne of mountain-
kings.

At first he could see little. He seemed to be in a world of
mist in which there were only shadows: the Ring was upon
him. Then here and there the mist gave way and he saw
many visions: small and clear as if they were under his eyes
upon a table, and yet remote. There was no sound, only
bright living images. The world seemed to have shrunk and
fallen silent. He was sitting upon the Seat of Seeing, on Amon
Hen, the Hill of the Eye of the Men of Númenor. Eastward
he looked into wide uncharted lands, nameless plains, and
forests unexplored. Northward he looked, and the Great
River lay like a ribbon beneath him, and the Misty Mountains
stood small and hard as broken teeth. Westward he looked
and saw the broad pastures of Rohan; and Orthanc, the pinnacle of Isengard, like a black spike. Southward he looked,
and below his very feet the Great River curled like a toppling
wave and plunged over the falls of Rauros into a foaming
pit; a glimmering rainbow played upon the fume. And Ethir
Anduin he saw, the mighty delta of the River, and myriads
of sea-birds whirling like a white dust in the sun, and beneath
them a green and silver sea, rippling in endless lines.

But everywhere he looked he saw the signs of war. The
Misty Mountains were crawling like anthills: orcs were issuing
out of a thousand holes. Under the boughs of Mirkwood
there was deadly strife of Elves and Men and fell beasts. The
land of the Beornings was aflame; a cloud was over Moria;
smoke rose on the borders of Lórien.

Horsemen were galloping on the grass of Rohan; wolves
poured from Isengard. From the havens of Harad ships of
war put out to sea; and out of the East Men were moving
endlessly: swordsmen, spearmen, bowmen upon horses,
chariots of chieftains and laden wains. All the power of the

Dark Lord was in motion. Then turning south again he beheld Minas Tirith. Far away it seemed, and beautiful: white-walled, many-towered, proud and fair upon its mountain-seat; its battlements glittered with steel, and its turrets were bright with many banners. Hope leaped in his heart. But against Minas Tirith was set another fortress, greater and more strong. Thither, eastward, unwilling his eye was drawn. It passed the ruined bridges of Osgiliath, the grinning gates of Minas Morgul, and the haunted Mountains, and it looked upon Gorgoroth, the valley of terror in the Land of Mordor. Darkness lay there under the Sun. Fire glowed amid the smoke. Mount Doom was burning, and a great reek rising. Then at last his gaze was held: wall upon wall, battlement upon battlement, black, immeasurably strong, mountain of iron, gate of steel, tower of adamant, he saw it: Barad-dûr, Fortress of Sauron. All hope left him.

And suddenly he felt the Eye. There was an eye in the Dark Tower that did not sleep. He knew that it had become aware of his gaze. A fierce eager will was there. It leaped towards him; almost like a finger he felt it, searching for him. Very soon it would nail him down, know just exactly where he was. Amon Lhaw it touched. It glanced upon Tol Brandir – he threw himself from the seat, crouching, covering his head with his grey hood.

He heard himself crying out: *Never, never!* Or was it: *Verily I come, I come to you?* He could not tell. Then as a flash from some other point of power there came to his mind another thought: *Take it off! Take it off! Fool, take it off! Take off the Ring!*

The two powers strove in him. For a moment, perfectly balanced between their piercing points, he writhed, tormented. Suddenly he was aware of himself again. Frodo, neither the Voice nor the Eye: free to choose, and with one remaining instant in which to do so. He took the Ring off his finger. He was kneeling in clear sunlight before the high seat. A black shadow seemed to pass like an arm above him; it missed Amon Hen and groped out west, and faded. Then all the sky was clean and blue and birds sang in every tree.

Frodo rose to his feet. A great weariness was on him, but his will was firm and his heart lighter. He spoke aloud to himself. 'I will do now what I must,' he said. 'This at least is plain: the evil of the Ring is already at work even in the Company, and the Ring must leave them before it does more harm. I will go alone. Some I cannot trust, and those I can trust are too dear to me: poor old Sam, and Merry and Pippin. Strider, too: his heart yearns for Minas Tirith, and he will be needed there, now Boromir has fallen into evil. I will go alone. At once.'

He went quickly down the path and came back to the lawn where Boromir had found him. Then he halted, listening. He thought he could hear cries and calls from the woods near the shore below.

'They'll be hunting for me,' he said. 'I wonder how long I have been away. Hours, I should think.' He hesitated. 'What can I do?' he muttered. 'I must go now or I shall never go. I shan't get a chance again. I hate leaving them, and like this without any explanation. But surely they will understand. Sam will. And what else can I do?'

Slowly he drew out the Ring and put it on once more. He vanished and passed down the hill, less than a rustle of the wind.

The others remained long by the river-side. For some time they had been silent, moving restlessly about; but now they were sitting in a circle, and they were talking. Every now and again they made efforts to speak of other things, of their long road and many adventures; they questioned Aragorn concerning the realm of Gondor and its ancient history, and the remnants of its great works that could still be seen in this strange border-land of the Emyn Muil: the stone kings and the seats of Lhaw and Hen, and the great Stair beside the falls of Rauros. But always their thoughts and words strayed back to Frodo and the Ring. What would Frodo choose to do? Why was he hesitating?

'He is debating which course is the most desperate, I think,' said Aragorn. 'And well he may. It is now more hopeless than ever for the Company to go east, since we have been tracked by Gollum, and must fear that the secret of our journey is already betrayed. But Minas Tirith is no nearer to the Fire and the destruction of the Burden.

'We may remain there for a while and make a brave stand; but the Lord Denethor and all his men cannot hope to do what even Elrond said was beyond his power: either to keep the Burden secret, or to hold off the full might of the Enemy when he comes to take it. Which way would any of us choose in Frodo's place? I do not know. Now indeed we miss Gandalf most.'

'Grievous is our loss,' said Legolas. 'Yet we must needs make up our minds without his aid. Why cannot we decide, and so help Frodo? Let us call him back and then vote! I should vote for Minas Tirith.'

'And so should I,' said Gimli. 'We, of course, were only sent to help the Bearer along the road, to go no further than we wished; and none of us is under any oath or command to seek Mount Doom. Hard was my parting from Lothlórien. Yet I have come so far, and I say this: now we have reached the last choice, it is clear to me that I cannot leave Frodo. I would choose Minas Tirith, but if he does not, then I follow him.'

'And I too will go with him,' said Legolas. 'It would be faithless now to say farewell.'

'It would indeed be a betrayal, if we all left him,' said Aragorn. 'But if he goes east, then all need not go with him; nor do I think that all should. That venture is desperate: as much so for eight as for three or two, or one alone. If you would let me choose, then I should appoint three companions: Sam, who could not bear it otherwise; and Gimli; and myself. Boromir will return to his own city, where his father and his people need him; and with him the others should go, or at least Meriadoc and Peregrin, if Legolas is not willing to leave us.'

'That won't do at all!' cried Merry. 'We can't leave Frodo! Pippin and I always intended to go wherever he went, and we still do. But we did not realize what that would mean. It seemed different so far away, in the Shire or in Rivendell. It would be mad and cruel to let Frodo go to Mordor. Why can't we stop him?'

'We must stop him,' said Pippin. 'And that is what he is worrying about, I am sure. He knows we shan't agree to his going east. And he doesn't like to ask anyone to go with him, poor old fellow. Imagine it: going off to Mordor alone!' Pippin shuddered. 'But the dear silly old hobbit, he ought to know that he hasn't got to ask. He ought to know that if we can't stop him, we shan't leave him.'

'Begging your pardon,' said Sam. 'I don't think you understand my master at all. He isn't hesitating about which way to go. Of course not! What's the good of Minas Tirith anyway? To him, I mean, begging your pardon, Master Boromir,' he added, and turned. It was then that they discovered that Boromir, who at first had been sitting silent on the outside of the circle, was no longer there.

'Now where's he got to?' cried Sam, looking worried. 'He's been a bit queer lately, to my mind. But anyway he's not in this business. He's off to his home, as he always said; and no blame to him. But Mr. Frodo, he knows he's got to find the Cracks of Doom, if he can. But he's *afraid*. Now it's come to the point, he's just plain terrified. That's what his trouble is. Of course he's had a bit of schooling, so to speak – we all have – since we left home, or he'd be so terrified he'd just fling the Ring in the River and bolt. But he's still too frightened to start. And he isn't worrying about us either: whether we'll go along with him or no. He knows we mean to. That's another thing that's bothering him. If he screws himself up to go, he'll want to go alone. Mark my words! We're going to have trouble when he comes back. For he'll screw himself up all right, as sure as his name's Baggins.'

'I believe you speak more wisely than any of us, Sam,' said Aragorn. 'And what shall we do, if you prove right?'

'Stop him! Don't let him go!' cried Pippin.

'I wonder?' said Aragorn. 'He is the Bearer, and the fate of the Burden is on him. I do not think that it is our part to drive him one way or the other. Nor do I think that we should succeed, if we tried. There are other powers at work far stronger.'

'Well, I wish Frodo would "screw himself up" and come back, and let us get it over,' said Pippin. 'This waiting is horrible! Surely the time is up?'

'Yes,' said Aragorn. 'The hour is long passed. The morning is wearing away. We must call for him.'

At that moment Boromir reappeared. He came out from the trees and walked towards them without speaking. His face looked grim and sad. He paused as if counting those that were present, and then sat down aloof, with his eyes on the ground.

'Where have you been, Boromir?' asked Aragorn. 'Have you seen Frodo?'

Boromir hesitated for a second. 'Yes, and no,' he answered slowly. 'Yes: I found him some way up the hill, and I spoke to him. I urged him to come to Minas Tirith and not to go east. I grew angry and he left me. He vanished. I have never seen such a thing happen before, though I have heard of it in tales. He must have put the Ring on. I could not find him again. I thought he would return to you.'

'Is that all that you have to say?' said Aragorn, looking hard and not too kindly at Boromir.

'Yes,' he answered. 'I will say no more yet.'

'This is bad!' cried Sam, jumping up. 'I don't know what this Man has been up to. Why should Mr. Frodo put the thing on? He didn't ought to have; and if he has, goodness knows what may have happened!'

'But he wouldn't keep it on,' said Merry. 'Not when he had escaped the unwelcome visitor, like Bilbo used to.'

'But where did he go? Where is he?' cried Pippin. 'He's been away ages now.'

'How long is it since you saw Frodo last, Boromir?' asked Aragorn.

'Half an hour, maybe,' he answered. 'Or it might be an hour. I have wandered for some time since. I do not know! I do not know!' He put his head in his hands, and sat as if bowed with grief.

'An hour since he vanished!' shouted Sam. 'We must try and find him at once. Come on!'

'Wait a moment!' cried Aragorn. 'We must divide up into pairs, and arrange – here, hold on! Wait!'

It was no good. They took no notice of him. Sam had dashed off first. Merry and Pippin had followed, and were already disappearing westward into the trees by the shore, shouting: *Frodo! Frodo!* in their clear, high, hobbit-voices. Legolas and Gimli were running. A sudden panic or madness seemed to have fallen on the Company.

'We shall all be scattered and lost,' groaned Aragorn. 'Boromir! I do not know what part you have played in this mischief, but help now! Go after those two young hobbits, and guard them at the least, even if you cannot find Frodo. Come back to this spot, if you find him, or any traces of him. I shall return soon.'

Aragorn sprang swiftly away and went in pursuit of Sam. Just as he reached the little lawn among the rowans he overtook him, toiling uphill, panting and calling, *Frodo!*

'Come with me, Sam!' he said. 'None of us should be alone. There is mischief about. I feel it. I am going to the top, to the Seat of Amon Hen, to see what may be seen. And look! It is as my heart guessed, Frodo went this way. Follow me, and keep your eyes open!' He sped up the path.

Sam did his best, but he could not keep up with Strider the Ranger, and soon fell behind. He had not gone far before Aragorn was out of sight ahead. Sam stopped and puffed. Suddenly he clapped his hand to his head.

'Whoa, Sam Gamgee!' he said aloud. 'Your legs are too short, so use your head! Let me see now! Boromir isn't lying, that's not his way; but he hasn't told us everything. Something scared Mr. Frodo badly. He screwed himself up to the point, sudden. He made up his mind at last – to go. Where to? Off East. Not without Sam? Yes, without even his Sam. That's hard, cruel hard.'

Sam passed his hand over his eyes, brushing away the tears. 'Steady, Gamgee!' he said. 'Think, if you can! He can't fly across rivers, and he can't jump waterfalls. He's got no gear. So he's got to get back to the boats. Back to the boats! Back to the boats, Sam, like lightning!'

Sam turned and bolted back down the path. He fell and cut his knees. Up he got and ran on. He came to the edge of the lawn of Parth Galen by the shore, where the boats were drawn up out of the water. No one was there. There seemed to be cries in the woods behind, but he did not heed them. He stood gazing for a moment, stock-still, gaping. A boat was sliding down the bank all by itself. With a shout Sam raced across the grass. The boat slipped into the water.

'Coming, Mr. Frodo! Coming!' called Sam, and flung himself from the bank, clutching at the departing boat. He missed it by a yard. With a cry and a splash he fell face downward into deep swift water. Gurgling he went under, and the River closed over his curly head.

An exclamation of dismay came from the empty boat. A paddle swirled and the boat put about. Frodo was just in time to grasp Sam by the hair as he came up, bubbling and struggling. Fear was staring in his round brown eyes.

'Up you come, Sam my lad!' said Frodo. 'Now take my hand!'

'Save me, Mr. Frodo!' gasped Sam. 'I'm drownded. I can't see your hand.'

'Here it is. Don't pinch, lad! I won't let you go. Tread water and don't flounder, or you'll upset the boat. There now, get hold of the side, and let me use the paddle!'

With a few strokes Frodo brought the boat back to the bank, and Sam was able to scramble out, wet as a water-rat. Frodo took off the Ring and stepped ashore again.

'Of all the confounded nuisances you are the worst, Sam!' he said.

'Oh, Mr. Frodo, that's hard!' said Sam shivering. 'That's hard, trying to go without me and all. If I hadn't a guessed right, where would you be now?'

'Safely on my way.'

'Safely!' said Sam. 'All alone and without me to help you? I couldn't have a borne it, it'd have been the death of me.'

'It would be the death of you to come with me, Sam,' said Frodo, 'and I could not have borne that.'

'Not as certain as being left behind,' said Sam.

'But I am going to Mordor.'

'I know that well enough, Mr. Frodo. Of course you are. And I'm coming with you.'

'Now, Sam,' said Frodo, 'don't hinder me! The others will be coming back at any minute. If they catch me here, I shall have to argue and explain, and I shall never have the heart or the chance to get off. But I must go at once. It's the only way.'

'Of course it is,' answered Sam. 'But not alone. I'm coming too, or neither of us isn't going. I'll knock holes in all the boats first.'

Frodo actually laughed. A sudden warmth and gladness touched his heart. 'Leave one!' he said. 'We'll need it. But you can't come like this without your gear or food or anything.'

'Just hold on a moment, and I'll get my stuff!' cried Sam eagerly. 'It's all ready. I thought we should be off today.' He rushed to the camping place, fished out his pack from the pile where Frodo had laid it when he emptied the boat of his companions' goods, grabbed a spare blanket, and some extra packages of food, and ran back.

'So all my plan is spoilt!' said Frodo. 'It is no good trying to escape you. But I'm glad, Sam. I cannot tell you how glad. Come along! It is plain that we were meant to go together. We will go, and may the others find a safe road! Strider will look after them. I don't suppose we shall see them again.'

'Yet we may, Mr. Frodo. We may,' said Sam.

So Frodo and Sam set off on the last stage of the Quest together. Frodo paddled away from the shore, and the River bore them swiftly away, down the western arm, and past the frowning cliffs of Tol Brandir. The roar of the great falls drew nearer. Even with such help as Sam could give, it was hard work to pass across the current at the southward end of the island and drive the boat eastward towards the far shore.

At length they came to land again upon the southern slopes of Amon Lhaw. There they found a shelving shore, and they drew the boat out, high above the water, and hid it as well as they could behind a great boulder. Then shouldering their burdens, they set off, seeking a path that would bring them over the grey hills of the Emyn Muil, and down into the Land of Shadow.